'Marry me.'

Eleanor froze. A thousand disconnected thoughts flew through her brain. A huge part of her screamed that this was the miracle she'd been longing for. Lord Whittonstall had asked her to marry him. But she also knew she didn't want him offering out of pity. She had her pride.

'I wasn't begging you for help. I was attempting to explain.'

'Is there something wrong with marrying me?' Ben stared at Eleanor Blackwell. He had not intended to ask her to marry him when he arrived at Moles, but now, seeing her here and hearing her story, he knew it was the right thing to do. The perfect solution to his problem and to hers. Mutual assistance.

She pulled away from him. 'You have no reason to want to marry me. Don't patronise me. I can't stand it.'

Ben watched the crown of her head. Her bravery impressed him, but he also wanted to touch her hair. His desire to kiss her had grown, not diminished. Most unexpected. He desired her.

AUTHOR NOTE

This book had two major inspirations. First, it amazed me when I learned that the finest swords in England during the Regency Period were manufactured in Shotley Bridge, County Durham. Second, I have been intrigued for a number of years by successful Regency businesswomen—women like Eleanor Coade, whose factory made the famous Coade Stone statues which so evoke gardening in this period, and Sarah Child Villiers, Lady Jersey, who inherited Child and Co from her grandfather because he disapproved of her mother's elopement.

Lady Jersey served as the senior partner from 1806-1867. She never allowed the men in her life to take an active part in the bank, and retained the right to hire and fire all the other partners. Lady Jersey was also the Lady Patroness of Almack's, and was responsible for popularising the French Quadrille—the precursor to traditional square dancing.

In 1812 in England fourteen women literally held licences to print money because they were senior partners in a variety of private banks. The two wealthiest bankers in London in the 1820s were the Peeresses—Lady Jersey and the Duchess of St Alban's, who was the senior partner at Coutts. However, for some reason Regency businesswomen have often been ignored or overlooked in the history books, and it is hard to find more than snippets about them. The sole biography of the Duchess of St Alban's dates from 1839. One of the best books on the subject that I have found is *Women Who Made Money: Women Partners in British Private Banks 1752-1906* by Dawes and Selwyn (Trafford Publishing, November 2010).

Hopefully you will enjoy my story of Eleanor Blackwell as much as I enjoyed writing it.

As ever, I welcome all feedback from readers.

HIS UNSUITABLE VISCOUNTESS

Michelle Styles

First published in Great Britain 2012
by Mills & Boon, an imprint of Harlequin (UK) Limited.
Large Print edition 2012
Harlequin (UK) Limited, Eton House, 18-24 Paradise Road,
Richmond, Surrey TW9 1SR

© Michelle Styles 2012

ISBN: 978 0 263 22540 2

Harlequin (UK) policy is to use papers that are natural,
renewable and recyclable products and made from wood grown in
sustainable forests. The logging and manufacturing process conform
to the legal environmental regulations of the country of origin.

Printed and bound in Great Britain
by CPI Antony Rowe, Chippenham, Wiltshire

Born and raised near San Francisco, California, **Michelle Styles** currently lives a few miles south of Hadrian's Wall, with her husband, three children, two dogs, cats, assorted ducks, hens and beehives. An avid reader, she became hooked on historical romance when she discovered Georgette Heyer, Anya Seton and Victoria Holt one rainy lunchtime at school. And, for her, a historical romance still represents the perfect way to escape. Although Michelle loves reading about history, she also enjoys a more hands-on approach to her research. She has experimented with a variety of old recipes and cookery methods (some more successfully than others), climbed down Roman sewers, and fallen off horses in Iceland—all in the name of discovering more about how people went about their daily lives. When she is not writing, reading or doing research, Michelle tends her rather overgrown garden or does needlework—in particular counted cross-stitch.

Michelle maintains a website, www.michellestyles.co.uk, and a blog, www.michellestyles.blogspot.com, and would be delighted to hear from you.

Previous novels by the same author:

THE GLADIATOR'S HONOUR
A NOBLE CAPTIVE
SOLD AND SEDUCED
THE ROMAN'S VIRGIN MISTRESS
TAKEN BY THE VIKING
A CHRISTMAS WEDDING WAGER
   (part of *Christmas By Candlelight*)
VIKING WARRIOR, UNWILLING WIFE
AN IMPULSIVE DEBUTANTE
A QUESTION OF IMPROPRIETY
IMPOVERISHED MISS, CONVENIENT WIFE
COMPROMISING MISS MILTON*
THE VIKING'S CAPTIVE PRINCESS
BREAKING THE GOVERNESS'S RULES*
TO MARRY A MATCHMAKER

*linked by character

And in Mills & Boon Historical *Undone!* eBooks:
THE PERFECT CONCUBINE

To my mother-in-law, Mary Styles.

Chapter One

May 1811, Durham County

What were the precise words you used when proposing marriage to a rake? Not necessarily the polite ones, but the words guaranteed to get results?

Miss Eleanor Blackwell paced Sir Vivian Clarence's library, banging the newly forged rapier against her palm.

Proposing to Sir Vivian had seemed straightforward back at the foundry. In fact the ideal solution to her current dilemma. She needed a husband and Sir Vivian had debts to clear. But as she waited for Sir Vivian to appear doubts warred with desperation and she fought against a rising sense of panic.

Even if she did succeed in her proposal, was Sir Vivian the sort of man she wanted to be married to?

Eleanor glanced up at a particularly lewd painting of a woman reclining on a bower of flowers while two men fought over her with swords. She rolled her eyes and made a disgusted noise. The painter had made a mistake with the swords. No one would ever be able to fight with their bodies contorted in that fashion. Physically impossible.

Staring at the painting did nothing for her already jangled nerves. She needed to sort her speech out. Once she'd heard the words out loud she'd know if they were right or if they needed to be altered.

'Sir Vivian,' she began, turning her back on the painting. 'Our previous acquaintance has been confined to business matters, but unfortunately my stepfather has died.'

Eleanor paused. There was nothing unfortunate about the manner of his death, brought on by eating far too many eels in direct defiance of the doctor's orders. The world was a better place without his selfish ranting and fits of extreme temper.

The unfortunate part was the wording of the will—a will she could not challenge as being un-enforceable without causing hardship to people she loved and rewarding her stepfather's odious nephew, Algernon Forecastle. What was worse, she'd discovered that her stepfather had left instructions for Algernon on how to challenge Eleanor's marriage should the unthinkable occur.

Even thinking about the clause and what failure would mean to so many hard-working people made a hard knot grow in her throat, and she found it impossible to continue with her speech.

Eleanor clenched her teeth. This was far from good. In order to propose marriage she had to be able to speak.

She tightened her grip on the sword. A new start with far less potential for emotional outbursts from her was needed. With the specifics about what she wanted and why. Facts and not feelings. This marriage was to be a business transaction without pretence to sentiment.

'My great-great-grandfather founded Moles Swords. Sword-making is in my blood. I have made Moles Swords into what is today. However, my mother remarried in haste, without a proper settlement, and under English law all her possessions belonged to her new husband. At my mother's deathbed my stepfather promised I would eventually inherit Moles. But my stepfather's will declares that unless I marry within four weeks I will lose everything. Being a man of honour...'

Her eyes were drawn back to the painting. This

time she noticed where the woman's hands were. A profound sense of shock shot through her and her cheeks flamed.

What sort of man gave that sort of painting prominence?

Even the porcelain vases seemed more appropriate for a brothel than a gentleman's residence. Did men of honour display such things in public rooms?

A severe pain pounded behind Eleanor's eyes. She was doing the right thing, coming here and demanding he honour his word. The note she'd found yesterday stated: *Name your price for your latest rapier and I will happily pay it, dear lady.* She would hold him to it. Her price was marriage.

The marriage made sense. He had debts. She had money. She would ensure a proper settlement which would allow her to control the business. It could be done in time. Just.

All she needed was the courage to put the proposal in a way that Sir Vivian would accept.

Eleanor thrust forward with the sword. Death to all doubts!

'Sir Vivian, it is imperative that I see you today. There is a matter which cannot wait.'

'Alas, Sir Vivian is unavailable, Mrs Blackwell,' a

deep voice said. 'I'm his cousin, Lord Whittonstall. Please accept my regrets for any inconvenience.'

She gaped at the man who strode into the library. With his curly black hair, olive-toned skin and hooded eyes, he was one of the most beautiful men she had ever seen. More a Greek statue come to life than an actual human being. The only flaw she could see was a tiny scar under his right eye.

'Unavailable?' she whispered, and her heart plummeted. Panic threatened to engulf her. How much had Lord Whittonstall overheard? It had to be very little or she'd sink to the ground in shame. Eleanor thrust the sword forward. 'He has to be available. He simply must be.'

At Lord Whittonstall's surprised expression she brought her hand down abruptly. The sword arced out of her hand, flew through the air and narrowly missed a particularly ugly Ormolu vase, landing with a clatter on the threadbare Turkish carpet. Eleanor stared at it in disbelief, biting the knuckle of her left thumb.

How could that happen to her today? Of all days?

She wanted the floor to swallow her. Or more preferably to be any place but here. But she knew she had to remain here and endure the humiliation. Without a successful marriage proposal her life would be worthless.

Lord Whittonstall briskly crossed the library and reached the sword before she had a chance to retrieve it.

'It is a Moles rapier. The latest model,' she said at his questioning glance. 'My grip must have been off. I had something else on my mind. It has never happened before.'

'I know the type of sword you make, Mrs Blackwell. Your reputation precedes you.'

His hooded gaze held hers. Dark with a guarded quality. It would be possible to drown in those eyes.

'Which is?' Eleanor asked. Her shoulders relaxed slightly. Everything would be fine. Lord Whittonstall knew who she was, had even used the courtesy title of Mrs, and no doubt held the swords her company made in the highest regard. She gulped a welcome breath of air.

'Swords for the sort of gentleman who wants his sword to be noticed rather than used in combat. For someone who is more concerned about style than the actual substance of the thing. I have seen your advertisements—"a sword for the truly refined". Nowhere do you mention its practicality.'

All thoughts of drowning in his eyes vanished. Eleanor struggled to retain a leash on her temper. He made it sound as if her swords were mere playthings. Didn't he understand how hard everyone had worked to make them? What good was a sword if you couldn't use it?

'Moles are the sword of choice in seven regiments,' she said, with crushing dignity. 'They combine practicality with aesthetic beauty. And perhaps a little fun. A Moles gentleman is someone who enjoys novelty.'

His thin lips turned up into an arrogant smile. 'They are your creation. You shape them, forge them from your own hands, and are therefore blind to their faults.'

'I don't actually make the swords,' Eleanor explained, aware that her cheeks flamed. She could count on one hand the number of women who were successful in a business such as hers. 'It is a common misconception.'

'Indeed. My mistake. You are the figurehead.'

'I run the business,' Eleanor said firmly. 'I know every inch of it. Each sword is the result of many men's labours, from the humblest coal-picker to the master cutler sharpening the sword. Each design goes through rigorous testing and modification. A sword which is merely for show has no purpose. Everything needs to have a purpose. A good sword can save your life, whatever amusement it might provide at other times. Now, may I see your cousin, please? I have an appointment.'

'With regret, my cousin remains unavailable. Your purpose must wait for another time.'

He obviously expected her to make her apologies and go. If she went Eleanor knew she'd never work up the courage to return. And the will specified her marriage had to take place within four weeks of its reading. That was in twenty-six days' time. The settlement would take time to finalise. It was today or never.

Eleanor dug into her embroidered reticule, searching desperately for Sir Vivian's note. 'I have an appointment with Sir Vivian. It was confirmed in writing. Yesterday.'

She shoved the crumpled note towards him and willed him to relent.

'I'm sorry for the inconvenience, but alas that is my cousin. Wonderful company but the attention span of a gnat.'

'But…' Eleanor looked at Lord Whittonstall in dismay. Tears of frustration pricked at her eyelids. After all her careful planning, it came down to Sir

Vivian *forgetting?* All her plans for the future?
Everything? Gone?

Her throat worked up and down but no sound
came out.

'You may leave a note for him,' Lord Whittonstall
said in a slow voice, as if he were speaking to a
child. 'I will personally ensure he receives it on
his return.'

'I need to see him in person.' Eleanor hated the
way her voice squeaked on the last syllable. Lord
Whittonstall couldn't turn her away—not while her
goal was so close. And the entirety of her scheme
was dependent upon her making her appeal in person. Leaving a note was impossible. She pulled
her shoulders back and looked at him with her
best closing-the-sale gaze. 'How long will he be?'

'Impossible.'

'But he will return. I understand he is in residence? I'm willing to wait.'

Lord Whittonstall tilted his head. His dark eyes
assessed her, sweeping from the crown of her black
feathered bonnet to the hem of her black silk gown.
His frown increased. 'A respectable woman in a
single gentleman's house?'

'Lady Whittonstall is not here?' Eleanor asked,
grasping for an amicable solution, and then winced

silently. His entire countenance had changed, becoming remote and forbidding. She had chosen the wrong words.

'My wife died years ago and my mother is elsewhere.'

'I'm sorry. Truly I am.'

If anything Lord Whittonstall became more granite-like, and Eleanor knew only some vestige of politeness prevented him from throwing her out of the house.

'You never knew her,' he said, in a voice which would cut through steel. 'What is there to be sorry about? Mawkish sentimentality is one of the more depressing features of modern society.'

The pain in Eleanor's head became blinding. She wanted to escape and hide under the bedcovers, start the day again. On a day that she needed everything to go right, everything was going wrong.

'An expression of politeness is never out of place.' She took a deep breath and hated how her stomach knotted. She couldn't afford any more mistakes. 'And it is never easy to lose someone who is dear to you. No matter how long it has been, it still hurts. Not a day goes by that I don't miss my grandfather and his wisdom.'

She finished with a placating smile and hoped. The ice in his eyes softened.

'Your expression of sympathy was far from necessary, I assure you. A tragic accident—or so they told me.' He inclined his head but his mouth bore a bitter twist. 'I thank you for it. I believe that is the response you require. Will you now depart?'

Eleanor kept her chin up. She refused to be intimidated and quit the field. 'If I go, the sword goes. You might discount Moles swords, but Sir Vivian is a keen customer. He wants the sword. Desperately. He wrote to me, begging for it.'

He balanced the sword in his hand before making an experimental flourish with it. 'Despite the workmanship of the hilt, it seems barely adequate. This sword would fly out of your hand in a trice— as indeed it did earlier.'

'Your grip is wrong.'

He raised an arrogant eyebrow. 'I beg your pardon?'

'You will lose your sword in combat if you are not careful, but it is a matter that can be easily solved.' Eleanor swallowed hard. She'd done it again. Spoken before she thought. Said the wrong thing. But she had started now. He deserved it for being pompous—and his grip *was* appalling.

She glanced up at him. There was a gleam of speculation in his eye. It was a small opening, a glimmer of a chance. She needed to capture his interest if she was going to remain in this house until Sir Vivian returned.

'You would lose any sword if your opponent possessed even a modicum of skill,' she said, trying to keep her voice steady as her mind worked feverishly.

'Excuse me?' His smile became withering. 'You sent this sword flying through air without any provocation and you are telling me that *my* grip is wrong?'

'If someone comes at you with a counterlunge you will struggle.' She gave a small pointed cough. He hadn't thrown her out yet. She had to take this one chance to convince him to allow her to stay. And in doing so, if she improved his technique, so much the better. 'They will be able to send the sword spinning out of your hand if they do a *moulinet*.'

'A *moulinet* is slow, and easy to twist out of if you know what you are doing. I doubt anyone could disarm in that fashion,' he said, as if he were addressing a child rather than the owner of the best sword manufacturer in the country. 'I must assume you know precious little about swords and the actual art of fencing, despite your position.'

White-hot anger flashed through Eleanor. Who did he think he was? 'Is that a challenge? Do you want me to prove my assertion?'

'If you like...' He shrugged out of his velvet cutaway coat and put it on the back of an armchair. 'Never let it be said that I am unwilling to accept criticism.'

Her hands undid her bonnet and tossed it on a table. The black feathers kept falling over the brim, making it impossible to see straight. And taking it off would make it more difficult for him to get rid of her.

'That sword is made to be held in a certain way and you are curling your fingers incorrectly,' she said, returning to his side.

'Indeed?' He arched one perfect eyebrow.

She stood beside him. His scorn was not going to intimidate her. His crisp scent rose around her, holding her, making her aware of him. Why did he have to be so beautiful? Eleanor swallowed hard and attempted to concentrate.

'Show me.' He held out the blade with the faintest trace of a smile. 'What is the correct grip, my *dear* Mrs Blackwell?'

Eleanor froze. Was he flirting with her? Or mocking her? Men like him didn't flirt with women like her. She knew her shortcomings. Her stepfather always catalogued them when he'd taken port—too tall, too thin, a strong chin and eyes far too big. No, Lord Whittonstall was being condescending, thinking to humour her and get her out of here.

'I'm not your dear,' she muttered finally.

'A mere figure of speech.' He looked at her through a forest of lashes. Men should not have lashes like that—particularly not arrogant aristocrats. 'I shall remember not to call you that.'

'You need to put your hand like this,' she said concentrating on the hilt of the sword rather than on his eyes. 'It is the slightest of adjustments but it makes all the difference.'

'As simple as that?' He curled his fingers about hers. 'I want to make certain I am doing this properly. I'd hate to think I've been holding my sword incorrectly for all these years.'

'You seek to mock me, sir.'

'Nothing could be further from my mind. I wish to learn and further my skill. Help me to understand, Mrs Blackwell, why your swords are held in such esteem.'

She focused on the sword rather than on how his fingers had accidentally brushed hers. 'A simple mistake, which is far too common amongst swordsman of a certain type for my liking.'

'A certain type?'

'Ones who failed to listen to their instructor.'

'Do I have it right now?' he asked. His voice flowed over her like treacle. 'I fail to see how this particular grip can make the slightest difference. Perhaps it is all in the pressure. Is that what you are attempting to say, Mrs Blackwell? I will inform my cousin when I see him.'

She let go of the sword so abruptly that it would have fallen to the ground had he not had his hand on the hilt. He placed it on the table next to her bonnet with a smug look on his face. He thought she was trying to flirt with him in order to stay! He wasn't taking her seriously.

Eleanor clenched her jaw. Very well. Lord Whittonstall deserved his comeuppance.

'Do you have another sword? Perhaps I could demonstrate, as my word is clearly not enough,' she said, striding away from him. Her body quivered with indignation. He wasn't taking her seriously. 'It is perhaps better that you see how it operates in actual practice. I can make any sword fly out of your hand in a few heartbeats.'

A muscle jumped in his jaw and she knew she'd hit a raw nerve. 'If you wish. But you should be aware I am considered to be one of the top swordsmen in the country. The great Henry Angelo considers me to be his equal.'

'Modesty is such an uncommon virtue that it takes my breath away when I behold it. I know the wrong sort of grip when I see it.'

'Allow me to get my weapon of choice. I can't allow such a challenge to go unanswered.'

Lord Whittonstall strode out of the room, his footsteps echoing down the corridor. Eleanor put a hand to her head.

What had she done? Gone mad? She'd challenged Lord Whittonstall to a duel with no certainty of winning.

She picked up the sword intended for Sir Vivian and balanced it in her hand. Holding the blade made her more confident. She should be able to do it. She *had* to do it—to wipe the arrogant look off his face and find a way to stay here until Sir Vivian appeared.

'Shall we see, Mrs Blackwell, who knows what they are about?' Lord Whittonstall asked, coming back into the library, carrying one of her competitor's swords. From the way he held it, she knew that he was far from a novice.

'I look forward to it.' She tucked an errant strand of black hair behind her ear and tried to quell her nerves. She knew how to fence. Better than most. And she could take advantage of his mistakes.

'May the best…person win.'

'You need to learn. *En garde,* my lord.'

Benjamin Grayson, the third Viscount Whittonstall, glowered at the black-shrouded creature standing before him, daring to lecture him on the inadequacy of his grip and challenging him to a duel. Did she actually think she'd win, or was she merely trying to prolong the time she was here, hoping to encounter his cousin?

If so, she was in for a shock. He'd defeat her in short order and the price of her defeat would be her departure.

The larger question, though, was why she was here at all. Had his cousin ignored the appointment, knowing it was going to be trouble, or had he truly forgotten?

He knew without a shadow of a doubt that this was about more than the sword Mrs Blackwell defiantly held in her hand. She had gone beyond the bounds of decorum to stay, and there was a faint air of desperation in her manner.

If he were a gambling man he'd be willing to wager a considerable sum that Mrs Blackwell's need to see Viv had to do with the wretched state of Viv's finances.

Viv and he had been close as boys, but had grown apart. His aunt's latest missive had entreated him to come and discover what the true situation was. The trip made a welcome relief from his mother and her increasingly strong hints about his duty to provide an heir and preserve the dynasty. She ignored the fact that he had tried once and lost his wife. Tragic accident? Maybe one day he'd believe it. Maybe one day he'd stop blaming himself.

What he'd discovered up north gave him pause. Viv needed funds. Unless something was done it was only a matter of time before the bailiffs came knocking and Viv had to flee the country. And he did not intend that to happen. Viv had helped Ben in his hour of need at Eton. Fighting his corner. Ben would repay the favour now. He'd solve the mystery before Viv woke from his port-induced stupor and teach Mrs Blackwell a lesson she wouldn't soon forget into the bargain.

'Shall we have at it, Mrs Blackwell?' he asked softly.

'Whenever you are ready.'

Their swords clashed. He parried easily and did a counter-lunge, blocking her move. She took a step backwards. A tiny frown appeared between her brows and she slightly readjusted her grip.

'Not as easy as you thought, Mrs Blackwell?' he said in a withering tone. 'You will see my grip needs no improvement. I am not a swordsman who wishes to have his sword disguised as a walking stick or festooned with frills, but a swordsman who spends hours practising my skill.'

'You are worse than I imagined,' she replied with the faintest trace of a smile. 'Do try to put up a fight, Lord Whittonstall.'

She half-turned and countered his move with a parry, forcing Ben on the back foot. He missed his stroke and it was only through sheer instinct that he blocked her sword.

'You *do* need some pointers. You have become complacent,' she said with a tiny laugh.

Ben stared at her, seeing her for the first time as a person rather than as an object of pity or a woman to be indulged. A brain existed behind those grey eyes. She knew how to fence and in all likelihood was better than him. He rejected the thought. As good as he was.

'Complacency? An interesting accusation,' he said finally, moving a step closer to where she stood, ready for the next onslaught. Their swords crossed. They circled around each other. Their breath intertwined. Their faces were no more than a few inches apart. He was suddenly aware of the magnificence of her grey eyes and the determination of her chin.

'But a true one. You play with skill but lack the heart. Every truly good fencer combines skill with a zest for life. Do you know where your heart is?'

Ben missed his step. He knew exactly where his heart lay—buried in a coffin with his wife and their baby who had never breathed. He remembered everything about the day when they had buried Alice and he had stood at the graveside, watching as the dirt slowly buried the coffin, listening to the sounds of sorrow, knowing that he'd never be whole again. Even the heavens had wept for his loss. He accepted that, but this—this had become about proving this woman wrong.

'I beg to differ. This has nothing to do with hearts and everything to do with skill.'

'An observation. But to truly rank among the greats you must fence with passion and fire.'

He redoubled his efforts, to show her that she was wrong. All it would take was his considerable technical skill.

She twisted her hand at the last possible instant. Sharp and to the right. His sword slid harmlessly past her shoulder, barely ruffling the black tendril of hair that had snaked loose from her bun.

He clenched his jaw. A mistake could happen to anyone at any time. The unpredictability was one of the things he loved about swordplay. But he had enough confidence in his ability to recover.

He concentrated on his next stroke. It was only a matter of time before her luck ran out and she made a mistake. Over-confidence would be her undoing.

She parried and then paused. Her long lashes swept down over her eyes, making dark smudges on her bright pink cheeks. The exertion of the match had transformed Mrs Blackwell from a colourless mouse into a vibrant creature.

He missed a step and barely recovered before he was forced to retreat backwards. He glanced over his shoulder as the table dug into his thighs. But he used it to propel himself forward and forced her on to the back foot. This time it was her sword which missed.

'You appear to be losing. Do you wish to ask for quarter?' he asked.

'Never!'

Ben stared at Mrs Blackwell. A series of ringlets had formed about her forehead, making her appear far more womanly than he'd first considered. She might have the advantage now, but he would regain it. It was a matter of concentrating on the sword rather than on her parted lips or her grey eyes. No more distractions.

'As you wish… I believe the time has come to end our bout.'

'I couldn't agree more.'

She lunged forward, twisting the sword and performing a perfect *moulinet.*

Ben moved his arm to block it a heartbeat too late. His grip shifted. He clung on—barely.

With a twist of her sword and the faintest hint of a smile she completed the move.

His sword arched out of his hand, landing embedded in her hideous coal scuttle of a bonnet.

Chapter Two

Ben stared at the sword where it lay. Disbelief swiftly followed by horror coursed through him. He went over the moves in his mind. It should have been impossible, but the evidence stared at him, quivering in the black bonnet. Mrs Blackwell had not boasted. He'd lost his sword.

He glanced at her, ready for tears or possibly hysterics at the loss of a bonnet. A small infectious bubble of laughter escaped from her covered mouth, swiftly followed by another larger one.

To Ben's surprise, a laugh loud and long exploded from him in response to the joyous sound of Mrs Blackwell's mirth. The sound made him pause. He couldn't remember the last time he'd spontaneously laughed with a woman. Probably before Alice died. He hadn't laughed much since then, and certainly not this all-consuming belly laugh.

'Oh, dear.' She dabbed her eyes with the back of her hand. 'It couldn't have happened to a nicer bonnet. You should have seen your expression when the sword flew out of your hand. Priceless.'

He sobered immediately. He'd misjudged her and over-estimated his own skill. He pulled his sword out of the now ruined bonnet. 'I owe you a bonnet and an apology. I was insufferably rude and pompous. It was uncalled for.'

She shook her head. 'The bonnet was far from my favourite, but it seemed appropriate to wear it. You owe me nothing and I thank you for the apology.'

'Appropriate to wear?' Ben eyed the hat. Rather funereal. The back of his neck prickled. What did Mrs Blackwell want to see Viv about?

'One must look proper when one makes an important business call.'

Ben regarded her upturned face, flushed from their exertions. Her eyes sparkled and her lips shone the colour of port. Mrs Blackwell was far more attractive than he'd first considered. He should send her away right now. It was the correct thing to do. But she intrigued him. He wanted to learn her secret. Why was Mrs Blackwell desperate, and why was Viv the only person who could help her?

'Viv remains, alas, unavailable. Can I assist you with this mysterious matter?'

Eleanor gulped. Lord Whittonstall's words pounded through her brain—*can I assist you*? She wasn't even going to think about confessing her predicament to Lord Whittonstall. Or asking for his help. She had nothing to offer *him*.

'It must be Sir Vivian,' Eleanor said, her stomach clenching. She hated the way she felt as if an opportunity had slipped past. 'It has to be him and no other.'

'You are doomed to disappointment.'

'I doubt that.'

'Then we must agree to disagree.'

Eleanor bit her lip. She had said the wrong thing—reminding him about the meeting, about why she was here. That moment of camaraderie and laughter they had shared vanished. And she wanted it back. She had to find a way before he manoeuvred her out through the door and her chance to ask Sir Vivian slipped away for good.

'Shall we fight again?' she asked as brightly as she could. 'Best out of three? Give you a chance to prove that it was luck on my part?'

'I know when to admit my mistakes.' He raised his rapier in a gesture of respect.

She returned the gesture, ending the bout. She searched her mind for another excuse to stay, but she seemed fresh out of ideas.

'I must congratulate you, Mrs Blackwell. You are a worthy opponent. And your swords are far more than mere decoration for the well-dressed gentleman.'

He took a step closer to her. Her sword would have dropped to the ground if he had not taken it from her slack grasp. He placed it beside his.

'We won't need these.'

'Yes. I believe I have proved my point.' Her voice sounded husky to her ears.

He stood a few inches taller than she was, but not too tall. His eyes were not coal-black, as she'd originally supposed, but full of a thousand different colours from the deepest black to light grey and every colour in between.

Her heart pounded in her ears and she knew she was far too breathless, far too aware of him as a man rather than as an opponent.

'You are a far better swordswoman than I considered possible.' His voice held a new rich note that flowed over her, warming her to the tips of her toes.

'Fancy that. You admitting defeat so easily.' She attempted a little laugh but it came out far too high. She winced and studied the folds of his cravat. Intently.

'I never hesitate to admit my mistakes. It is part of my charm.'

Charm? He was trying to flirt with her after she'd bested him? Eleanor struggled to get her breathing under control.

'Is it?' she whispered through aching lips.

This had been all about proving that Lord Whittonstall had underestimated her rather than a prelude to flirtation. But right now all she could think about was him and the way his lips moved. All she had to do was move forward a pace and she'd be in his arms.

She lifted her eyes.

Their gaze locked. He lifted a hand and touched her forearm.

Somewhere a door banged, bringing her back to reality.

Eleanor jumped backwards. Shocked. She had nearly stepped straight into Lord Whittonstall's arms and destroyed everything she held dear.

Her proposal to Sir Vivian needed to happen. It was her best chance of securing Moles' future. Everything would be lost if she was discovered in this man's arms. Her employees—the men who literally sweated over an open fire to make the swords—depended on her getting this right. Saving the company. This marriage was not about *her;* it was about giving them a future. Guilt washed over her. How could she have forgotten what was at stake for a single instant?

He stood staring at her, not moving a muscle.

She bent her head and pretended great interest in the hilt of the sword. Pointing to it, trying to get back to some semblance of normality, she said, 'Lord Whittonstall, as you can see, I had the correct grip and the sword has stayed in my hand.'

'Is fencing all you can think about?'

His voice sent a warm tingle coursing down her spine. She ruthlessly ignored it. Lord Whittonstall wasn't interested in her. Men never were. If her stepfather were to be believed she possessed no sense of refinement and all the charm of a rogue bear.

'It will do for now.'

'And for later?'

She tried not to think about Lord Whittonstall

drawing her into his arms and kissing her thoroughly. She'd accepted her fate a long time ago.

'Are you seeking a rematch, Lord Whittonstall? A chance to prove you can learn from your mistakes?' She lifted her head.

His dark gaze held hers. 'When the time is right. I want to see if there is anything else I need to learn.'

She found it impossible to look away. He was going to kiss her. Every fibre of her being told her so. Against everything logical, he was going to do it. He was going to actually kiss her and she wanted him to.

'Do you believe me now…about the grip?' Her voice sounded far too breathless and reedy. 'How that subtle change can transform your prospects of success?'

'You have challenged a number of notions today. And I will accept your word on the swords. I had misjudged them.'

His hand smoothed a curl from her forehead before brushing her skin—a feather-light touch, but one that sent an unfamiliar jolt of heat through her. She wanted him to lean forward and… She flicked her tongue over her lips.

'What is going on here?' a high-pitched male

voice asked, and she froze. 'Why wasn't I informed that there was swordplay in the library? *My* library?'

'Nothing is injured, Viv. All things in moderation,' Lord Whittonstall said, smoothly moving away from her.

'Yes, but my Ormolu vases! My carpet! I might not read, but I like my books to look as if I do.'

Lord Whittonstall's dark eyes shone with mischief. 'Everything survived except for Mrs Blackwell's bonnet—and that was her own fault.'

Lord Whittonstall retrieved his black velvet cutaway coat and put it on, becoming utterly correct again. The moment of intimacy slid away as if it had never been.

Eleanor struggled to fill her lungs. Saved from scandal. She was here for a purpose, a business transaction. Not some sort of tryst where she'd end up humiliated. Her hands shook slightly.

She should be relieved, but a stab of disappointment went through her. Lord Whittonstall wasn't going to kiss her.

She shook her head. Desiring to be kissed had no part in her plans. All it did was make her look as ridiculous as her unlamented bonnet.

She grabbed her ruined bonnet and twisted it. One of the feathers snapped in two.

'Is this what you mean by moderation in all things, Ben—duelling in my library?'

Eleanor half turned and saw her true quarry—Sir Vivian Clarence. Her heart sank. With reddened eyes and a sallow cast to its skin, his face showed distinct signs of hard living. An odour of stale wine hung about him—a stench that reminded her of her stepfather. Worse still were Sir Vivian's voice, his mincing gestures with his hands, and the overly fussy way he wore his cravat. And he had the beginnings of a bald patch. He repulsed her. Utterly and completely repulsed her.

She could not imagine why she had ever thought he might be a suitable candidate.

How could she have forgotten his voice and his mannerisms? Why had she focused solely on his offer?

She could not even imagine asking him to escort her across the road, let alone become her husband and all that entailed.

It simply showed what a foolhardy scheme it had been in the first place. It should make her feel better, but somehow it didn't. Her problem remained. She needed a husband desperately—but not that desperately. She wasn't going to suffer her mother's fate.

Eleanor gave Lord Whittonstall a panicked look. What if she begged *him* to marry her? He was a widower. They would have kissed if Sir Vivian hadn't come in.

Instantly she rejected the idea—why would he accept her, or her proposition? And to be turned down would be far too humiliating. She had little desire to know if that moment when she'd thought he was about to kiss her had been real or not.

Neat footwork was required here. There was no way she could put her proposition to either of them. There had to be another way to find a bridegroom. Giving up and allowing her stepfather and Algernon Forecastle to win was not an option.

It was there on the edge of her brain, just waiting. She kept her eyes on the stone floor and concentrated, but her mind remained frustratingly blank. All she could think about was how Lord Whittonstall's breath had fanned her cheek. She needed to return to being the sensible businesslike Mrs Blackwell this instant.

'I was merely attempting to see what was so wonderful about Moles swords. Mrs Blackwell has made me a convert.'

She glanced up, startled. Lord Whittonstall made a bow and held out the sword. His eyes challenged her. The time to deliver the sword had arrived. She had to explain why she'd been so insistent that the interview take place.

Eleanor put her hand to her throat but no words came out.

'The sword is a gift from you, cousin?' Sir Vivian's cheeks became tinged with pink. 'You should have said, Ben. I thought you only wanted to berate me for spending my money like water and you've bought me a top-drawer sword. We *will* have that talk—the one I have been avoiding. I need to do you the courtesy of listening.'

'Not from me,' Lord Whittonstall said, inclining his head. 'From Mrs Blackwell. But her purpose in giving it remains a mystery. She insists on speaking to you and only you. The mystery has me flummoxed.'

'From Moles…for your birthday,' Eleanor said quickly, before she gave in to her impulse to flee. This whole thing had turned into a nightmare. How could had she have blocked Sir Vivian's voice from her memory? She should have remembered it from their previous meetings. And the fact he drank port to excess!

'But you were duelling in my library!' Sir Vivian squeaked, turning a strange shade of puce.

'Lord Whittonstall believed that Moles' swords were mere flash.' Eleanor kept her voice steady. If she skated around the reason why she was even here at Broomhaugh Hall she might be able to think up an acceptable excuse, something she could believe in. Anything but the unvarnished truth. 'I sought to change his view. I regret that you were caused even a moment's discomfort about the contents of your library.'

Sir Vivian pursed his lips. 'And did you succeed in changing his view? My cousin's views are notoriously steadfast.'

'I relieved him of his sword. It became embedded in my bonnet.' She held up her bonnet and wiggled her fingers through the gash.

'Ben lost his sword?' Sir Vivian shook his head. 'Impossible. You are seeking to make fun of me.'

'But true,' Lord Whittonstall commented. 'Mrs Blackwell accomplished it, proving the value of her sword design and the defects of my sword grip. I humbly apologise, Viv, for thinking your choice of sword was more to do with fashion than function.'

A warm glow filled Eleanor at Lord Whittonstall's unexpected words.

Sir Vivian raised his quizzing glass. 'Ben is the best swordsman I know. Equal to the great Henry Angelo. The last time you lost a sword was at Eton, Ben.'

'Just afterwards. In Bath. Exaggeration does no one credit, Viv.'

Lord Whittonstall made a bow while his eyes danced. Eleanor wondered why she had thought them cold and lifeless. Or lacking in passion.

'Mrs Blackwell will tell you that I made elemental mistakes with my grip and anyone who knew could exploit the weakness. Mrs Blackwell does possess more than a modicum of skill.'

'I saw an opportunity and took it. Luck.' Eleanor shrugged. 'Once you correct your grip you will be a formidable opponent.'

'Luck had nothing to do with it. It will be the sword.' Sir Vivian rubbed his hands together. 'Will I have a chance of beating my cousin as well?'

'It is Moles' latest design,' Eleanor said, suddenly knowing what she had to say—and why. 'It combines practicality with a certain flair for the discerning gentleman, such as yourself.'

'Why give it to me for my birthday now? My birthday isn't for another two months.'

Eleanor winced. That long? 'I know what…what

an influential figure you are. How people look up to you and admire your taste. I hope you will help spread the word about our new design, and I wanted to take the opportunity of your thirtieth birthday to ask for your assistance…with the matter. Personally. While you are still up here in the north. Rather than sending a note which might get mislaid when you are in London.'

'You want me to use this sword and give your creation the exposure it needs? Like the great Beau does for his tailors?'

'Yes, precisely.' Eleanor kept her head up as sweat started to trickle down the back of her neck. He'd accepted her explanation. There was no need to linger. She could go and never see Lord Whittonstall again. Never know if he would have kissed her or if it had been a figment of her imagination. 'I know how much influence you have with those who really matter. A number of people have mentioned your name when they have purchased one of our swords.'

She breathed slightly easier. Not exactly a lie, but not the whole truth either. Sir Vivian had been influential in getting *some* custom in.

Sir Vivian turned the sword over in his hands. His cheeks went quite pink. 'You best be on guard,

Ben. I shall beat you every time now. No one will believe a harridan like Mrs Blackwell gave *me* a sword! But she has, and she has entrusted me to spread the word.'

Lord Whittonstall coughed. Pointedly.

Sir Vivian hung his head. 'Sometimes my poor tongue gets ahead of my brain, my dear Mrs Blackwell. Far too much port last night. You could never be a harridan. It is simply your reputation that is quite fearsome. It is not every day one encounters a woman sword-maker—a woman who forges swords with a delicate hand.'

Eleanor forced a smile. So she had a reputation as a harridan? At least she'd been saved from suffering the biggest humiliation of her life. All she wanted to do now was slink off and lick her wounded pride. Tomorrow she'd puzzle out some suitable man to marry her. 'Now that I have said my little piece, I should go.'

Lord Whittonstall's large hand clamped about her elbow, pinning her to her spot. 'And this is all you came to say?'

'Yes. As Sir Vivian has quite clearly said, he would not have believed it if I left the sword. I had to have his agreement, and now I have it.'

His gaze became more hooded and a muscle

jumped in his jaw. Eleanor had the uncomfortable feeling that he saw through her tale. That he'd heard her rehearsing her proposal when she'd thought she was alone.

'And you will show me the move that bested my cousin?' Sir Vivian asked. 'Before you depart?'

'I can show you that,' Lord Whittonstall said. 'We have undoubtedly delayed Mrs Blackwell for far too long.'

'I do have a business to run.' Eleanor paused in the doorway. 'Good day to you both.'

'Mrs Blackwell, there will be a rematch. I have my reputation to think of.'

Eleanor ignored the tremor of excitement. Fencing with Lord Whittonstall was off the agenda. It would only lead to heartache. She had other more important things to think about. And she would never forget her quest again.

Ben watched Viv march around the terrace, making various lunges at unsuspecting bushes.

'Would you mind telling me what is going on? You avoided my questions all over luncheon. Fobbing me off with nonsensical answers.'

Viv completed his lunge. 'I am sure it is as Mrs

Blackwell indicated. She has seen how much business I have sent her way and wants me to help her.'

'You may drop the pretence. How bad are your finances?'

Viv made a disgusted noise. 'We don't all have your financial acumen, Ben. If you weren't my cousin I'd hate you. What with your title, your fortune and your excellent looks. Plus a reputation for lively and intelligent conversation.'

'That would be the side of me the public sees. My father died before I was born and my pregnant wife in a tragic accident. My fortune was squandered by rapacious financiers that my mother mistakenly trusted. I worked hard to rescue it.'

Viv dropped his gaze. 'My debts will be paid some time. I have never not paid a debt of honour. Temporary cash problem.'

'Is it that bad, Viv?'

'My luck has changed, Ben.' Viv poured two glasses of port and held one out to him.

Ben shook his head. Viv downed both of them in quick succession.

'Mrs Blackwell came here for another purpose,' Ben said, tapping his fingers together. 'Her pretty speech about you being a rival to the great Beau was concocted on the spot. Nobody could take that assertion seriously. Before she knew I was there I overheard her practising a speech to be directed at you. And when I tried to send her on her way she insisted it was imperative she see you today. She thought that wearing a coal scuttle bonnet was appropriate for her task.'

'The sword was obviously for me.' Viv held it out. 'See—on the blade she has had my name engraved. You must have misheard her.'

Ben turned the blade over and saw the engraved name. He had dismissed it earlier as fancy scrollwork. Eleanor Blackwell *had* planned to give this sword to Viv, but it didn't make him believe the explanation she'd given—her colour had been too high and her manner too abrupt. Everything about her had been too much at odds with her desperation before they'd fought. Was she in some sort of trouble? Why did she need Viv's help in particular? And, more importantly, what had changed her mind?

He handed the sword back to Viv.

'Mrs Blackwell did intend to give it to you. But your birthday is not for another few months. She could have come back any day. But it had to be *today* that she saw you. Why?'

'You have far too cautious a mind, cousin. I'm

London-bound at Mrs Blackwell's specific request. Going to meet my destiny.' Viv rubbed a hand along his stubble and belched. 'And while we are there you can introduce me to all the heiresses that your dear mama has lined up for you. She possesses a certain flair for discovering heiresses. Don't deny it! My mother constantly writes of the despair you cause your mother.'

Ben knew precisely what Viv meant. Every season since Alice's death his mother had made it her mission to sniff out a possible replacement. She liked to pretend that the way Alice had died had no bearing. A tragic accident, best forgotten.

No matter where he went in London she arranged for accidental meetings with women she deemed suitable. While all the while remaining deaf to his arguments that he wanted to choose his own bride in his own time, or indeed that he had a good enough heir in Viv. Every time he rejected one of her protégées she'd sigh and remind him how his father would want him to do his duty if he were alive, and how as his mother all she wanted was the best for him.

The truth was, none of the debutantes excited him. And what was the point in indulging in a meaningless affair with some piece of Haymarket ware? He knew what he'd shared with Alice. He also knew that it was in spite of his mother rather than because of his mother that he'd fallen for Alice. And he'd vowed that any bride of his would not have to suffer what he'd inadvertently caused Alice to suffer. Never again. He could not make it up to Alice, but he could prevent it from reoccurring.

There had been a spark, a flash of chemistry between him and Mrs Blackwell. And he could have murdered Viv for interrupting him. He'd wanted to see if it was real. If her lips did taste as sweet as he'd imagined.

'Is there a Mr Blackwell?'

'I'm speaking of the bright lights of London and pretty heiresses and you want to discuss Mrs Blackwell?' Viv gave him a quick indulgent smile. 'Well, I believe she is an ape-leading spinster. Her father's name was Blackwell. He was alive when Papa bought me my first sword. Now, enough of the woman. I'm much more interested in strategy. Do I wear my plum waistcoat or my emerald-green with the sword?'

'Strategy?'

'When Mrs Blackwell placed this sword in my hands I knew I was accepting her trust and admiration. I plan to fulfil her request. This sword needs to be seen and it will be—with all the bravado I can muster.'

Ben tapped his finger against his lips. His sense of unease increased.

Why the pretence? What had been Mrs Blackwell's true intention in coming here today?

He forced his mind away from the duel they had shared. If Viv had not interrupted she would have been in his arms, looking up at him with her marvellous eyes. That jolt of energy coursed through him again at the mere memory. He'd thought that part of him dead, but it was there and alive. And she was the cause.

'You are sure you know of no other reason why Miss Blackwell would seek you out?' he asked.

'Relax, cousin, and accept good fortune when it comes your way.' Viv made another flourish with his new sword. 'It might seem a large thing, even insurmountable, to Mrs Blackwell, but it is something I am delighted to do.'

'You're mistaken. She needed your help with something else, but after she spoke with you she changed her mind.'

Viv rolled his eyes. 'You can believe what you want. It is my sword now, and I shall enjoy it.

You're bad-tempered because she chose me over you. Because someone proved you were merely human at fencing. You had to lose some time. Be grateful it was in private. Face it. Mrs Blackwell did us both a favour.'

He stalked off with the sword tucked under his arm, leaving Ben standing there.

'We are far from finished, Eleanor Blackwell,' Ben muttered, reaching for his walking stick. 'Whatever trouble you are in, giving Viv that sword has only increased it tenfold. You must trust me on this.'

'I failed, Grandfather.'

Eleanor regarded her grandfather's portrait, which hung next to her great-great-grandfather's sword in the office at the foundry. Always when she re-entered the office she spoke to the painting. It made her feel as if she wasn't the only one left who cared about the company.

Ever since she'd returned from Sir Vivian's she'd been trying to work up the courage to come into this room. In many ways the office still felt as if it belonged to her grandfather and she was only borrowing it, even twenty years after his death. Her father had lacked the courage to change it, and

Eleanor had never wanted to. She always found inspiration and peace in the old leather chair, the walnut desk and the various swords hanging on the walls. But today everything stood in mute rebuke. Even the Villumiay clock her grandfather had won just before he died seemed to pause and frown, as if it knew how far her failure extended. She'd lacked the courage even to ask.

Eleanor had always considered herself the saviour of the firm, the protector of its heritage. She was the one who had rescued it when it had been on the brink of collapse after her father died. She was the one who had made the business what it was today—thriving, and one of the biggest employers in Shotley Bridge. She had kept her stepfather out of the day-to-day running of the company and ensured it flourished. But today she'd learnt it was all an illusion. When it really counted she'd put her personal aversion to Sir Vivian before the needs of the company.

She hadn't even asked the question! Hadn't given him a chance to refuse!

'I failed today, Grandfather, but tomorrow I will find another way.' She blinked rapidly, keeping back the tears. Whatever happened, she refused to give in. She wouldn't feel sorry for herself. She enjoyed challenges. She thrived on them. 'I *will* succeed. This company is my heritage, not anyone else's.'

'Ah, there you are, Eleanor. I have been searching everywhere for you. It was most remiss of you to go off without informing me.'

Eleanor dabbed her eyes with her handkerchief. Just what she needed—the Reverend Algernon Forecastle, her stepfather's nephew, making an appearance. He slithered into the room and deposited himself at her grandfather's desk.

'When I am in charge of this benighted company one of the first things I'm doing is sacking that man in the patched waistcoat and frayed trousers. He is *not* the sort of person we want representing Moles. He told me to mind my business and go and practise my sermons on the cows, sheep and other animals in the field, rather than bothering honest folk who were going about their daily business. The cheek of the man! I only preach on Sundays.'

Eleanor breathed deeply and reminded herself that getting angry with Algernon wouldn't help anyone. He wasn't responsible for her failure. She was. But he made it sound as if running a business was easy, when she had dedicated her life to making sure that it didn't fail. Even now, despite all her success, she woke up in a sweat, having dreamt that somehow her actions had destroyed the company.

'That man is Mr Swaddle, who is in charge of steel production,' she said steadily. 'He always wears his lucky clothes when he is trying out a new method of tempering steel. Something that requires immense concentration and is of untold value to the company. We are very close to discovering the lost formula that my great-grandfather used.'

'That doesn't matter. He is making the entire place look untidy.' Algernon put his boots on top of the walnut desk. 'You should get rid of him immediately. You make it sound as if running a company is difficult. It's not. You don't have to do much—just issue orders. Uncle was far too soft.'

'Your uncle was quite happy for me to run the company as I saw fit.'

'Uncle never properly applied his mind to the problem. If a woman can make this company prosper, just think of what a man could do on a few hours a week. It is not *you,* Eleanor, that made this company. You simply take the credit unnecessarily. You have ridden your luck. That's all.'

'Thankfully, for the future of Moles, I remain in charge.' Eleanor crossed her arms. If she needed any further proof that Algernon was completely and utterly unsuitable for running the company, this was it. Who cared about a few patches on his clothes when Mr Swaddle was a genius with steel? At least her stepfather had understood why Moles made money and who made it happen. 'And, given Mr Swaddle's expertise, he can wear whatever he likes. Moles is the better for having him as a foreman.'

Algernon blew on his nails. 'So you say.'

Eleanor rested her chin on her hand. There was something more than pleased about Algernon Forecastle today. He couldn't know about her failure with Sir Vivian, so what was it? 'What are you doing here, Algernon?'

'I demand to see the latest ledgers. It is my right.'

'Your *right*?' Eleanor stared at him in astonishment. 'You have no rights here. This company does not belong to you. You ought to go and compose a sermon. Won't your parishioners want to hear one this Sunday?'

He gave her a pitying glance. 'I bought a complete book of sermons, and I am only halfway through the third reading.'

'How resourceful.'

'Yes, it was.' Algernon began to preen like the prematurely balding otter that he was. 'I learnt about the book from a classmate at Oxford. It means I can spend my time doing other more important things.'

'Visiting the poor and the sick?'

'You must be joking, Eleanor.' Algernon paled. 'The great and the good. The poor can fend for themselves. And I've no wish to come down with some horrible disease.'

Eleanor forced a smile. She should have remembered that Algernon had a hide tougher than most forms of steel and seemed impervious to sarcasm. 'That may be so, but you still don't possess the right to bother my employees, to demand the ledgers or to put your muddy boots on my great-grandfather's desk. Remove your boots from there immediately.'

He made a show of wiping the dirt off with his linen handkerchief. 'Satisfied? I plan to replace this with something more modern when I take over.'

'I doubt that will ever happen.'

'Miss Varney says it is about time I stood up for myself and became actively involved.'

'And who, pray tell, is Miss Varney?' Eleanor asked.

'Miss Lucinda Varney is my intended.' His sneering gaze travelled up and down her. 'You didn't think I would marry *you?* Despite what my uncle counselled.'

'I take it that my stepfather remained in blissful ignorance about your matrimonial plans?'

'Uncle would not have understood. I need a truly refined wife—one who will be in keeping with my new station in life.'

His words about refinement stung far more than they should. Eleanor gritted her teeth. She knew why she'd turned her back on parties and balls. The reasons were all around her and in the very air she breathed. She was proud of her accomplishment, even if it was far from what was expected of a lady. And even if the company was not the bustling family that she'd dreamt of when she was a young girl.

'I hope you and Miss Varney are very happy,' Eleanor said when she trusted her voice. 'But you must relinquish all notions of inheriting the business or any of its investments.'

'My uncle put that codicil in to tease you. What sort of man would marry *you?*' Algernon's smile grew oilier. 'My uncle even left me instructions on how to challenge your marriage if necessary. He did specify banns, Eleanor. Do you have the time?'

'I never doubted that for an instant.' Eleanor kept her back ramrod-straight. 'But the fact remains that until you do inherit, the company belongs to me and I shall run it as I see fit.'

'You have twenty-six days left. Banns take at least twenty-one days. Ordinary licences take the same.'

'There are always special licences.'

'Do you know how difficult it is to get a special licence? They are called special because you must give an excellent reason.' Algernon stuck his thumbs in his waistcoat. 'I wonder what reason you will give, Eleanor? To the Archbishop of Canterbury, no less. Did you know that I know his son? What connections do *you* have? Or indeed do you have a man who would wish to marry you?'

Eleanor fought against the rising tide of panic. She refused to give in. 'I have twenty-six days, Algernon. At the end of that time, if you inherit, you may do what you like with the ledgers and my grandfather's desk. You may even sack valuable members of staff and cut this company's throat. But until that time keep your boots off the desk and your fingers off the ledgers. And your opinions of my employees to yourself!'

'You will regret this.'

'I think not.'

'Mrs Blackwell.' One of the junior clerks rushed in with a panicked expression on his face. 'There is a gentleman here to see you. He wants to see you now.'

'I don't have any appointments—' Eleanor began.

'We have unfinished business, Mrs Blackwell,' Lord Whittonstall said, coming to stand beside the clerk. 'And it will be completed today.'

Chapter Three

Eleanor pressed her hands to her eyes and counted to ten, hoping that Lord Whittonstall was some apparition or fevered fantasy.

When she opened her eyes he remained standing in the doorway to the office. He looked positively immaculate in a frock coat and sand-coloured breeches, with a top hat perched on his head. Every inch the London gentleman.

Eleanor was very aware that she hadn't taken any time to change and remained in the same hideous black gown that she'd worn earlier. Worse, her hair, instead of staying firmly in its bun, had come loose and several tendrils now fell about her shoulders. She must look like some demented creature rather than a respectable businesswoman.

Of the bad outcomes that could possibly happen, this beat everything hands-down. Lord

Whittonstall stood before her, glowering. He obviously hadn't accepted her garbled explanation to Sir Vivian, and Algernon was right behind her, listening to every word.

'And you are...?' Algernon asked rudely.

'Benjamin Grayson, third Viscount Whittonstall.' Lord Whittonstall's gaze pierced Algernon's. 'I take it from your attire you are a vicar?'

'Of this parish.' Algernon's smile became oily and ingratiating as Lord Whittonstall's identity slowly penetrated his brain. 'I do hope we will have cause to see each other on Sunday.'

'Your flock undoubtedly requires your attention. I wish to speak with Mrs Blackwell alone on a matter of urgent business.'

'This entire company will belong to me within the month. My uncle ensured it with his will.' Algernon narrowed his eyes and puffed out his chest. 'You may wish to deal with me instead of Miss Blackwell. I am sure all you require can be provided for. Moles does enjoy an excellent reputation for its business dealings. How can I assist you?'

'What are you doing, Algernon?' Eleanor cried.

Algernon flushed. 'I was merely trying to apprise Lord Whittonstall of the true situation. So he isn't inadvertently misled into thinking you have something to do with Moles' future.'

'My business is with Mrs Blackwell,' Lord Whittonstall said evenly. 'I don't believe a third party is necessary.'

'Our business is concluded, Reverend Forecastle,' Eleanor said pointedly. 'Should the need arise, I will inform you of the outcome of my discussion with Lord Whittonstall. But until this company actually belongs to you, pray remember I am in charge.'

'Very well. I'm going.' Algernon jammed his hat on his head. 'Eleanor, remember I am wise to your tricks. I, too, have friends in high places.'

Eleanor's insides seethed. As if she'd stoop to game-playing!

'*Does* Mrs Blackwell play tricks?' Lord Whittonstall asked, in a quiet but deadly voice.

'Normally I despise game-playing. The truth always comes out. One way or another,' Eleanor replied steadily. 'You may leave us, Reverend Forecastle. I am safe, I assure you. Lord Whittonstall is a gentleman who is held in the highest regard by all who know him.'

Algernon shook his head. 'And you wonder why any decent, respectable man would refuse to marry

you, Eleanor. You wilfully engage in intimate conversation with strangers. Alone. I fear for you.'

Eleanor waited until she heard the outer door
slam. Every particle of her was aware of Lord
Whittonstall. How much had he heard? And
guessed? She wasn't attempting to play some game
with him. It was simply that he did not necessarily need to know the whole truth.

'I suppose I should thank you for getting rid
of the Reverend Forecastle in such short order.'
Eleanor smoothed the pleats in her black silk gown.
'I had feared that he intended to spend the afternoon here, going over the ledgers and generally
disturbing the staff.'

'He believes he is the new owner of Moles?'

'He isn't. The Reverend Algernon Forecastle
has no connection with Moles and he never will,'
Eleanor said pointedly, hoping to end the discussion. 'You must trust me on this. He would ruin
it in six months—nine at the outside. I refuse to
allow it. I will fight with everything I can to avoid
that situation. The employees of Moles look to me
to save them.'

'And who will save *you?*' Lord Whittonstall
asked softly.

Eleanor's heart thudded in her ears. She must

have misheard the words. She shook her head, attempting to clear it.

'I don't follow.'

'You are prepared to fight to your last gasp of breath. I suspect if your employees feel the same way about you as you do about them they wouldn't want you to suffer that fate.'

'You are talking fustian nonsense.' Eleanor gave a quick smile. But his words filled her with a warm glow. She hated to think how long it had been since anyone other than her employees had asked about her welfare. 'I know what I have to do. And I intend to do it. The Reverend Forecastle will be disappointed, but life is full of disappointments.'

'That is good to know.'

She gestured to a chair and he sat down, crossed one leg over the other, displaying immaculate black riding boots that barely contained his muscular calves. Here was a man who didn't spend his time lifting cards and drinking port to excess, but instead rode and fenced. Why did he have to look like that? And make her pulse leap?

'About this business you claim is unfinished...' Eleanor shifted uneasily on her chair. What did he think unfinished? Their fencing? Or the kiss they had nearly shared? She firmly dragged her mind away from the tingle of awareness. That had only ever been in her imagination. 'I must disabuse you of any notion you have. Everything has been concluded between us. Your cousin has his sword and that is the end of the matter.'

'If your stepfather has left the Reverend Forecastle the workings in his will there is little you can do,' he said, watching her through narrowed eyes. 'Particularly if he is your stepfather's next of kin. Even if you succeed in challenging the will it must still go to him. I take it that Moles did belong to him?'

'You give legal advice?'

'It is best to know how the law works. False hope leads to bitterness.'

Eleanor put her hand on her stomach. Somehow it made things harder, having Lord Whittonstall being concerned. Right now all she wanted to do was to crawl home, go to bed and pull the covers over her head. Tomorrow she'd begin her fight back with a new and better plan.

'Yes, if you are interested. Moles *did* belong to my stepfather. My mother neglected to make a proper settlement when she married. Everything became his when they married. Still, we had an arrangement.'

'An arrangement?'

'My stepfather enjoyed spending money rather than making it. He permitted me to run Moles as I saw fit and to invest the profits. I did so on the understanding...' Eleanor held up her hand as she struggled to keep her voice calm. 'No, on the expressed *promise* at my mother's deathbed that he'd leave me the company when he died.'

His eyes widened with astonishment. 'Your stepfather broke his promise? Wasn't he an honourable man?'

Eleanor clasped her hands together. The last thing she wanted was to break down in front of Lord Whittonstall. 'My stepfather has left me Moles and all its investments provided certain conditions are met.'

'And they are...?' He waved a hand, inviting her confidence.

Eleanor bit her lip. Did she dare confess? With his warm eyes regarding her, the temptation grew. She glanced up to where her grandfather frowned down. *One didn't air one's troubles to strangers. One kept them in the family.* She drew a deep breath and wrapped her pride about her.

'Of no concern to you. But they will be met.'

'The Reverend Forecastle seems to believe otherwise.'

'Algernon is an ass. Always has been. Always will be. Hopefully his new wife will make something of him.'

'He is getting married? Was that something your stepfather envisaged?'

'I am sure you came here for reasons other than to discuss the terms of my late stepfather's will or his nephew's matrimonial status, Lord Whittonstall.' Eleanor picked up her fountain pen and pretended to make a notation. She'd regained control of the situation now. She'd moved the conversation away from the dangerous shoals of the will and back to the less dangerous one of why he was there and what he wanted. 'Shall we discuss *your* business? I am sure it is far more interesting.'

He leant forward. His eyes sparkled with hidden fire. 'Why did you give my cousin that sword? What was so desperate that you had to see him today? What sort of trouble are you in, Mrs Blackwell?'

'I explained that at the house.' Eleanor set down the pen with a shaking hand. It was as if they were fencing again, but this time she was the one with a poor grasp of the rules. She'd given her excuse.

He should have accepted it rather than coming here and asking questions. 'For his birthday. Sir Vivian understood.'

'His birthday is not for another two months. It is unusual to give such a gift early.' Lord Whittonstall lifted a solitary eyebrow.

The heat crept up Eleanor's cheeks. If she kept calm he might ignore the blush. *Please let him ignore it.* Confessing the whole truth would be a lesson in abject humiliation. The more she thought about it, the more pathetic and naive she had been even to try. She hadn't understood how wrong it might have gone. What a mistake she'd nearly made. And how could she explain about that moment when she'd thought Lord Whittonstall was going to kiss her? No. Anything but that.

'I wished him to take it to London,' she said, when she considered that she'd mastered her emotions. Those few extra heartbeats had helped her to formulate the perfect answer. 'To show it off. If I had waited for his birthday he would have departed. Gentlemen such as your cousin never stay long in these parts.'

'Until you gave him the sword my cousin had no plans to quit the county. He'd retired up here with his tail between his legs. A gaming debt. But

I don't think your visit had anything to do with his finances. It had something to do with you and your current predicament.'

She shuffled paper about the desk. Against all reason she wanted to lay her head on his chest and confess. She shook her head. She could just imagine his recoiling from her, and that was a thousand times worse. The last thing she wanted was pity from him.

'It was a straightforward request, Lord Whittonstall,' she said briskly. 'I don't see why you think it a mystery.'

'Have you given swords away before?' he asked, tilting his head to one side.

'It is a new initiative.'

'How new?'

'Very new.'

Eleanor pushed away from the desk, stood up, and began to pace the room, stopping in front of her grandfather's portrait. The compulsion to confess grew with each passing heartbeat. But she simply couldn't. It would be opening up a Pandora's box of questions. And she might inadvertently blurt out how she'd wanted him to kiss her. She bit her lip. How much she still wanted him to kiss her. She couldn't remember ever being this aware of a man before. And she'd met hundreds during her fifteen year tenure running Moles.

'A sudden inspiration,' she said, in a tone that few within Moles would question. 'I'm so pleased and relieved your cousin agreed to the scheme. It solves a multitude of problems.'

'How good to know that my cousin was the first to receive your largesse in this manner.'

Eleanor glanced over her shoulder and he gave her an ironic bow.

'A genuine request from my heart, Lord Whittonstall,' she said, putting her hands on her hips. 'I believed when I went to his house, and I still believe now, that Sir Vivian can help this company to succeed. All he needs to do is show off the sword, hold it in combat as I taught you, and the rest will follow.'

She drew a breath. She had told the truth in a roundabout way. Nothing to be ashamed of. She waited for him to concede the point.

'You were desperate for his help—so desperate you were prepared to risk your reputation. You even challenged me to a duel so that you could remain in that library. Then Viv arrived and you made your milksop request. What did you *truly* want from him? What were you afraid to ask for?'

Eleanor stopped and faced her grandfather's portrait. His stern features frowned down on her. She hated the feeling of being judged and found wanting. She had never considered that Lord Whittonstall would be so perceptive.

'It no longer matters because all I want from him now is to publicise the new sword.' She turned and smiled triumphantly. Her point was the killer blow.

Lord Whittonstall took a step towards her. Their eyes met and she became intensely aware of him—his long fingers, the way his dark hair curled at the nape of his neck and his scent. Especially his scent. Extract of masculinity. Her pulse increased its speed and she knew her cheeks flamed. But it didn't matter. She'd won. He'd have to back down.

'I believe it had to do with your stepfather's will. You wanted help with the conditions your step-father has imposed. But once you saw Viv you changed your mind and invented this scheme.'

Eleanor stared at him, astonished. He'd accomplished the verbal equivalent of sending her sword flying through the air. 'How did you know?'

'I am far from unintelligent, *Miss* Blackwell. The truth, if you please. Why did you go to see my cousin? How did you think he could help you? And why did you decide he couldn't?'

Eleanor stared at Lord Whittonstall. He'd guessed, but he couldn't know everything. For a wild moment she considered lying but knew she couldn't. It would only make Algernon's accusations true. And she had no wish to play those sorts of games with Lord Whittonstall. Only the entire humiliating truth would do.

'I went to see your cousin to ask him to marry me, but I decided against it once I had met him again. We would not suit.'

'You would *not* suit,' Lord Whittonstall agreed. A dimple played in the corner of his cheek. 'Why on earth did you think you would?'

'I was desperate.' She clasped her hands together and tried to keep the panic at bay. 'Absolutely and completely desperate. Your cousin had sent a note, begging for the new sword. It fell out of a ledger when I came back from the reading of the will. Serendipity, I thought. I suspect I wasn't thinking clearly or I wouldn't even have tried. I am sorry if you were caused any discomfort by my feeble attempt to solve the problem. I should have known better.'

He gave her a sharp glance. 'What does marrying my cousin have to do with your stepfather's will? Start at the beginning, Miss Blackwell, and perhaps I will understand.'

'In his will my stepfather gives me Moles and all its investments provided I marry. If not, everything goes to Algernon. He also left instructions for him on how to challenge any marriage.'

Lord Whittonstall's eyebrows drew together. He was puzzled more than angry. 'Why would he do that?'

'To taunt me and keep me in my place. To create the illusion of keeping his promise.' Eleanor gave a light shrug to show that she was over the hurt. 'He knew my feelings on the subject of marriage and the inequities that women can suffer. I'm not very good at holding my tongue, but he tolerated me because he enjoyed the prosperity I brought to Moles and his purse.'

'You are not overly enamoured of marriage?' He gave a little nod of understanding. 'Perhaps he was acting for the best. Most parents want their children or indeed their stepchildren to be secure within the confines of marriage. Perhaps he had your best interests at heart and chose to show them in a unique fashion.'

'I saw how my stepfather treated my mother.' Eleanor caught her bottom lip with her teeth. There was no need to catalogue her stepfather's verbal cruelties. He might have abstained from physical violence after she'd threatened him with a sword but his tongue had been razor-sharp and he had had the unerring habit of finding weakness.

'That is a shame.' He regarded her with sorrowful eyes.

After this interview she doubted if she'd ever see Lord Whittonstall again. But his pity was the last thing she wanted or required.

'Until my stepfather's will was read I was determined never to marry. I wanted to put my energy into the family firm, rather than into hating him.'

'Not all men are beasts like your stepfather,' he remarked, his face becoming resolute.

She knew then that he understood.

'I am sure you will find someone. But what is the hurry? Why did you rush out and contact my cousin? The instant after you returned here from the will-reading you must have sent the note. It is the timing, Miss Blackwell.'

'You would make a good detective. One final twist.' Eleanor clasped her hands together and struggled to keep her voice even. 'I have to marry within the month.'

Lord Whittonstall's eyes had opened wide.

Thank heavens! He finally understood the truly shocking nature of the will. All the nervous energy flowed out of her.

'There would not be time for a proper settlement if you had to marry within a month,' he said. 'Lawyers are notoriously slow about such things. They often take longer than posting the banns.'

'You appear remarkably well informed.'

His lips turned up in a smile. 'I've a variety of cousins. Some of my female cousins are more headstrong than others and have wanted to marry quickly out of devotion to their fiancés. But it would be financial suicide. Their interests have to be protected. Fortune-hunters are ten a penny in London these days.'

A warm glow filled Eleanor. Against all hope or expectation Lord Whittonstall understood the obstacles she faced.

'I see you appreciate the crux of the problem. I know only too well what happens when there is no proper settlement.'

'You do?'

'My mother married too quickly. I think she wanted to erase the shame of my father's death from her conscience. She was the sort of woman who wanted to be married and have a home.'

Eleanor bit her lip. All her mother had wanted to be was petted and admired. A decorative object rather than something useful. Eleanor's strength was her brain rather than her beauty, and therefore she trod a very different path from her mother.

'But why did you stay if you found the situation intolerable? Surely you could have started a new company? Or, failing that, found a job elsewhere.'

'I gave a promise to the employees when my father died,' she said, needing him to understand her reasoning. 'I promised them that if they stuck with me and the company I would give my all for them—and I have. Moles has more than prospered in my tenure.'

'These men are all skilled. They could easily find jobs elsewhere. Would they do the same for you?'

'A promise, Lord Whittonstall, is a promise.'

'And you were prepared to compromise your life for a business?' His eyes showed his incredulity.

Eleanor pressed her hands together and held back a frustrated scream. It wasn't just a business. It was her heritage. Something that had been built with the sweat and blood of her forefathers. It was the only thing of her family's that she had left. She was the last one. It was the only place where she truly belonged.

Suddenly she knew what she had to do. She had to make him understand. Then he'd see why she'd changed her mind, and that it had nothing to do with her reaction to him.

'Come with me. See the forge. Meet the men who work here and then you will understand.'

'I doubt I will.'

'You doubted I could best you at swords.'

He gave a sudden barking laugh. 'I stand corrected.'

Giving in to her impulse, she led him out of the office and gave him a brief tour of Moles. She showed him where the iron was kept, how it was made into steel, and then how the swords were made. All the while, whenever they encountered anyone, she introduced him to the men who made Moles—from the most junior errand boy to Mr Swaddle, who was busy with his experiments. To her great relief Lord Whittonstall asked intelligent questions and didn't patronise her. He seemed genuinely surprised to learn how long some of the men had worked there, and of their hopes for the future.

'There,' she said, when the tour was done and they had stopped outside the office building, underneath the apple tree that her great-grandmother had planted. The blossom was late this year and had just started to open. 'Do you understand now?'

'They certainly hold you in high esteem. When the blacksmith needed you to inspect the latest shipment of iron Mr Swaddle took me aside to explain about how you had single-handedly rescued this company.'

'Mr Swaddle is given to exaggeration. We worked together. Everyone did. The men did the physical labour. I simply did the accounts and worked to get the swords where they would be appreciated. If a fifteen-year-girl could do it, how hard could it have been?'

She found it hard to keep the bitterness from her voice. She shook her head. Algernon's pompous pronouncements had affected her more than she'd thought possible.

'And you have continued to do it for the last fifteen years?'

'It has become a habit.' She ducked her head. 'I enjoy my work and enjoy working with the men. Mr Swaddle, for all his eccentric dress, is a genius with steel.'

'He doesn't like Algernon Forecastle. Doesn't trust him. He made that quite clear.'

'These people depend on me. I can't allow Algernon to ruin their lives.' Eleanor drew a deep breath. 'I went to see your cousin to secure their future. I went to offer to pay his debts in return for a marriage on paper. But I couldn't do it. And I shall have to live with my selfish decision for the rest of my life. When the time came I was a coward and couldn't even say the words. So I asked your cousin for his help in another way. It may do some good. There—now you know the truth and my reasons. I hope you are satisfied.'

'You care a lot about these people?'

'Yes, I do.' She stood with her feet firmly planted on the ground and dared him to make a derogatory comment.

A light breeze blew a strand of hair into her mouth. She pushed it away and still he looked at her.

He put a hand on her arm, keeping her there. His brows drew together and his eyes darkened to coal black. 'Marry *me*.'

Eleanor froze. A thousand disconnected thoughts flew through her brain. A huge part of her screamed that this was the miracle she'd been longing for. Lord Whittonstall had asked her to marry him. But she also knew she didn't want him offering out of pity. She had her pride. 'I wasn't begging you for help. I was attempting to explain.'

'Is there something wrong with marrying me?' Ben stared at Eleanor Blackwell. He had not intended to ask her to marry him when he'd arrived at Moles, but now, seeing her here and hearing her story, he knew it was the right thing to do. The perfect solution to his problem and to hers. Mutual assistance.

She pulled away from him. 'You have no reason to want to marry me. Don't patronise me. I can't stand it.'

'It is far from a joke.'

A deep frown appeared between her delicate brows. 'But why would you want to marry me?'

'You mean I'm no wastrel and therefore don't need your money?'

She bent her head and picked at her glove. 'Something like that.'

'I took an irrational dislike to the Reverend Forecastle.'

'Enough to marry someone to spite him? I doubt it.'

Ben watched the crown of her head. Her bravery impressed him, but he also wanted to touch her hair. His desire to kiss her had grown, not diminished. Most unexpected. He desired her. 'You want the truth?'

Her grey eyes met his. 'I find it best. You could marry anyone. Why me? Why now?'

How to answer her? He could hardly explain about the spark and his desire to pursue it. It remained far too new and tenuous. In any case, this marriage was not about desire or romance; it was about the possibility of companionship and duty. A new start—one in which he'd atone for old mistakes. He didn't want to make false promises.

He pushed the unwelcome thoughts away and concentrated on the apple tree behind her.

'Like you, duty drives me. In this case my mother has impressed upon me the necessity of marriage. I need a wife. You need a husband. It is quite simple. For my part, it solves a multitude of problems which show every sign of increasing rather than diminishing.'

'Things are never that simple.' Her brow furrowed as if she was trying to find a hidden flaw.

'I'm a widower, Miss Blackwell,' Ben said slowly. 'I loved my wife, but she died before we had children. I have an heir in Viv but my mother keeps pressing me to marry. Her demands are growing in strength with each passing year.'

'And you listen to your mother? You hardly seem the type.'

Ben paused. After her revelations, she deserved an explanation. She didn't need to know about Alice, or the way she'd died. All that was in the past. However, he *could* explain about what drove his mother.

'My father died before I was born. Mama devoted her life to raising me. Within reason I try to listen to her. And each year the season has become more intolerable as she artfully arranges for me to meet more eligible young women. Each year the age gap grows and I find less and less in common with her protégées.'

'Why don't you tell her to let you choose your own bride in your own time?'

He captured Miss Blackwell's hand and raised it to his lips. 'You are very alike in your determination. Do your employees say no to *you* after all you have done for them?'

She withdrew her hand and moved away from him, turning her back on him. Her black dress hung limply about her body, emphasising her slender angularity and the straightness of her back. Ben found it impossible to discern what she was thinking. Silently he willed her to accept his offer.

'And you would agree to a settlement in which I keep control of Moles?'

'It will be hard to do within the timeframe, but I have no objection.'

'And you want it to be a paper marriage? If you find someone else we could part amicably. It can be done.'

'It won't be,' Ben said shortly. He tore his mind away from the past. There would never be another woman like Alice. He wasn't looking for that heady feeling. That part of his life had finished five years ago, and he knew ultimately whose fault it was.

Her cheeks went pink. 'I am well aware that this will be a business arrangement. I want you to understand that I wouldn't stand in your way...should it happen.'

'Is it settled? Will you stop being stubborn?'

'But you don't live here. And I can't leave Moles.'

'That will solve another problem. Viv needs funds. I have no wish to return to Leicestershire. I will purchase his property. That should put you near enough for those times when you are needed.'

He waited. Suddenly tense. This was far removed in many ways from the manner in which he'd proposed to Alice all those years ago. Then he had laughed and kissed her. She'd asked him what had taken him so long before throwing her arms about his neck. He glanced at the apple tree in front of the office building. Funny, the apple trees had hung heavy with blossom then as well. He suspected Alice would have approved, even if this marriage was to be unorthodox.

She held out her hand. It trembled under his fingers. 'Then I accept with gratitude. You have been more than kind, Lord Whittonstall. You have saved my company from an awful fate.'

'Please call me Ben...as we are to be on intimate terms, Eleanor.'

Her tongue wet her lips, turning them the colour of unopened apple blossom. 'Intimate?' she whispered.

'Try it.'

'Ben.' She gave him a level look. 'We are speaking about a marriage on paper. I have no expectation of anything else.'

He reached out and pulled her firmly into his arms. As her body collided with his he registered the fact that she was less angular than he'd supposed. He lifted her chin slightly and regarded her face. The more he looked at her, the more he found to appreciate.

He brushed her lips with his, intending it to be

a quick demonstration. But the instant his mouth encountered hers he knew that he wanted more. He gathered her more firmly in his arms and drank. She parted her lips. When his body thrummed with desire he put her away from him. They both stood there, chests heaving and blood pumping far too fast.

'It will be a proper marriage, Eleanor. My mother expects an heir and I have no intention of denying her.' He put two fingers to his hat. 'Good day to you. The banns will be posted. You will meet your stepfather's conditions.'

Eleanor wandered back into her office. The men studiously avoided her gaze, pretending interest in the ledgers and other bits of paper.

Her fingers explored her mouth. Lord Whittonstall...*Ben*...had kissed her in full view of everyone. Put his mark on her. She'd never dreamt a kiss could be like that. Heart-stopping. Exciting. And absolutely meaningless to him. He'd been trying to prove a point.

Eleanor hugged her arms about her waist. A real marriage. With the possibility of children. Someone to carry on after her. She'd not bargained for that. She'd never even considered it. Ever since she was fifteen she'd concentrated on Moles, and now this...the domestic side of things and all it entailed. It shook her.

She carefully closed the door behind her and glanced up to where her grandfather frowned down at her.

'I must make a success of it, Grandfather. How hard can it be? To be a viscountess and all that entails? If I can run a company, I can do that. I have to. I've given my word.'

Chapter Four

Any task was much simpler when its components were written down. More straightforward, less daunting.

Eleanor surveyed her latest list—the seventeenth she'd penned since she woke. Only half-past eleven and she'd already crossed off five items. Progress at speed.

Sleep had been next to impossible, so she'd worked through the night. She'd gone over Moles' accounts and made lists and schedules of everything that had to be done in the next few weeks. Her appointment with her solicitor was scheduled for tomorrow. His reply had arrived with the first post.

She'd already sent over an outline of what she wanted, and once she knew it was in hand she'd arrange for the banns to be posted.

Eleanor tapped her pen against the table. Could she trust Algernon to fulfil the duties of his office and read out the banns? Did she even want to be married in his church? The thought of Algernon officiating at her wedding made her nauseous. She put a big question mark beside 'banns' and regarded the next item: 'find a suitable dress'.

'What do you think you are playing at, Eleanor?' Algernon said, pushing past Jenkins the butler and coming into the breakfast room. 'I'm not one of your suppliers who gives you extra time to pay because you sigh and bat your eyelashes. Or one of your competitors who feels sorry for you when the new furnace doesn't arrive on time. Oh, yes, you needn't look so surprised. Uncle told me all about how you saved Moles and why. They *pitied* you, Eleanor.'

Her butler gave her an apologetic look when she raised an eyebrow. The last thing she needed today of all days was an interruption from Algernon.

Why couldn't he be like normal vicars and be interested in his parishioners, or failing that some esoteric academic study? Why was he coming to plague her—and so early in the day?

One would think he'd have the decency to wait until the afternoon, or better not even to appear without sending a note round. And, from the belligerent set of his jaw, it appeared he intended to stay awhile.

'Ah, Algernon,' Eleanor said, forcing her voice to stay calm and pleasant. 'I see you have inherited my stepfather's bad habit of twisting history. It had nothing to do with my feminine charm—something that you *always* accuse me of lacking. It is precisely because I pointed out the financial opportunities to Mr Smith and Mr Oley that Moles flourished and became the company it is today. Moles bought all of Mr Smith's iron ore until he retired and then we bought his business. We continue to share transport with Mr Oley—only now his swords are shipped with ours, instead of the other way round. It saves costs and benefits everyone. Business, not pity.'

She finished with a brilliant smile.

Algernon opened and closed his mouth several times as he went his special shade of puce. 'I will take your word for it.'

'Why are you here, Algernon? I feel certain it is not to go over my various triumphs in business. However, if you insist, I must warn you it will take some considerable time.'

'Francis Percy, the curate at Broomhaugh, contacted me about your pathetic scheme this morning.'

The back of Eleanor's neck prickled. Her life needed fewer complications, not more. 'Who is Francis Percy, and why should he contact you about me? Does he wish to purchase a sword? If so, I would suggest he go through the proper channels. We do have a backlog of work and cannot make exceptions…even for your friends.'

Algernon jabbed his finger at her. 'There has been a query about posting banns for one Eleanor Blackwell.'

'Has there?' Eleanor laced her fingers together and rested her chin on them. It would appear Ben had wasted no time. She should have thought of holding the wedding at the Broomhaugh church. It would solve a multitude of problems. 'Fancy that.'

Algernon stuck his nose in the air. 'Merely posting the banns with some unknown does not mean you will fulfil Uncle's will. I have instructed Percy to ignore the request.'

'You have instructed him to ignore the request?' Eleanor gripped the table and struggled to breathe. Was she going to have to fight everyone for this wedding? 'Will he do so?'

'I have every reason to suspect he will. He

thought the enquiry a bit unusual, as the man was unknown to him and you don't live in the parish. He asked for my advice, and I was happy to give it.'

Eleanor's heart thudded. If Ben had waited she would have had it all organised and done before Algernon started creating complications. 'Your advice was worthless. Do you know what you have done?'

'It may surprise you, Eleanor, but I'm held in the highest regard in certain circles. My advice is actively sought. Even the bishop—' Algernon stopped and tapped the side of his nose. 'Your ploy is painfully obvious.'

'Ploy?' Eleanor stared at him. 'Why would making an enquiry about posting banns be a ploy? I am attempting to follow your reasoning here, Algernon.'

'You intend to plead a broken heart,' he said with a huge sigh. 'Left at the altar in the last moment and therefore in need of more time. However, I have hardened my heart and I intend to enforce the will to the letter. The very letter. You need to post banns and marry like a good Christian woman— in the church where you intend to worship.'

Eleanor stared at Algernon. Was it just her or did he think that *all* women lacked intelligence?

'What happens to members of the clergy who wilfully refuse to post genuine banns? What sort of sanction is sued against them?'

'That is not the case here.' He gave an insufferable sigh. 'I know you went over to that area yesterday. And Percy has indicated that it was a note, rather than an actual face-to-face meeting. He has no knowledge of the intended bridegroom. Neither you nor this phantom bridegroom lives in that parish. Why should banns be posted there?'

Eleanor choked back angry words. Algernon was a duplicitous snake, but becoming angry with him would not solve her problem. Calm. Cool. Collected. Her grandfather had always told to hold her temper. Knowing about a problem was halfway to solving it.

'It is good to know that you are having me watched and are so busy blackening my name, but it was my intended who made the enquiry, not me,' she said finally, when she'd mastered her emotions. 'He currently resides with Sir Vivian at Broomhaugh Hall.'

'Eleanor, Eleanor, Eleanor... Stop spinning fantasies. Who would marry *you?*' Algernon's lip curled as he examined her up and down. 'Someone blind and deaf? Feeble-minded?'

Eleanor struggled to keep her voice even. Losing her temper was precisely what he wanted her to do. Years of dealing with her stepfather had taught her that if she lost her temper, he thought he'd won. 'Lord Whittonstall. You met him yesterday.'

'You seek to flannel me, sending me off on a wild goose chase.' He shook his head, tutting. 'How many times must you be told that *gentlemen* don't marry women like you? They require a bride of a different stamp, someone of delicacy and refinement.'

'Algernon Forecastle! You...you...' Eleanor drew a deep breath and tried to search for the words that would display the correct amount of contempt for this creature. The man's arrogance was truly staggering.

Algernon gave a tiny pleased smile. 'I suspect you are annoyed that your little scheme has been discovered so readily. Next time try something a little less transparent.'

'I'm annoyed that my highly productive morning has been interrupted for an asinine reason. Go! Get out of my sight!'

'Very well.' Algernon rocked back and forth

on his heels. 'I shall go and confront Lord Whittonstall. You are merely using a member of the aristocracy because you think I won't challenge you if you are pretending to marry someone powerful.'

Eleanor bit the knuckle of her thumb. The easiest thing would be to allow Algernon to confront Ben. However, the last thing she wanted was to seem like some feeble woman, running to Ben every time she hit the slightest hiccup. It would appear as if she could not handle the situation, and she'd spent her entire adult life handling *everything.*

She straightened her shoulders and lifted her chin, meeting Algernon's pig-like expression of overstuffed smugness full on.

'Lord Whittonstall is very well connected and you are about to insult his choice of life partner. You should consider the consequences of such a move very carefully. I tell this to you as someone who knows you and wishes to stop you from appearing foolish and blighting your career. You know how your uncle used to warn you about that.'

Algernon puffed out his chest. 'I won't make an ass of myself. I never do. Uncle was wrong—completely wrong about me. Miss Varney says...'

'You are giving a pretty good impression of foolishness thus far.' Eleanor crossed her arms. The man would try the patience of a saint. 'On second thoughts, why should I want you to stop? Go ahead! Go and see Lord Whittonstall. As I said, he is staying with Sir Vivian Clarence. Ask him. Inform him of what you have done!'

Algernon's nostrils flared. 'I am sure he does not realise what you are like. How unnatural you are! You possess nothing of true refinement, Eleanor. You have no charm to entice a man of any standing or wit.'

Eleanor stood up and advanced towards him, shoulders back and head up so that she emphasised their height difference. Once, many years ago, after she had discovered him abusing the downstairs maid, Eleanor had challenged Algernon to a duel, bested him in short order, but only extracted an apology when he had stumbled, trying to run away, and the tip of her sword had pointed at his fat neck. After that he'd left the maids alone…at least in her household.

She reached for one of the swords on the sideboard.

Algernon blanched and took two steps backwards.

'I *will* be getting married,' she said between

clenched teeth. 'You are *not* going to sabotage this wedding. Is that understood?'

'I wish to save you from folly and embarrassment.' He raised his hands. 'You are so used to being shocking, Eleanor, that you fail to realise what you are doing. For that reason I forgive you. No harm is done as your scheme has been discovered and is at an end. We part as friends.'

Eleanor stared at Algernon in astonishment.

'You are very pompous, Algernon,' she said, gesturing with the sword for emphasis.

'Lord Whittonstall would never marry someone like you.' Algernon scrambled to put a dining chair between them. *'Ever.'*

'I heard raised voices. Are you in trouble, Eleanor?' Ben appeared behind Jenkins. His shoulders seemed almost too broad for his frock coat and his tan breeches followed the contours of his thighs perfectly. Her pulse leapt.

Relief quickly followed by horror flooded through her. Ben had discovered her chasing Algernon around the room with a sword. Did Algernon's words have a ring of truth? *Was* she truly so shocking and lacking in refinement?

Hastily she retraced her steps and returned the

sword to its normal place. Why had he appeared at that moment? Why not earlier?

'You should be careful, Reverend Forecastle. My fiancée has a way with swords.'

'You mean it is true? The rumour?' Algernon squeaked.

'Very true,' Ben replied. He wandered over and picked up the sword, balancing it on his hand before making an experimental flourish with it. 'Well-balanced but flexible. A prototype, Eleanor? The hilt is a bit old-fashioned, though.'

'My great-grandfather's. He used a special formula of steel which has been lost. It normally rests there to remind me of the possibilities and all that I have still to achieve. It never gets used.'

'Ah, I see. Pity.' He set the sword back down on the table. 'And what did the Reverend Forecastle do to deserve being chased with the sword? Is it something I can assist you with?'

Eleanor's heart beat faster and the heat on her cheeks grew. It was wrong of her to be pleased that he was here and taking care of the Algernon problem. She had wondered when they would see each other...

She'd even made a list of possible reasons why he would stay away—a list that peeked out from under the others. Eleanor hurriedly straightened her papers. All the while her heart kept singing— Ben was here, living proof that she would be getting married. She wasn't alone any more. It made things easier, but she had no desire to become dependent on him. And it certainly didn't mean that she wanted to give up fighting her own battles. It just made victory that much sweeter.

'Algernon has heard about our impending nuptials.' Eleanor hated the way her voice sounded breathless. She swallowed hard and tried again. 'Apparently enquiries have been made at Broomhaugh parish which he believes are a harum-scarum attempt to circumvent my stepfather's will.'

'I thought it best.' Ben inclined his head and his eyes burnt fiercely. 'Churches are notoriously difficult to book. My cousin Isabella had dreadful trouble a few years back. To my mother's annoyance she ended being married in Hampstead rather than in St James's.'

'*You* m-m-made the enquiry?' Algernon tugged at his stock.

'I wish to marry Eleanor as soon as possible.' Ben lifted an eyebrow. 'Miss Blackwell is far too rare a prize to allow to slip through my fingers through tardiness on my behalf.'

Algernon shrank under the ferocity of that gaze. Eleanor fought against the temptation to punch the air in triumph, clasping her hands behind her back and attempting to keep a bland expression.

'I believe there might be some parishioners who wish to see me. Urgently.' Algernon slithered towards the door.

'It surprises me that Broomhaugh's vicar should be so indiscreet.' Ben's voice became glacial, stopping Algernon in his tracks.

'Not the vicar. It was the curate who wanted advice, apparently. Algernon is well-known within his circle for the quality of advice that he gives,' Eleanor said, fixing Algernon with a steady gaze. 'Algernon has informed him he must ignore the request. However, I suspect Algernon will now inform Mr Percy that he made an error of judgement.'

Algernon tugged at the bands about his neck, his watery eyes blinking furiously. 'He is a friend of Miss Varney's and wanted to keep me apprised of the situation. I have known Eleanor for years and she has never had even the faintest whisper of an offer before. The timing seemed too good to be true.'

'Miss Varney is Algernon's fiancée,' Eleanor explained at Ben's perplexed expression. 'A very recent acquisition.'

'I must offer you felicitations, Reverend Forecastle.' Ben made a deep bow. 'When is the happy date?'

All the gesture did was increase Algernon's discomfort. 'It isn't settled. Miss Varney is of a delicate nature, and negotiations with her father are proving difficult.'

'I can only surmise that a part of the reason she accepted him was his inheritance from my step-father—or rather what he supposed he would inherit,' Eleanor confided. 'A terrible thing to be married for your money—isn't that what you said to me, Algernon?'

'I may have done,' Algernon admitted reluctantly.

'You should find someone who wants to marry you for who you are now, Reverend Forecastle, and not for your expectations,' Ben said with a severe frown. 'Expectations have a way of slipping through one's fingers.'

Algernon threw back his shoulders. 'Miss Varney

is the sweetest of women, and her parents are naturally desirous of an excellent station for her in her married life. Expectations maketh the man. My uncle only put in that blasted codicil because he promised Eleanor's mother on her deathbed. He didn't actually expect Eleanor to fulfil it.'

'In my opinion, character and integrity is what makes a man,' Ben said pointedly.

A tremor of pride went through Eleanor. Ben had demolished Algernon without raising his voice or giving way to temper.

'Expectations count for very little.'

'They count for something with Miss Varney and her mother!' Algernon replied haughtily.

'Confiding about your good fortune before you've actually acquired it generally leads to humiliation, not to acceptance,' Ben said coolly.

Algernon blinked furiously. 'Miss Varney might have accepted Francis Percy's offer, and I couldn't have had that! She will be my ideal companion for life.'

'Indeed. And the ends justify the means.' Eleanor suddenly understood the young curate's desire to best his rival. It did not have anything to do with trying to stop her marriage or seeking advice but with underlining the precariousness of Algernon's position. A stab of pity went through her, but it was something that Algernon had to solve on his own and without jeopardising Moles.

'Your rival told the truth,' Ben said, looking hard at him. 'Miss Blackwell is doing me the honour of becoming my wife.'

'Why? Why marry someone like her?'

A deathly silence fell over the room. Even Algernon had the grace to look embarrassed as the full rudeness of his outburst slowly but inexorably dawned on him. Ben's look of astonished disbelief spoke volumes.

'It is none of your business, Algernon,' she said into the silence.

'Surely you must have a reason?' Algernon persisted.

Eleanor hated the way her stomach tensed. The last thing she wanted was for Ben to give Algernon a detailed explanation about the reasons why they were marrying. It was a business transaction. That was all. No finer feeling or romance. It was no good her suddenly becoming attached to him.

'Because I want to,' Ben explained, in a voice that dripped with long-suffering patience. 'Isn't that the reason that most people do things?'

Algernon's Adam's apple bobbed. 'Huh? I don't follow. You *want* to?'

'I shall leave you to puzzle that out for yourself.' Ben looked Algernon up and down. 'I am not a man you wish to cross, Reverend Forecastle. I advise you to remember that. I trust that our banns will be posted in good order and that there will be no more attempts at sabotaging this marriage. I know where the blame would lie.'

Algernon looked as if he'd swallowed a particularly nasty plum. 'Sabotage is a harsh word.'

'Next time, Algernon, make an appointment.' Eleanor waited a beat and added, 'Please.'

Algernon gave a great *harrumph* and seemed ready to argue. But another glance from Ben made him scamper out of the breakfast room, muttering under his breath as he went.

'I believe we have seen the last of him,' Ben said with a smile.

'He is very determined.' Eleanor sank down on her chair. Her limbs trembled as if she'd fought a long bout.

'He has no idea how determined *I* am.' A muscle in Ben's jaw jumped. 'Eton was full of bullies like him, and some far worse. I learnt to fight my corner.'

'Thank you for your help.'

'The banns will be read. We will be married before the time runs out. I gave you my word.'

A warm tingling rushed through Eleanor and she fought the desire to throw her arms about his neck. Rather than drowning in his eyes, she concentrated on the pile of papers.

'It is good to know,' she said when she trusted her voice.

'I regret you found out in that way.' Ben's fingers curled around hers. 'I hadn't considered that the curate might be indiscreet. I was seeking to do the most expedient thing. And I suspected that the Reverend Forecastle might be installed in a parish around here.'

She pulled away. His apology did strange things to her insides, making her want to kiss him once more. But she also wanted him to know that she could stand on her two feet quite ably. She didn't expect or require his help. 'You weren't to know. Algernon would have found another excuse to ruin my morning. Hopefully now he will understand that his inheritance is only the small legacy my stepfather left him.'

'You need to contact your solicitor for the precise wording of the codicil.'

She glanced up at him, startled. 'We are getting married. That should suit.'

'Best to avoid any contest to the marriage. Moles could be tangled in chancery for years if we are not careful.'

Eleanor began to rearrange the pens and papers. He was actually concerned about Moles and its prospects. That should be enough. It would be so easy to start to have feelings for him, but that wasn't what this marriage was about. It was purely business. 'Algernon is not that clever. Bombastic and full of his own importance, but he wouldn't resort to something like that.'

'He is desperate, and desperate men do desperate things,' Ben said.

Eleanor concentrated on the inkwell rather than watching his mouth and the way the dimple flashed in and out of his cheek. Later, when she was alone, she knew she'd go over each gesture, but for now she wanted to appear calm and collected. 'I will keep that in mind.'

'You haven't asked me why I am here.' He dug into his pocket and withdrew a tiny box. 'I saw it in the jeweller's in Consett. It seemed appropriate. It reminded me of you.'

With trembling fingers, Eleanor opened the box.

A small pearl was embedded in a simple band of gold. Not showy, but definitely expensive. Tears pricked at the back of her eyelids. She blinked rapidly and took an unsteady breath. For the first time she allowed herself to believe. It was going to happen. Ben would make it happen. Moles would remain hers. She'd fulfil her promise to those people who mattered.

'Why?' she breathed.

'To forestall awkwardness such as you just encountered. I hadn't anticipated a lovelorn curate seeking to score points from his rival.' A smile transformed his face. 'Put the ring on. See if it fits.'

She slipped it on. The ring made her hand feel heavy and alien, as if it belonged to someone else. 'It fits.'

'I am a reasonable judge of size.' Ben frowned. 'Do you like it?'

'It is most unexpected.' She turned her hand from side to side, trying to marshal her thoughts. She wanted to like the ring. She knew it was important to wear it. And yet she felt like a fraud, as if she was claiming to be something she was not. 'It will take some getting used to. I'd never anticipated wearing a wedding ring. Let alone an engagement ring.'

'Most brides do wear one.'

'Ours will be a different sort of marriage. We both know why it is happening and that there is no pretence towards finer feeling.' The words came out in a rush.

He shrugged. 'But it will be a marriage all the same, and you shouldn't have to explain to everyone why there will be one. It will put your employees' minds to rest.'

Eleanor closed her hand about the ring. Not only her employees. The ring made it seem far more real to *her*. It was tangible proof that he intended to honour his commitment. And she knew that in the middle of the night, when she worried, all she had to do was to look at the ring and believe.

She hadn't expected kindness from him. Most of the other aristocracy she'd encountered never seemed to bother about the small details. They expected someone else to do it for them. 'Was that the only reason why you came over here?'

A smile tugged at his features. 'A picnic seemed in order.'

'A picnic?' Eleanor glanced out of the window, hoping for a good excuse to refuse. He was being kind, but with every heartbeat she found him more attractive. His words from yesterday thrummed in her mind—this marriage was about duty. She'd be wrong to hope for anything more. The late-morning sun shone down. The sky was the sort of blue that only happened in the spring and only a few clouds dotted the sky. 'What sort of picnic?'

'Eating outside. Being out in the fresh air...with me.'

'There are things I have to do at the forge,' she said quickly, before she gave in to temptation.

'You employ a foreman. Is it a crisis? Why not take time to enjoy the day?'

Eleanor considered telling him that it was a crisis, but knew if it was serious she'd already be there. And, what was more, she guessed he knew that as well.

She averted her gaze. 'I like to keep to a routine. Prevent crises before they happen. My men need me.'

'Why not try trusting your men? For the afternoon?' He lifted an eyebrow. 'You could consider it a meeting if you must. We'll discuss the wedding and other serious matters.'

Eleanor held her breath. Did she dare spend more time in his company? She shouldn't, as it would be too easy to pretend that it meant something more than a business transaction. 'Yes, I will.'

She stopped. She had meant to refuse.

His eyes twinkled with hidden lights. 'You won't be sorry.'

Eleanor took another look at the ring, turning her hand this way and that. The girl who had once longed for a real marriage and family threatened to escape from the box she placed her in all those years ago, when she'd discovered her father dead in the office and his suicide note by his side. She slammed the box shut.

'One time only. Moles must come first.'

Chapter Five

Ben relaxed against the dark blue horsehair cushions of his carriage while Eleanor sat bolt upright facing him. Her hands were holding a heavily beaded reticule, and a bonnet marginally less ugly than the one he'd destroyed was perched on her head, shielding her expression.

He hated not seeing her eyes, not having a clue about what she thought. To his surprise, he wanted to know.

He blamed himself for Forecastle's intrusion earlier. But now all that was behind them and he could concentrate on Eleanor. Every time he saw her he found something more to look at—yesterday it had been her eyes that had haunted him, today it was the shape of her lips and the way her hands moved.

'Have you been on many picnics?' he asked, to keep from reaching out and drawing her to him.

The spark from yesterday had grown, not diminished. He wanted to taste her lips and see if they were as sweet as his memory of them. But he also wanted her to trust him and learn more about her. She intrigued him. He'd never met anyone like her before. What sort of woman sacrificed her life for business? Particularly one who seemed to hold such passion for life?

'Not many. There hasn't been time recently.' She picked at the beads of the reticule. Ever since they'd left her house she'd seemed nervous and uncertain. Answering his questions with the minimum amount of words and keeping her head down, only allowing him the briefest glimpses of her amazing grey eyes. 'But I haven't just worked. I *do* enjoy myself.'

She gave a little nod, as if the subject was closed and satisfactorily explained. Ben drummed his fingers on the seat. His guess of this morning was correct. Eleanor Blackwell had had very little frivolity in her life.

'Name a ball you've been to.' He leant forward so that their knees brushed. 'The one you remember the most.'

She laced the reticule strap between her fingers.

'Go on,' he urged. 'Which one holds the most precious memories?'

'Before my father died I went to the Assembly Rooms in Newcastle,' she said in a low voice. Her bonnet tipped backwards, revealing her face. 'When I entered the grand ballroom it was as if I had entered a magical place, touched by a mysterious fairy glamour, something that couldn't exist in the real world.'

She gave a long sigh. From where he sat Ben could see her eyes glow with the memory. It transformed her face, softening it and making her seem vulnerable and heart-stoppingly beautiful. Only the memory of a doomed romance could have made her look like that.

Hers was not a conventional beauty, not like Alice's had been—fair and sweet—but striking, with more than a hint of latent passion. He struggled against the temptation to pull her into his arms and lose himself in the depths of her mouth. Eleanor was to be his wife, not his mistress.

'Go on,' he said, not wishing to think about the man who had made her look like this. 'Why was that ball at the Assembly Rooms magical?'

'I have never forgotten the profusion of colours.

How the dresses shimmered like a sea of rainbows and the chandeliers twinkled like stars.'

'Was that all?' Ben tilted his head and regarded her shining eyes. Surely there was more? 'No clandestine meeting with a handsome man who swept you off your feet? No fairytale romance?'

She wrinkled her nose. 'Mama became upset because one of the candles dripped on my new gloves and insisted we leave before the ball was over.'

'And later...?'

'Someone had to make sure that Moles was properly run.' A firm note in her voice implied any further discussion of romance was unwelcome. 'There wasn't time to attend balls at the Assembly Rooms. My mother and stepfather went to Newcastle or Durham several times, but I stayed at the foundry where I was needed. Balls meant so much more to Mama.'

Ben silently vowed that Eleanor would have the time to enjoy life now she was under his protection. She had given her youth for her employees and her selfish mother and stepfather. Once her period of mourning for her stepfather was up he intended to make sure she possessed a wide range of dresses in any colour she chose. Along with hats and bonnets that complemented her face and colouring rather than draining the vitality out of her.

Unexpected guilt tugged at him. He knew the heady feeling of falling in love and being loved back. He'd experienced it once with Alice. But Eleanor would never experience it. She'd have to settle for second-best—friendship. He pressed his lips together. Yes, he could be Eleanor's friend and make life easier for her, more pleasant and perhaps a little more frivolous.

'How many balls have you been to since the Assembly Rooms?' he asked when Eleanor didn't answer his question.

Eleanor crossed her arms and glared at him. 'I have been to a number of dinners for the guild of swordmakers. They have dances as well. It wasn't all work. In any case, attending any function with my stepfather was always a trial.'

'And did you dance?'

'Very rarely.' She shifted slightly on her seat, sitting bolt upright. 'I wanted people to think of me as Mrs Blackwell, the woman who runs the best sword manufacturer in the world. Not Miss Blackwell, the one who can't get the steps to the Harlequin right or whose lace has slipped.'

Ben smiled at the picture. Somehow he doubted

that Eleanor's lace ever slipped. 'I'm sure dancing would not upset your dignity or the regard the world holds you in.'

'Will it be necessary for your wife to dance?'

'I would hope my wife would enjoy it.' He closed his eyes and clearly saw Alice's flushed and happy face shining up at him as they exited the dance floor at Almack's. The memory was not as painful as it once had been. Surprisingly. 'Alice adored dancing. She was an excellent dancer. There was always a queue of men wishing to dance with her. But she always saved the Roger de Coverley for me.'

'Are you a good dancer?' Eleanor asked, bringing him back to the present.

'Passable,' Ben admitted. 'I do have vouchers to Almack's, and Mama insists that I take lessons in order to know the latest figures and sets. She doesn't want people to comment that her son is a disappointment.'

She fiddled with the clasp of her reticule. 'Your mother sounds very involved with the social whirl.'

'Mama is. It is her lifeblood,' Ben confirmed. His mother had a different way of dealing with grief than he did. She was determined to enjoy life and to play her full part. As soon as she had been able to she'd re-entered society, and spent her nights flitting from one party to the next. Instead he had discovered the pleasures of solitude since Alice's death.

'My mother used to enjoy such things as well, but...' She gave a small shrug. 'Providing a living for the men had to come before everything.'

'The truth, Eleanor. You used your employees as an excuse.'

'At first I couldn't take the risk of people commenting. Everyone expected me to fail. Giving them something to whisper about was not an option. I had to work twice as hard as a man.'

'And later...?'

'Later I had better things to do with my time.' There was no mistaking the firm note in her voice.

But Ben wondered about the tone. Was there an underlying fear? Anyone who could fence as well as Eleanor had to be able to dance. Ben gave Eleanor an indulgent smile. The memory of Eleanor's eyes when she spoke about the sea of rainbows and the chandelier twinkling niggled and pulled at his conscience. Eleanor deserved better than she had had. She deserved a chance to enjoy those things, a chance not to work twice as hard as a man.

'My mother will smooth your way if you require it. Mama has a kind heart, and is always looking for someone to sponsor. In recent years she has regularly sponsored one or two young ladies.'

'Has she indeed?' she asked in an arch tone.

'Mama will look on it as her duty to introduce her new daughter-in-law to society. Only the best will do.'

Silently he vowed that was *all* his mother would do. Eleanor had the strength of will to withstand his mother, and he had learnt from the past—his wife would know whose part *he* took.

She dipped her head so that he could see only the crown of her bonnet. A vague disquiet filled him. It was what she wanted, wasn't it? For Alice, society had been everything. She'd lived for the social whirl—or he had thought she had.

'Yes, when we go for the season I will ask her advice…if I require it.'

Not the enthusiastic response he'd been looking for, but it meant that he didn't have to warn Eleanor about his mother's tendency to take over. Eleanor had far more backbone than Alice.

The memory of how Alice had excitedly caught his hands, twirling round and round, after she'd learnt of his mother's proposed sponsorship assaulted him. On the other hand Eleanor seemed less than pleased. Retreating back into her shell, becoming Mrs Blackwell again instead of the passionate woman he wanted to see.

'You've been to London before?' he said carefully, attempting to understand what was wrong.

'Ben, my company sells swords,' she said with a forced laugh. 'London is a major market. I've been to London before. I generally go several times a year. I know many members of the ton. Personally. I know how to behave in the correct manner and have no need of a *nursemaid*.'

'What is the problem?' he asked, perplexed at her vehemence. 'My mother would only want to help. Alice used to lean on her for advice. Mama has exquisite taste, and Alice endeavoured to emulate it.'

'There isn't a problem.' She turned her head and gazed out of the window. 'Where we will be having the picnic? Is it far?'

'Not too far.'

'Good, I want to go to Moles afterwards. It wouldn't feel right if I missed a day.'

Ben pressed his lips together. She had neatly ended the conversation. But it wasn't over. He would give her the things she had missed. He'd ensure that she took her proper place in society when the time came. She deserved a bit of frivolity in her life, something to make her eyes sparkle.

Eleanor dusted the final crumbs of poppyseed cake from her fingers. True to his word, Ben had laid on a splendid repast on the banks of the Derwent River, right near Broomhaugh Hall. She had eaten everything, determined to enjoy it rather than worry about the proposed visit to London where she'd be sponsored by his mother.

A shudder went through her at the mere thought of an endless round of parties, lunches and dancing, surrounded by some of the brightest and most beautiful. She'd been to London and seen what they were like—the wit, the beauty and the up-to-the-minute fashions.

How could she possibly leave Moles for so long? How would her employees cope? The season took months and months.

And there were the hours of dancing lessons and fittings to consider. *Exquisite taste.* Her stepfather's words flitted through her brain—*awkward, lacking in any grace, two left feet.* And the final insult, when she'd had a new ballgown last year— *a beanpole wrapped in gaudy rags.* Somehow she had to find a way to avoid that fate. She wanted

Ben to like her, rather than highlight her short-comings.

Would he kiss her again, as he'd kissed her yesterday? Her body tingled in anticipation at the mere thought.

'Another slice of poppyseed cake for your thoughts?' Ben asked, holding out a tempting piece of cake.

Eleanor shook her head and pulled her lace shawl tighter about her shoulders. The brilliant blue sky of earlier had grown dark with clouds. 'The first was enough—more than enough. I'm fine. Truly a wonderful meal.'

'Shame to let the last piece go to waste.' Ben waved the piece of cake before leaning back in his chair and stretching out his legs so that they brushed her skirt.

Eleanor stilled, uncertain what she should do next. Flirtatious games happened to other women. She knew how to be charming, and how not to take various gentlemen's remarks seriously. But that was part of doing business and had to do with Moles swords rather than with *her*. What Ben was doing was about her, not her swords.

'I'm completely full.' He had to know that her skirts were there. The pressure of his leg against hers was exciting, daring. What was the proper way to respond? She didn't want to seem forward, or for him to laugh at her. They were marrying for duty rather than because of a mutual attraction. 'I've eaten far too much as it is. I can't remember when I last had such a delicious meal.'

'Viv will have to allow us to keep his cook.' He paused and looked directly at her. The piece of cake still rested in the palm of his hand, tempting her. 'Unless you'd prefer to bring your own?'

'Mrs Nevin serves both as my housekeeper and cook,' Eleanor said, trying to rein in her wayward thoughts. Keep the topic on everyday things and not ask him to feed her. 'I normally eat simple meals and she is looking to retire. You must have that last piece.'

'If you insist, it will be my pleasure.' He devoured the piece, licking his fingers to get the last crumbs.

Eleanor's stomach tightened. There was something sinful in the way he seemed to take so much enjoyment from it.

'I have an idea.' Eleanor pleated her napkin and ran it through her fingers, trying not to think about how he had sucked the final crumb from the tip of his finger.

Ben rested his chin on his hand. Something fluttered inside her at the look. He made her feel as if she was the only person in the world. She ruthlessly quashed the feeling. Theirs was to be a marriage of convenience. He had no need to flirt with her. She was misinterpreting things. And if she started to think otherwise she'd be disappointed.

'Do tell. Does it have to do with cake?'

'It has to do with introducing you to the area. Making sure that everyone meets you. You are certain to be the talk of the region. It is not often a viscount removes himself here.'

A mutual helping out. Nothing more. She refused to become one of those love-starved females that various men made jokes about. Moving in a man's world had taught her a few lessons about the necessity of guarding her heart. She didn't want the disappointment or the inevitable failure.

'I suspect they will want to meet you more than me. It will happen in time. Don't be over concerned with it.'

'We'll be spending the better part of the year up here rather than in London. Society can't be neglected.' She attempted to get her thoughts in a coherent order and not suddenly blurt out something about the length of his lashes or how his fingers tapered. 'Once the mourning for my stepfather is over I think we ought to have a ball here, to introduce you to our neighbours.'

She knew her voice was far too breathless and reedy.

'That is a splendid idea, Eleanor. Truly splendid.' His face broke into a wide smile which warmed her all the way down to her toes. 'And it solves a few other problems. Mama and her schemes will have to give way. We shall not go to London this season. *Bravo,* you! I knew marrying you was a good idea.'

He raised her hand to his lips. The soft touch made her knees go weak and she was glad that she was sitting.

Was it so wrong of her to want to be a success and see his eyes light up because of something she had done? If she made it exciting enough they might be able to forgo the season altogether.

She withdrew her hand and picked up another linen napkin, dabbing her mouth to hide the heightened colour on her cheeks. 'It is decided. Once I can go out in society again properly, without causing comment, we will have a ball up here. It shouldn't take long to organise.'

His eyes turned sober. 'If that is what you want.

Balls are a huge undertaking. My mother always complains that I fail to appreciate the enormity of the task. Will you have time?'

'I will make time. I am more than capable of organising it as well as looking after Moles.' Eleanor crossed her fingers. She ran a company. How hard could organising a ball be?

'You have experience with such things?'

'Did Sir Vivian agree to you acquiring the house?' she asked, changing the subject. 'Otherwise we shall have to be sure to acquire a house with a ballroom. The house I shared with my stepfather only has a good-sized parlour.'

His eyes danced, as if he knew exactly why she was changing the subject. 'Viv isn't sure if it is entailed or not. But he is quite willing for me to lease it and refurbish as I see fit. There is no hurry, and the lawyers can sort it out in due course. I trust it meets with your approval as Broomhaugh does have a large ballroom?'

'The interior is…' Eleanor searched for the right words.

'Not in keeping for a married couple?'

'Precisely.' She smiled back, pleased he'd understood what she had been trying to say. 'I'm not criticising his taste.'

'Perish the thought.'

'It is just that something with perhaps more dignity would suit the married condition better.'

He burst out laughing. 'What bothered you so much?'

'The picture with the swords,' Eleanor blurted out, before she thought. She wanted the ground to open up and swallow her.

'I suspect Viv is fond of that picture and will be taking it with him.' His eyes twinkled. 'It is interesting that an unmarried lady should take note of it. Let alone mention it.'

'I'm not just any unmarried lady. I noticed the swords in the picture first of all. They were holding them all wrong. No sense of balance.'

He let out an infectious roar of laughter. 'Only you, Eleanor, would notice the swords first!'

'What is wrong with that?'

'Nothing at all. It is refreshing. Very refreshing.' He leant forward and touched her cheek. His breath lightly tickled her skin. 'You missed a crumb. Just there.'

'Did I?' she whispered. Her entire body seemed infused with fizzy bubbles and everything was concentrated on him. He was going to kiss her again and she wanted him to. She wet her lips in anticipation.

'It's gone now.' His voice sounded deep, but he didn't move towards her.

'I should be getting back.' Eleanor stood up and managed to knock her bonnet askew in the process. She rapidly undid the ribbons and tried to straighten it. Only making matters worse. All the while he watched her with a dark gaze. She hated how much she wanted him to kiss her. How the only thing she could think of was how she'd wanted to turn her face towards the palm of his hand. It was probably something that most women did naturally, but she knew that if he rejected her gesture she'd curl up with shame. It was better not to try.

She took two steps backwards—and stumbled over a tree root.

'I've kept you from your work for long enough,' he said, putting out a hand to steady her.

Eleanor picked at the seam of her glove rather than looking him in the eye. She didn't even want to think about the possibility of being kissed. 'Do you mind?'

'Your hard work has made Moles into what it is today.' He straightened her bonnet. She stood completely still, hardly daring to breathe. 'And I had best take you back there.'

'Yes, you must. We shall have to do this again some time.' Eleanor's voice faltered at his look. Once back on familiar ground she would be fine, but right now she wanted to sink down to the ground and die of embarrassment. She'd asked for too much.

'I look forward to it,' he said with extreme politeness.

'As do I.'

Eleanor's heart thudded in her ears. The first drops of rain hit her bonnet. Everything would work out well. She could cope and she wouldn't borrow trouble. But she wasn't going to go on another picnic tomorrow. The weather would be in her favour.

'The picnic was very pleasant,' Eleanor said as she stood beside the carriage, carefully keeping her skirt out of the mud. The sharp shower had stopped and various puddles dotted the yard.

Ben leant forward. His lips brushed her forehead. A chaste kiss, but one which sent warmth pulsing throughout her body. 'More than pleasant.'

'It is good the wedding is settled,' she said, concentrating on a particularly large puddle.

'Shall I pick you up here or at the house to-morrow?'

'Tomorrow?' she squeaked. 'The rain...'

'Having discovered such a charming luncheon companion, I am determined to repeat the performance. I dare say I can find a summer house or somewhere to shelter. After all, we are allies in the fight against Algernon Forecastle.'

Eleanor bent her head and pretended to fiddle with the beads of her reticule. She had an ally. She wasn't alone in the fight. She'd been alone for such a long time that it felt strange. 'I would enjoy that...very much.'

He brushed her cheek. 'Until tomorrow.'

Eleanor watched as the carriage rumbled away. Was it wrong of her to want to be more than a friend? Even the dream of such a thing seemed impossible. She concentrated on the sign above the office door. She was marrying to save her business, not marrying because he was attracted to her. To lose sight of that simple fact was the road to heartache.

Hours later, long after Ben had returned Eleanor to Moles, he sat in his dressing room at Broomhaugh, holding a miniature of Alice.

The most amazing thing about today was that he'd been able to speak about Alice without a sharp pain running through him, without that awful sense of guilt washing over him.

Alice's pale features with their rosebud mouth peered up at him. The miniature of Alice had been done for her first season, and she hadn't wanted it done at first, preferring to be his valiant follower, a girl he tolerated. His mother had taken her under her wing and produced a lovely, gracious woman—someone who had totally bowled him over as she'd walked down the stairs and graciously extended her hand. From then on he'd worshipped the ground she trod on. But until he'd read her journal after her death he hadn't understood the pressure she'd felt from his mother. In her way Alice had coped, but Ben wished he'd known.

Even as he looked at the miniature Ben found his thoughts returning to Eleanor and her mobile mouth. He loved watching the way her face reflected her moods and how passionate she was about the making of swords. When she forgot herself she became positively radiant, glowing with vitality.

Did he really want his mother changing that? Did he want another Alice when he had loved the first one so much? Eleanor had a stronger backbone, more determination. His mother might be able to help her, but she wouldn't be able to change her.

He put his fist to his forehead. He hadn't expected the pull he felt for Eleanor. How much he'd wanted to kiss her again. The passion bubbling up inside unnerved him. He'd thought he'd never feel like this about another woman. Alice wouldn't have wanted it.

Looking at Alice's picture, he knew he was wrong. She would have wanted him to go on and choose another bride. Just as he would have wanted her to choose another husband. He'd seen his mother's loneliness. His mother had spoken of it so many times that he'd become tired of hearing it. But, unlike his mother, Alice would have wanted his bride to be one he chose.

'She's nothing like you, Alice, but I think we could become friends and allies.'

A friend and an ally. It wasn't the same as what he'd had with Alice but it could work. He wanted it to work. All he knew was that he liked Eleanor's spirit and the way she kept fighting for her cause. His feelings for Eleanor were different from his ones for Alice.

He carefully put Alice's miniature in the mahogany box he used for handkerchiefs. He didn't need it to remind him of his loss. He carried that in his heart.

Eleanor would have all the advantages of being his wife except the romance. He would be her friend and give her the life she'd missed.

Chapter Six

The blistering heat from the foundry's furnace beat against Eleanor's face. It felt good to be doing something practical, rather than sitting in her office waiting for the sound of Ben's carriage.

If Mr Swaddle could produce the sort of steel she hoped for she looked forward to presenting Ben with a new sword as her wedding gift—a sword curled inside a hat, sharp enough to be used, just like the one family legend proclaimed her great-great-grandfather had made.

She knew the precise design of the sword, but the exact composition of the steel had eluded her in six attempts over the past three weeks. Last night, as she'd sat packing various keepsakes for her move, the solution had come to her—they needed to use a different-shaped crucible. She'd brought in her grandfather's favourite one and insisted on using it for good luck.

'Just about ready to pour, Mrs Blackwell,' Mr Swaddle said. 'You and Timmy might want to stand well clear. I wouldn't want anything to happen to either of you two.'

'Nothing will.' Eleanor forced her mind away from Ben's absence today and back to the most dangerous part of the operation—pouring the steel in the bar mould. She tried to gauge if the steel was ready to pour. Too soon and it wouldn't set correctly. Too long and the metal would froth up like milk and be completely spoilt. 'I know what I am doing.'

'All the same, Mrs Blackwell, it is best to be cautious. I don't want you getting hurt. You and Timmy stand on the other side of me.' Mr Swaddle wagged his finger at his young grandson, who had recently started working at Moles. 'And mind you, Timmy—none of your tricks. Not a blessed peep out of you once I start pouring. I want to concentrate.'

Eleanor moved closer to where Timmy stood and held the skirt of her new white muslin dress with its triple ruff away from the furnace. Normally she'd have worn leather breeches, but the chance that Ben might appear and whisk her away for lunch remained—even though it was long past the dinner hour—so she had covered the dress with a heavy leather apron and worn heavy leather gloves. Safety first, just as her grandfather had taught her.

'Do you think my slight tweak of the formula worked?' she asked, standing on one foot, trying to improve her view of the crucible. 'And the slightly different-shaped crucible? I'm sure that is the very one my grandfather used when he wanted a more flexible steel. I found it stuffed in the bottom of a drawer at home.'

'Could work. The crucible appears sound. I can't rightly remember why we stopped using that one.' Mr Swaddle made a considering noise. 'Don't get your hopes up, Mrs Blackwell. Steel can be a tricky thing. I've tried for years to recreate this here particular formula. Sometimes I think the secret died with your great-granda and sometimes I'm certain it did.'

She ignored Mr Swaddle's pessimism. After fifteen years she was used to his gloomy forecasts. 'A more flexible steel is needed to keep up with the requirements of today's swordsmen and possibly other people.'

'Not thinking of branching out, are you, Mrs

Blackwell?' The elderly man laughed. 'I can remember the speech you gave that first day, about
how swords were our business first, last and
for ever. Real stirring it was, too, Timmy. And
I thought, Mrs Blackwell here might be young,
but she is just like her grandfather—dedicated
to sword-making. My God, she even fashioned
swords with her own hands to start with.'

'Not many,' Eleanor hastened to add as Timmy
looked at her open-mouthed. At the start she'd had
to prove herself, and she'd done it in the only way
she knew how—demonstrating to the men that
she intimately knew every facet of the business.

'Your father thought new-fangled machines were
the answer. How many times did that grindstone's
leather strap break afore you scrapped it?'

'Merely a thought,' Eleanor said, putting her
hands behind her back and crossing her fingers.
She knew what her grandfather had thought about
new-fangled machines but he wasn't in charge any
longer. *She* was. And times were changing. They
were in a new century. Swords would always be
their main business, but it would be good to find
new markets just in case. She'd get Mr Swaddle
used to the idea. Slowly.

'What would you use the new steel for?' Mr

Swaddle shook his head. 'Sides making this right fancy sword for Lord Whittonstall's pleasure, like? How many people will want swords that fit in their hat? Have you thought about that? Where's the market you are always talking about?'

'Lord Whittonstall and I have had a discussion about the possibilities of travelling engines,' she said, trying another tack. 'I wondered about machine parts and if our steel could be used to make coils and other springs. Lord Whittonstall believes the age of the machine is dawning. And he's very interested in steel's potential.'

Mr Swaddle shook his head and made an irritated noise. Eleanor raised an eyebrow, willing him to answer. If he stated his objections she could counter them.

'You shouldn't be doing this just to please Lord Whittonstall,' he said finally, using the same indulgent tone he used with Timmy when he wanted to coax the lad into doing something new. 'What does *he* know about steel and the like? He's an aristocrat—probably never worked a day in his life.'

Eleanor clamped her mouth shut. Mr Swaddle made it seem as if the only reason she wanted to pursue this was to please Ben and that wasn't true. It did make sound business sense.

Under her glove, she twisted her engagement ring about her finger. It was strange how in a few short weeks, she'd become used to its weight. Her hand now felt naked if she didn't wear it.

Ben did know. He wasn't some brainless dandy like Sir Vivian. She'd learnt that much during their picnic discussions. He made her think, and she enjoyed the way her blood fizzed when he was around. Somehow life was more sparkling and full of possibility after she'd seen him.

'Sword-making is our business. Same as it's always been,' Mr Swaddle said, warming to his theme. 'We don't need no jumped-up peacock of an aristocrat saying we should do this or that. When did *he* ever make swords?'

'You go a bit far, Mr Swaddle. Lord Whittonstall *is* my intended.'

'Begging your pardon, Mrs Blackwell, but I don't want to see you get your head turned by a fine pair of eyes. You've always done what is right for the firm, I know that, but you have a man in your life now. I…that is the men here want you to keep making the decisions. We don't want to see you get hurt. Now I've said my piece, as I told Mrs Swaddle I would. We've worked together long enough, and I respect you and your judgement, but I will reserve judgement about *him*.'

Eleanor forced her angry retort down her throat. Mr Swaddle was being over-protective about the firm. She wasn't going to get hurt. And she most definitely wasn't about pleasing Ben. It made sound business sense to see if their steel could be marketed elsewhere—if they could take advantage of new markets.

'Lord Whittonstall is remarkably well informed. He thinks there will be a travelling engine soon, on account of the war and grain prices. The coal-owners will demand it. He knows of a couple of factories out near Wylam working on it,' she replied evenly. 'I want Moles to grow and take advantage of this potential market. The new formula could be key. Strong, but supple.'

'*Bah,* a locomotive engine will never happen—not in my lifetime. Wishful thinking. You might as well ask for wings while you are at it.' The elderly man rolled his eyes to show his incredulity. 'If God had intended us to fly along at unnatural speeds he'd have given us wheels or wings or something like that. That's what I always tell my son, Davy, when he starts on with that twaddle.'

Eleanor squared her shoulders and stared directly into Mr Swaddle's face. She had thought it would be simple to expand in that direction, particularly as Ben seemed enthusiastic about the prospect. She'd have to figure out a way to bring her men along with her. An unhappy and suspicious workforce would balk if she tried to force change through. She'd learnt that to her cost in those first few months after her father had died. But she could do it, and she could get Ben interested in the business. It bothered her how much she wanted their conversations to continue after they were married and how much she feared he'd lose interest.

'Thank you for your opinion, Mr Swaddle. I shall keep it under consideration as I always do.'

'You know I'm right, Mrs Blackwell.' Mr Swaddle gave a sudden smile. 'Stick to what we are good at and the company prospers. You've always said that. Swords first. You were the one who wanted to take Moles back to the days of your grandfather and what a powerful lot of good that has done. Moles makes the finest swords. Orders are flooding in. How many months do people have to wait now?'

'Three months,' Eleanor admitted. At Mr Swaddle's look, she added. 'More like five.'

'There—you see? We don't have time, Mrs

Blackwell. You keep us doing what we do best, just as you have always done, and we will be right fine.'

'Right fine,' little Timmy echoed.

'But we could *try*…to see if it's possible. If there is another market for our steel…' At Mr Swaddle's astonished look, she added, 'Moles produces some of the finest in the world. Why shouldn't it be put to other uses?'

'Aye, we could, but we have too much on with the new sword range and all. You wanted a light-weighted lady's rapier and that is done—all except the hilt.'

Mr Swaddle busied himself with the crucible of metal, twisting it this way and that before starting to withdraw it from the fiery furnace. Eleanor clamped her lips shut. Pouring the molten metal was always the trickiest bit. From childhood Eleanor had been trained to keep completely silent.

The bright yellow-white liquid trickled from the pot, sending sparks shooting through the air. She took a step closer and crossed her fingers. The new formula *had* to work!

'Eleanor! Are you in there?' Ben's voice resounded in the shed. 'Eleanor!'

Her heart did a funny leap. Ben had arrived after

all. She would see him today. But he couldn't come in here. It was far from safe. Once Mr Swaddle had finished the pouring she'd go out and greet him.

'Ben! Wait there. I will be out. Give me a moment,' Eleanor called out. 'Stay where you are!'

'Eleanor?' Ben appeared in the doorway. 'This place looks like a scene from Hades! What the blazes are you doing in here in a dress?'

Mr Swaddle swung the pot, missed his timing. A tiny bit of metal fell on the ground, hissing and spitting, narrowly missing her foot. Timmy ducked and curled up in a ball, as his grandfather had undoubtedly taught him. Instinctively she caught her skirts and held them away from the metal. Mr Swaddle *had* to right that crucible before any more spilled. It was behaving almost as if…as if the crucible had a crack.

Her mouth went dry. A white line had appeared on the side of the crucible—a sign that the worst was about to happen if Mr Swaddle didn't put the crucible down.

'Mr Swaddle!' she shouted. 'The crucible!'

Mr Swaddle paid no heed and started to pour the molten liquid into the ingot mould. The metal bubbled through the ever-growing crack, hitting Mr Swaddle's wrist. His agonised scream echoed around the shed. The air filled with steam and the acrid smell of burning. And all the while molten steel poured out of the top like milk pouring out of a jug.

Ben started to move from the doorway.

'No!' Eleanor shouted, holding up her hand to stop Ben. 'Stay where you are, Ben. Don't move a muscle. It's far from safe. Drop the crucible, Mr Swaddle. Do it *now!*'

Ben watched in horror as the molten metal bubbled and spewed out of the crucible, flowing onto the floor. Mr Swaddle's agonised screams bounced off the walls. Time slowed. Images froze on his brain. Eleanor's white dress. The brilliant yellow-white of the metal. The young boy cowering beside the table. The elderly man reaching out towards her as more metal spewed out.

'Drop the crucible, Mr Swaddle! Drop it, I say!' Eleanor shouted.

'I daresn't, Mrs Blackwell. Your dress! You'll go up like a light!'

Eleanor shot Ben an agonised glance.

Ben stumbled forward—half running, half falling. He grabbed the man's arm. 'Do as she says! Drop that crucible! Now!'

'But you don't understand!' the man shouted. 'If I drop this the metal might hit Mrs Blackwell.'

'Mr Swaddle!' Eleanor shouted. 'Ben! Turn the crucible towards the furnace!'

Without hesitating Ben shoved the man's hand forward, forcing him to let go of the crucible.

More metal spilt on the ground, hissing and spitting, narrowly missing Ben's boots as the crucible hit the floor and broke into two.

Ben grabbed a bucket of water and plunged Mr Swaddle's hand and wrist in. For an instant the man's wrist seemed to be silver. Then the metal dropped to the bottom of the bucket, leaving behind an angry red and white mark.

Over Mr Swaddle's grizzled head Ben caught Eleanor's eye and saw her mouth *thank you*. He itched to pull her into his arms and check that she was fine, that no particle of her delicate skin had been marred by the hot metal.

'How bad is the burn, Mr Swaddle?' Eleanor asked, coming to stand beside Ben.

His eyes roamed over her. She appeared slightly shaken but uninjured.

'Hurts like the very devil!' Mr Swaddle gasped as he sank to the ground. 'I ain't done something like that in I don't know how long. Blasted thing.

Begging Your Lordship and Mrs Blackwell's pardon. It were the noise, like. I told you Mrs Blackwell—no noise when I am pouring. It's the rule. Isn't it, Timmy?'

The young lad clamoured that *he'd* kept quiet as a mouse.

'It wasn't the noise,' Eleanor said with great firmness. 'You get that straight out of your mind, Mr Swaddle.'

'What was it, then?' the elderly man demanded.

Eleanor knelt on the dusty floor beside Mr Swaddle, keeping his arm in the bucket. Her white dress contrasted with the gloom. Her face became very earnest. 'The crucible split. I saw the line of fracture as it went. A white line snaking up the crucible just before the metal started frothing.'

Both the elderly man and the young boy went pale.

'Lord Whittonstall saved your life,' Eleanor continued. 'You think about what could have happened if you had kept hold of that crucible when it finally went.'

'Way-aye, you're right, Mrs Blackwell,' the young boy piped up. 'Lord Whittonstall is a hero— not some jumped-up know-nothing popinjay like Grandfather said.'

Ben tried to catch Eleanor's eye. Had she been defending him? She'd never said that some of her workforce thought him akin to Viv, but it made sense.

'I'm pleased I was able to stop the accident from getting worse.'

'If you want to blame someone, blame me,' Eleanor said.

'You weren't to know, like, Mrs Blackwell. It looked fine.'

'Do crucibles normally break like that?' Ben asked carefully.

'They are made of clay. Prevention is best—always checking when they are warm and discarding any which are unsound. It is near impossible to tell when they are cool,' Mr Swaddle said. 'But sometimes it happens. Moles has a good record. Better than most. Mrs Blackwell insists on it. Like her grandfather on that, she is. Other foundries… well…men die.'

'We will have to do an inspection of all the crucibles,' Eleanor said, a frown developing between her brows. 'I won't have Moles getting a bad reputation. Or more men getting hurt.'

'It can wait until you are better, Mr Swaddle,' Ben said decisively. Eleanor still appeared shaken.

The last thing he wanted was for her to put Moles above her own needs now. 'The important thing is to get that burn properly tended.'

'I'm right grateful to Your Lordship. There's not many men who'd have done what you did. You are no popinjay, but a right honest-to-God gentleman like me young grandson said. I'm sorry I ever thought otherwise.'

'Do you have any honey?' Ben asked, ignoring the praise. 'My nurse swore it was the best thing on God's green earth for burns. Without treatment that burn will be nasty.'

'My wife's mother swore the same. I will see to it when I get home.'

'And you are going home *now*.' Eleanor nodded towards where the young lad cowered, obviously too frightened to move. 'Timmy, take your granda home. Your granny will know what to do.'

'But I can't leave this mess.' The elderly man appeared close to tears. 'My tools…the new steel…'

'It will be cleared up,' Ben assured him. 'I will make sure.'

'*I* will clear it up,' Eleanor said in a firm tone, and Ben could understand why she was obeyed. A duchess could not have said it with more authority.

'Timmy! The metal has stopped falling. You are safe now. Your grandfather needs you.'

'But you are in your pretty white dress, Mrs Blackwell. I can wait while me lad does it.'

'You are far more important to me than any gown, Mr Swaddle.' She made a shooing motion. 'The dirt will wash clean. Now, go. And, yes, I know—next time I'll wear my breeches.'

'Accidents do happen, Mrs Blackwell,' Timmy said. 'I am sure Lord Whittonstall would rather you were safe. You could have gone up in flames. It won't take me hardly any time.'

'But I didn't. Now, go and take your grandfather home, Timothy Swaddle.'

The elderly man and his grandson went off, leaving the shed in silence. Ben pressed his lips together. He hadn't fully appreciated how respected Eleanor was.

Rather than asking him about why he was there or suggesting they leave, or more importantly looking after herself, Eleanor went straight to work, scraping the spilt metal off the floor.

'Like the lad said, someone else can do it.' Ben started to grab her arm.

'I told Mr Swaddle I would. It has to be put in

the correct place. There is a proper order to things. He wouldn't have departed so easily if he thought otherwise.' She pulled away from his grasp and bent a small piece of steel. Her red lips frowned. 'All that work and the steel is still far too brittle.'

'You are in a dress,' he argued. 'It is the sort of dress that deserves a picnic, from what I can see of it under your apron.'

He waited for her smile and her agreement to his scheme.

'I'm keeping away from the furnace.' Eleanor shook her head. 'Mr Swaddle worries too much. Normally I wear breeches but…anyway, it doesn't matter. Today was a reminder of what needs to come first.'

Ben's stomach twisted. She'd worn the dress because of him. 'I'm sorry I was late, but…'

'Serves me right for being vain,' she said, not letting him finish. 'It won't take me long to clean up. I gave my word to put this part of my world to rights. You can wait in my office. We'll go then.'

'Is there anything I can do?' Ben asked, refusing to let her dismiss him. 'It will be quicker.'

'I can handle it on my own.' She took off her gloves and placed them on the bench. Her engagement ring gleamed in the shadows of the shed. 'It won't take me long. I know where everything goes.'

'But I want to help.'

'It is not necessary.' She quickly and efficiently picked up the tools and placed them in a large wooden box. As she moved her apron slid over her curves, highlighting the fact that she was very much a woman rather than some burly steelworker. 'Truly it is not. I know what I am doing. It is not as if I am a novice. I grew up in this place.'

'Then I will stay and keep you company. I want to.' Silently Ben willed her to understand. He wasn't about to leave her after what she'd just been through. Someone needed to look after her. It amazed him how important she'd become to him in the past few weeks.

'Nothing else is going to happen, if that is what you are worried about.' She gave an irritated shake of her head which only served to emphasise the difference between her femininity and this place. 'I'm almost done. Mr Swaddle's favourite chisel has rolled under the table in the confusion. Once that is retrieved we can go.'

She knelt down in the muck and dirt, reaching

forward, then gave a muffled curse and drew back her arm sharply.

'What's wrong, Eleanor?'

'Listen to me prattling on about safety,' she said, rubbing her wrist. 'I wasn't paying attention and my arm has knocked the crucible.'

'How bad is the burn?'

She lifted her head towards the ceiling and blinked rapidly. 'Today is far from my day. Give me a moment. I will be fine.'

'Let me see,' Ben said. 'Show me and let me be the judge.'

She reluctantly held out her wrist. He could see a fading red mark, as well as three faint scars obviously from other similar accidents. It tore at his heart to see her delicate flesh marked in that fashion. Silently he vowed that he'd do everything in his power to make today the last day that such a thing happened.

'You've burnt yourself like this before?'

'Not for a long time.' Her unflinching gaze met his. 'When I first started I had to prove that I could do everything. It was the only way I could gain the men's respect.'

'And when you were burnt? What happened then? Did they respect you more?' he asked softly.

Her lips turned up in a tiny smile. 'I made sure that I didn't give way to hysterics and that did it. It is far from easy to run this sort of place if the men don't respect you. My grandfather taught me that.'

'But you have their respect now. You don't have to try any more.'

'My wrist has stopped hurting.' She lifted her arm. 'All gone.'

He shuddered to think of what she had gone through. She was making light of it, but he knew it had to have been hard. If anything the knowledge renewed his determination to make her life easier. He wanted her to understand that she didn't have to stand alone any more. She didn't have to pretend to be better than a man any more. He was there to help her.

He rubbed his thumb over the inside of her wrist. The silky-smooth skin slid under the pads of his fingers.

'It doesn't seem too bad, but allow me to bathe it in cold water. Put my mind at ease.'

She pulled back. Her eyes became fierce. 'You don't have to. I can look after myself. Always have done. Consider it a fiancée's prerogative.'

'I insist. You have me to look after you now.'

'When you put it that way…how can I refuse?'

He lifted a ladleful of water and dribbled it over her wrist. The mark faded to nothing. He brought the wrist to his lips and was unable to resist licking an errant drop of water from her skin. Her skin tasted of heat and of something pure Eleanor. 'There, you see—all better.'

Fighting his instinct to take her in his arms and kiss her, he forced himself to step away from her and to remember where they were.

She stood gazing at the broken crucible as she cradled her wrist. 'It was my fault, you know, despite what Mr Swaddle said.'

'The accident? How could that be your fault?' he said as lightly as he dared.

'I was the one who insisted on using that particular crucible. I brought it from home,' she said with a tremor in her voice. 'I thought it would be good luck. And now Mr Swaddle will be off work for weeks. It was my stubbornness. I wouldn't listen when he suggested that we use another crucible. Only that one would do. It was wrong of me!'

'Hush, it is over now.'

'It can be so hard to forget.' Her hands started to shake.

He reached out and drew her into his arms. She drew a shuddering sigh and laid her head against his chest. He closed his eyes and held her tight. Her body quivered, but slowly she relaxed and stilled.

'All better now, Eleanor?' he murmured against her hair.

'I forgot to put the chisel away,' she said, leaning back against his arms. Her cheeks flamed a bright pink. 'Mr Swaddle will be upset if everything is not properly put away.'

'You talk too much,' he said, inhaling the floral scent of her hair. He wound a strand around the end of his finger.

'Do I?'

Her lashes framed her grey eyes and her mouth had turned a particularly appealing shade of deep rose. He lowered his mouth and tasted. He'd meant it to be a gentle touch, but the instant his lips met hers a wild heat surged through him. Hot. Molten. He knew he had to drink his fill, but he also knew where they were. *Patience.*

He placed a kiss on the corner of her mouth, intending to stop. She twined her arms about his neck and pulled him closer, brought his mouth back to hers. There was a faint desperation in her kiss, as if she were battling demons.

Her lips opened under the pressure. His tongue touched hers. Rather than drawing back, her tongue played with his, tangled and teased. Life-giving, but awaking a deep-seated hunger within him—a hunger he had been sure had vanished. He wanted to devour her and sink into her softness. He wanted to spend time exploring and unwrapping her, bringing her to the heights of passion. But not in a dusty shed, and not now.

He froze, and the realisation that he'd failed to explain why he was late hit him. Eleanor needed to know now. Before anything else untoward happened.

'We must stop,' he murmured in her ear, trying to cling to his final breath of sanity. 'There is something you need to know. Something I should have said earlier.'

'Hmm?' She buried her hands in his hair and pulled his mouth back to hers. 'It can wait.'

'Benjamin!' an aristocratic woman's voice thundered from just outside the shed door. 'When are we going to meet this fiancée of yours? You promised.'

Chapter Seven

Eleanor jumped back from Ben's arms. Ice-water splashed through her veins. A woman was outside the shed, looking for him! She'd never have kissed him like that if she'd thought... And certainly not if she'd known that he'd brought someone with him.

'Who's that?' she asked in a panicked whisper, looking over her shoulders towards the open door.

'My mother. Mama arrived for our wedding this morning. Unexpectedly.' Ben tilted his head to one side. 'That is why I was late. Why I was looking for you. I wanted you to meet her.'

The news thudded through Eleanor. His mother! Here! Somehow, when she'd thought about it, meeting Ben's only parent had always been going to happen some day in the distant future, when Eleanor was beautifully dressed and thoroughly in control. Certainly not today and like this. Today was lurching from one disaster to another.

Eleanor put her hand on her stomach to quell the butterflies. This was far worse than dealing with something concrete, like Mr Swaddle's injury or a slight burn to her wrist. This was about dealing with a woman who was used to operating in the highest echelons of society. And she wanted to make a good impression. Her stepfather's taunts thudded through her—*scarecrow, ragamuffin, distinctly lacking in any grace.* Apt descriptions of how she must look at the present time.

'But you should have said when you first saw me,' she said, scanning his face to see if she could discern how big a fright she looked.

His hand smoothed a tendril of hair from her forehead. 'Other things took precedence. My mother is very anxious to meet you. You intrigue her. I can't remember when she has been this insistent about going somewhere.'

Eleanor's heart thudded. Ben's mother was *here.* In the yard. Surrounded by all the daily activity of the foundry. With expectations! And he was acting as if it were the smallest thing. He should have given her notice. A week. No, two. Lady Whittonstall was probably the sort of woman who ferreted out the smallest infraction and the slightest hint of bad taste.

Eleanor covered her aching mouth with her hand, well aware of the picture she must present—hair tumbling down her back, soot-stained, and now thoroughly kissed. More street urchin than lady. Her face flamed.

'This is the worst possible time!' Eleanor frantically tried to find a hairpin to twist her hair up, while trying to remove the heavy apron and wanting the earth to swallow her all at the same time. 'How could you allow this to happen?'

A smile tugged at his mouth and his eyes darkened to warm embers. 'We were busy. First with Mr Swaddle's burn and then yours...'

'You know what I mean,' Eleanor whispered. 'What is going to happen now? Whatever shall I do?'

A smile tugged at his mouth. 'Meet my mother. She has come all the way from London for the purpose.'

'Impossible!' Eleanor squeaked. She knew she wasn't ready to meet Ben's mother. An excuse. She needed an excuse. She saw Mr Swaddle's toolbox and knew she had it. Iron-clad and copper-bottomed. Her breath came a little easier.

'Absolutely impossible. The foundry is terribly busy. You know what's happened. Mr Swaddle will be out for weeks. Men will have to be reassigned. We need to keep the steel production up. We have a five-month waiting list as it is. I can't possibly have visitors poking around today. There are a million things I have to do. I am behind schedule.'

He put a finger against her lips, stilling her. 'Eleanor, Mama wants to meet you—not do an inspection of your men and your business. Rather than resting at Broomhaugh, she came in the carriage with me to fetch you. She is bustling with excitement at the prospect.'

'But—'

'Take it as a compliment. I don't think she has ever met a businesswoman before.'

Compliment? Lady Whittonstall would be looking for a reason to criticise. Eleanor knew it in her bones. She'd come up here to cause mischief and possibly to stop the wedding. She'd guessed immediately that a businesswoman would not be the right sort of material for a viscountess. That was why she'd demanded to see Eleanor immediately, rather than arranging a mutually convenient time.

Why hadn't he presented his mother with a *fait*

accompli? Or come up with a way to stall her? Eleanor chewed her lip.

'Benjamin! I can hear you in there! Are we staying here in this…this yard, or are you going to take me to your fiancée?' The imperious voice became more insistent.

He lifted an eyebrow. Eleanor shook her head and started to back away. His finger clamped around her wrist, lightly holding her there.

'Take a deep breath and greet her. What do you have to be ashamed of?'

Eleanor stared at him. He didn't understand. She knew the way such women judged other women. She knew what society thought of women who worked. Algernon's attitude was typical—she was a freak of nature. But she was successful at her chosen job. And she wanted her future mother-in-law to see what a success she was—even if that success was outside his mother's usual notions.

'Why is your mother here at all?' Eleanor whispered in a furious undertone. 'We've agreed on a quiet wedding. You might have let me know she was arriving. You must have known.'

'Once she heard the news Mama moved heaven and earth to get here.'

Ben's eyes crinkled at the corners and Eleanor

could tell that he was pleased to have his mother there. But the information only increased her disquiet.

'Her arrival this morning was a complete surprise. Is that a problem?'

'Yes! My dress! My face!'

He peered down at her and his smile increased. 'You look delightful. Stop worrying.'

Eleanor's heart did a small leap. He thought her delightful. As quickly as the thought came she quashed it. A delightful scarecrow was more like it. She tried to smooth her hair and knew she'd only succeeded in making it worse when the entire ensemble tumbled about her shoulders.

'You are impossible! Let me go. Give me five minutes and I will make myself decent.'

'Mama will be impressed by what you do here and everything you have accomplished. What you look like doesn't change that.' Ben put his hand in the middle of her back and propelled her towards the door and out into the yard.

An immaculately dressed woman who appeared to be fresh from the pages of *La Belle Assemblée* or one of the other fashion magazines stood in the centre of the yard. A fairy creature from another world. It was hard to believe that she was Ben's mother. At first glance she appeared barely old enough to be his sister.

Eleanor winced as Lady Whittonstall's gaze travelled around the foundry's yard. Her increasing frown told Eleanor all she needed to know about what she must think of Moles. Eleanor wished she had had time to make sure the various bits of metal, old grindstone and broken lathes were cleared away. On her great-grandmother's apple tree the browning blossom was far more noticeable than the new leaves. To add insult to injury, the carriage had stopped beside a large muddy puddle. Lady Whittonstall's kid boots were now less than immaculate.

If she wanted a primer on how to make a poor impression upon someone who could be very important in her life, this was it.

'There you are, Benjamin. I've been calling and calling for you,' Lady Whittonstall pronounced, daintily stepping around the puddle. 'That wretched footman hasn't returned and you left me. Abandoned me.'

'I had to find Miss Blackwell,' Ben replied evenly. 'I hardly abandoned you, Mama. Exaggeration fails to become you, as you used to always say when I was a boy.'

Eleanor moved behind Ben's bulk. The day was turning into a disaster of epic proportions. She tried to smooth her skirts, twist her hair up—everything and anything. She put her hand to her cheek and noticed it came away dark with dust. Hardly an advertisement for a successful and prosperous woman—someone who was worthy to be a viscountess.

If she retreated slowly there was a slim possibility that she could make it to the office before Lady Whittonstall truly registered who she was. Once there, she could make herself decent. Cowardly, yes, but utterly necessary. She took a step backwards.

'And this is where Miss Blackwell works?' Lady Whittonstall's face bore a look of studied interest, the sort of practised expression she must use when her musicians played out of tune. 'So much activity. So many workers. So much…*industry*. It is all terribly intriguing. I had no idea. And Miss Blackwell runs everything with her own fair hand? Is this paragon of virtuous industry about, or is she busy elsewhere?'

With the slightest curl of her lip the dowager Lady Whittonstall made the words *virtuous industry* sound like something unmentionable rather than something to be proud of. Eleanor continued her retreat.

'This is Eleanor Blackwell—my intended.' Ben's hand was planted firmly in her back, preventing her from slinking further away.

Lady Whittonstall's gaze travelled up and down Eleanor and Eleanor knew that it instantly took in everything—from her dishevelled hair to the stains on her gown. She raised a delicate eyebrow when her gaze rested on Eleanor's dirty hands. Eleanor hurriedly put them behind her.

'There was a slight incident with the furnace,' Eleanor began. 'We are at sixes and sevens. I must apologise for the disorder. Normally—'

A single raised eyebrow stopped her. 'You take an active role in the business? Incredible.'

'Someone has to, Mama,' Ben explained. 'What Miss Blackwell has accomplished is nothing short of phenomenal.'

'When you said your intended was a business-woman, I expected something...something else.' Lady Whittonstall gestured about her. 'I had imagined something genteel—something quaint and charming. This—this is a large concern. Your fiancée is a captain of industry, Benjamin.'

'The best sword manufacturer in England,'

Eleanor said, keeping her head up. Would Ben's mother have preferred that she live in poverty, perhaps sewing a few seams and existing on snippets of toast? 'Moles is one of the largest employers in the area.'

'And is everything all right? Have we come at a bad time? Benjamin, you should have told me. All one has to do is look to see that something is amiss.'

Eleanor crossed her arms and hoped that she could retain a leash on her temper. Lady Whittonstall's tone implied that the foundry must have been hit by a great tragedy, given its state. 'There was a problem with a crucible of molten steel breaking. Ben assisted me in preventing it from getting worse. There are not many men who would do what he did.'

Lady Whittonstall's eyes glowed at this praise of her son. Eleanor risked a breath. Lady Whittonstall was proud of her son. Perhaps everything would be all right after all. Perhaps she was jumping to conclusions.

'Ben is like that. Always doing things for others without regard to his own safety or prospects.' Lady Whittonstall gave a heartfelt sigh. 'Why he hasn't been snapped up on the marriage market before now remains a profound mystery to me.' Her gaze narrowed and she looked hard at Eleanor. Her gaze lingered on Eleanor's dress. 'So many women have tried, my dear, but he has remained oblivious...until now. Little did I guess that a veritable captain of industry would be what was required!'

Her faint laugh grated on Eleanor's nerves.

Eleanor stared at Lady Whittonstall, feeling as if she'd stepped into a play that she didn't understand. Ben *had* told her about the reasons for their marriage, hadn't he? Or had he let her think it another sort of alliance? She could hardly ask Ben in front of his mother.

Eleanor put her hand to her mouth and tried not to panic. 'There are not many of us about,' she gasped out, trying to make it into a joke. 'It must be that.'

There was no answering smile from Lady Whittonstall. If anything, her expression became distinctly glacial. 'Yes, I can see you are quite unique.'

'Eleanor and I are getting married on Monday, Mama.' This time there was no mistaking the hint of steel in Ben's voice.

'That is why I am here.' Lady Whittonstall gave a delicate cough.

Eleanor's heart sank. One final unexpected hurdle. His mother disapproved.

'To attend the wedding of my only child. Even if you insist on behaving in such a harum-scarum fashion. Why do you need to get married with such undue haste? We could have a large wedding. When you married Alice practically the entire ton was there. The Prince Regent along with two of his brothers attended. But now—marrying up here in the middle of nowhere! There is no one of any import! How *could* you, Benjamin?'

'I have my reasons,' Ben replied. 'Eleanor's stepfather recently died. I explained that in my letter.'

'A large wedding would hardly be appropriate,' Eleanor added as Lady Whittonstall's frown increased. 'The last thing we want is untoward gossip.'

'Of course, of course.' Lady Whittonstall waved a dismissive hand. 'I trust my son to do the right thing. But a hasty marriage, Benjamin…people will talk.'

'People always talk, Mama. That is the first rule you teach your protégées, isn't it?'

A teasing note had entered Ben's voice and Eleanor knew that it had to be a long-standing joke between them. A stab of envy went through her. She couldn't imagine ever teasing *her* mother, and certainly not teasing someone who appeared as formidable as Lady Whittonstall. That was the difference between someone who was born to privilege and wealth and someone who had to work for them.

'You have to control what they talk about rather than allow the talk to control you.' A furrow appeared between Lady Whittonstall's delicately arched brows. She gave a slight cough. 'And your bride must be appropriately dressed—as befits someone who is marrying into one of the most respected families in London society. There will be a report in the papers. Imagine what the people at Almack's would say if Miss Blackwell appeared in…in her work clothes!'

The dimple in Ben's cheek deepened. 'I trust Miss Blackwell has a dress that she can wear, but I have no wish to tempt fate by demanding to see it before the wedding day. Although I am given to understand that Miss Blackwell often wears breeches when she works, for safety reasons.'

Lady Whittonstall's mouth opened and shut several times. Ben gave a snort of barely suppressed laughter. Eleanor smiled back at him.

'Your intended wears breeches in public?' Lady Whittonstall said in a faint voice.

'I hardly plan to traipse down the aisle in breeches. I know the proper place to wear them,' Eleanor retorted, and then quietly died at Lady Whittonstall's astonished look.

'There—you see, Mama. Miss Blackwell is highly sensible. But I will stop teasing you now. However, you must understand I am marrying Miss Blackwell and couldn't care less what your friends at Almack's say. Besides, think about the various women you have helped over the years. Many of them had far less than Miss Blackwell.'

'Some people need more help than others,' Lady Whittonstall said.

'But the challenge makes it all the more rewarding.'

Eleanor's stomach sank. It was one thing for her to worry and quite another for Ben to confirm it. He didn't like her dress sense. In the back of her mind she heard her stepfather's laughter and her mother's despairing cries about nothing fashionable ever suiting her colouring or her figure. She'd hated everything that her mother suggested. Buying clothes with her mother had been a chore to be endured and not enjoyed. She much preferred to wear things that she knew were presentable and in keeping with her status.

'You will allow yourself to be guided, Miss Blackwell? I have years of experience.' Lady Whittonstall cleared her throat. 'I have made successes out of more unpromising subjects…it would be a privilege and an honour to assist you.'

'I know my own style,' Eleanor replied. The last thing she wanted was a repetition of the situation she'd had with her own mother.

'Miss Blackwell is not one of your debutantes, Mama.' Ben placed his hand on Eleanor's shoulder. The simple touch warmed her. He smiled grimly. 'Just so you remember, Mama. Eleanor will be my wife, and not your protégée. You can give her advice but not insist.'

Silently Eleanor blessed Ben. She hadn't expected him to rush to her defence like that. Some day, she promised herself, she would make him proud of her. He wasn't proud today. She knew that. How could he be? How could anyone be? She'd made a fool of herself, she looked like something the cat had dragged in, and she'd completely jumped to the wrong conclusion. The knowledge washed over her and silently she vowed that she would do better. She would succeed. She would show Lady Whittonstall and most of all Ben that she was worthy of being a viscountess, that she could do both—be a viscountess *and* run a successful company. That she wasn't some unsophisticated girl but a mature businesswoman who could move effortlessly in any situation. Then she'd be worthy of Ben's admiration.

The dowager Lady Whittonstall had the grace to flush.

'You make me sound like a dragon. I'm hardly that. I am simply a mother who wishes the best for her only child,' she said with a smile that did not reach her eyes. 'It will give me great pleasure to look after Miss Blackwell. Society can be such a tricky thing when one is ignorant of its ways.'

Eleanor concentrated on breathing steadily. In and out. What could she say in answer to that?

'If you will give me a few moments I will make myself presentable—' Eleanor began, but was interrupted by one of the cutlers who needed to speak to her urgently about his grindstone and a broken leather strap.

'I'm sure that someone else can deal with this man's enquiry.' Lady Whittonstall gave an elegant wave of her hand. 'Benjamin has promised me a picnic. You must join us, my dear. I am all ears to learn how you manage your…business.'

'I'm sure someone else can't, Lady Whittonstall,' Eleanor said between gritted teeth. 'That is why he came to me.'

'We have disrupted Eleanor's routine, Mama,' Ben said. 'She is needed here. She has business to attend to. She made that quite clear to me earlier. Business must come first. The picnic must go on without her today.'

'If you are too busy I will understand,' Lady Whittonstall said. 'We don't wish to interrupt and be bothersome. After all, I am merely your prospective mother-in-law.'

'Moles is my reason for marrying your son, Lady Whittonstall. It has to come first,' Eleanor said, and hurried away before either of them could say another word. Before she burst into tears at the humiliation of it all. That would ruin everything.

She paused on the threshold of the office and looked up at her grandfather's portrait. He seemed sterner than ever. As if he knew that rather than facing Lady Whittonstall down she'd relied on Ben's assurances and had been tempted to neglect her duty. Somehow she had to keep from falling in love with Ben. Somehow she had to remember that Moles was the most important thing in her life, constant and unchanging.

'There was no cause for you to be rude to Eleanor this afternoon,' Ben said, handing his mother her pre-dinner glass of port.

Three of her Pomeranian dogs circled about her feet. His mother, like her friend Queen Charlotte, was an enthusiastic breeder of Pomeranians and rarely travelled without at least three of the little dogs.

'Was I rude?' His mother gave a discreet signal and all three dogs sat, wagging their tails, waiting for their pre-dinner treat. From a silver tray, his mother fed the dogs slivers of meat. After completing her task, she turned and gave him a beatific smile. 'I wanted to meet my prospective daughter-in-law and was presented with a woman who looked like a street urchin. And that dress is two seasons out of date. Who wears *frills* these days? My girls—'

'Eleanor is not one of your girls,' Ben said, cutting her tirade off before his mother started. 'She never will be.'

'But she has absolutely no fashion sense. There

is so much to be done with Miss Blackwell before she is fit for society.'

Ben tapped his finger against his own glass of port. He knew his mother's bad impression was his fault. He should have warned Eleanor. But he suspected his mother would have found fault whatever the circumstance. Eleanor was as far from his mother's protégées as possible. And he wanted it that way.

'Eleanor will be my wife, and you should treat her with respect. She is not clay to mould as you see fit.'

'And are you telling me that I shouldn't be concerned?' His mother gave one of the dogs a pat on the head, before taking a considering sip of her port. 'You are about to humiliate the entire family by marrying someone whom polite society will laugh at. Benjamin, I truly believe you are rushing into things without considering the consequences...for everyone.'

'The consequences are my concern, not yours.'

'And you want me to give my blessing to this little enterprise of yours?'

'Not particularly, as it is *my* marriage.' Ben kept hold of his temper. His mother should know better. She was merely upset because he hadn't decided to marry one of her protégées. Once she became better acquainted with Eleanor she'd be reconciled to the fact. He had to admit that he hadn't anticipated her antipathy, or that she'd travel up north at such a speed. Or that there would be an accident at the foundry.

Viv, who had just come in the drawing room, smothered his laugh with a cough. Ben merely raised an eyebrow. But it was helpful that his cousin saw the humour in the situation.

'That woman has no sense of propriety. She will be a disaster in London. You mark my words. Everyone will see and comment.' His mother began to warm to her theme, punctuating her words with rapid jabs of her hands.

Ben exchanged a wry glance with Viv.

'Aunt Violet,' Viv said, his face no longer bothering to hide his dismay. 'Miss Blackwell enjoys an excellent reputation in certain quarters. You are overly worried. I, for one, have faith in Miss Blackwell's judgement, and in Ben's sense in marrying her.'

'There is so much I could do for her...if you would allow me but a few weeks. I could completely transform her. Postpone the marriage and allow me to work my magic.'

'What sort of magic is required?' Viv gave a laugh. 'I have seen Miss Blackwell blossom over the past couple of weeks. It is a pity that I hadn't appreciated her charm before she became engaged to Ben. Otherwise he'd have a run for his money. There is something so pleasing about a woman who can converse on subjects that interest a man.'

His mother's hand froze with the glass of port halfway to her lips. 'Her dress had far too many ruffles. It was more suitable for a debutante in her first season rather than an aging spinster like Miss Blackwell.'

'Miss Blackwell is younger than me,' Ben answered, his amusement fading.

'You could have married a hundred women who would have done you proud. Who would dance gracefully and know what is expected of a viscountess. Can your Miss Blackwell do any of those things? Is she even capable of it? And what about producing a child?'

Ben drew a deep breath and counted to ten. His mother was obsessed with her dynasty and future generations. A cold chill ran down his back at what might happen. But this time he knew where he'd made mistakes. 'That is in God's hands. Surely you are not going to presume...?'

'Benjamin, don't blaspheme. I take your point. You are marrying the chit and you refuse to save her from humiliation. For your sake I will attempt to be her friend.' His mother put her port down with a bang.

The dogs all gave a sharp bark. At Ben's look they hid their faces behind their paws, showing only the tips of their bat-like ears.

'I hope you know me well enough to agree that I try very hard to be kind. I want to save the chit from herself.'

'Once you get to know Eleanor I am sure you will find many things to admire,' Ben said, pinning her with his gaze. 'I'm pleased you have decided to try.'

'Now, shall we speak of something more pleasant?' his mother said. 'I want your advice on a new carriage. I need something stunning for when I take the morning air in Hyde Park. My dogs demand it.'

Ben mentally sighed. Her dogs wanted a new carriage? Sometimes his mother stretched the bounds of credibility.

Since his mother had arrived she had kept up a steady stream of requests for little things that she needed him to do, or things she needed his advice on. Nothing onerous, but things she could easily do herself—things he suspected she would do if he was not within earshot. But because he loved her he'd made sure her port was poured, the books she wanted were placed by her bedside, and that her maid understood how his mother liked things unpacked. Although Marie had been with his mother for the last ten years, and if she didn't understand by now she never would. He'd even made sure that the cook had provided the right diet for her dogs.

'I trust you to know your dogs' taste, Mama. You always seem to.'

'But I can't possibly make such an important decision without your input.' She paused, and two spots of colour appeared on her cheeks. 'Of course if you are too busy I will give way.'

'I'm not sure what you mean, Mother. You will get whichever carriage suits your fancy as you always do,' Ben said, when he knew he'd be able to answer evenly and without rancour.

'But I like knowing that you agree with me. But you are obviously too busy with your fiancée's company. After all you saved the day today. That company is in a sorry state.'

'How could you tell?'

'The amount of rubbish everywhere.' His mother

waved an airy hand. 'She's looking for someone to take over and has latched on to you. You have other duties, Benjamin. You can't go running something like that as well.'

'You mistook Eleanor's words, Mother.' Ben inclined his head. He was proud of the way Eleanor had coped today. Alice would have given way to hysterics and demanded that he handle everything. It was refreshing not to have someone cling to him, but he didn't want Eleanor to have to shoulder her burdens herself. The memory of the three scars on her wrist haunted him.

'I'm sure I didn't.'

'Eleanor is more than capable of running her company. She doesn't need to ask my advice. Furthermore, she will be able to negotiate society's shoals without a problem. You simply caught her unawares at a bad time.'

'Your wife needs to be so much more than a woman who can simply avoid problems. Any number of women can do that. You need someone who can be at your side and push your advantage. You come from a noble lineage and you will want your descendants to have the same advantages you enjoy.' His mother laid a hand on his arm and looked up at him with eyes the exact replicas of his. 'I don't want you to be hasty. I worry, Benjamin. You enjoy playing the white knight, but should you ruin your life?'

Ben covered her hand with his. His mother wanted what she saw was best for him. But long gone were the days when he'd done things solely to please her. Alice had always insisted on keeping his mother contented, deferring to her constantly. After Alice had gone he'd found her private journal, where she'd confided her hopes and fears. Until he'd read that he hadn't realised the extent of his mother's meddling, and how she had dictated that Alice should always give in to his demands and let him win. 'It is my life. I thought you were keen on me marrying again. My *duty,* you called it the last time we spoke on the subject. I've given Miss Blackwell my word.'

His mother's eyes narrowed. 'Tell me the truth. Were you caught with her? How far has this gone? Her waist is slender, but...'

'Good God, no.' Ben ran his fingers through his hair, attempting to tear his mind away from an image of a well-kissed Eleanor. Her lips had plagued his dreams for the last few nights, and the dreams were growing more and more explicit. Each time he saw her he wanted more of her. Had they not been interrupted, he dreaded to think what would have happened, what scandal they could have caused. 'Do you truly think so little of me that I would seduce a respectable woman?'

'I saw you holding her through the open door of that building! And if I saw you think about how many other people might have seen you.'

'We are engaged,' Ben said, as steadily as he could. With his mother in this mood he had little appetite for confessing why he had made his offer for Eleanor. His mother didn't need to know about the will. 'There was nothing wrong in that, and Eleanor had just survived an accident. What is wrong in offering comfort?'

'You were kissing your fiancée in the open after an accident? Imagine!' Viv said in an overly pleased tone.

His mother once again put her glass down with a bang. The three dogs cowered. 'In full view, Benjamin. I gave you time to let her depart, but the brazen hussy stood there. She has no shame.'

'My fault, Mother, not Eleanor's. I refused to allow Eleanor the chance to retreat. If you wish to blame someone, blame me.'

The room fell silent as his mother digested this news with a face like a sour plum. Silently Ben kicked himself. He should have known better. And his mother was right—but not for the reason she thought. The last thing he wanted to do was undermine Eleanor's position with her men.

'Do you love her?' his mother asked in a low tone. 'You loved Alice once I'd made her into the perfect wife.'

'Is that *any* of your business?' Ben countered. 'And I married Alice in spite of your tutelage, not because of it. Alice knew that. I wonder that you've forgotten.'

He might have seen Alice in a new light when she'd made her debut, but it had been when he'd discovered her sobbing in the morning room, afraid to go to a musicale and play the complicated piece his mother had requested, that their real courtship had started.

His mother blinked rapidly. 'I want you to be happy. How can you be happy if your wife makes mistakes? If your friends gossip about her? I want to help, Benjamin. Allow me to help. You *will* let me help her, guide her. I know I can make her into so much more than she is. Please give me some time.'

Ben regarded his mother. He'd known her long enough to understand that when she attempted to manipulate people most of the time she did it out of love rather than malice, but she could be over-bearing. He'd seen her do it to Alice many times, and had finally stepped in over the weeks before Alice's death. And then there were all her proté-gées, who seemed interchangeable. It wasn't going to happen to Eleanor. Eleanor made him forget that life. Eleanor was far from afraid to win.

'To turn Eleanor into another Alice? You think that is what I want? My wife *died,* Mother.'

She had the grace to flush. 'Until I altered Alice you thought of her only as a little girl. All puppy fat and pigtails.'

He shook his head. His mother's outrageous re-mark was not worth replying to. 'I like Eleanor as she is.'

His mother gave an exasperated sigh. 'Have you told her about Alice? About the baby? Does she truly understand what you lost? Why it is so im-portant for you to produce an heir? Does she un-derstand what will be required of her?'

Ben drew in his breath. His mother hadn't men-tioned Alice's advanced state of pregnancy for years. He'd begun to hope that maybe she never would and somehow the guilt would begin to fade.

'They are in my past, Mama. Eleanor knows I was married before. It is enough.'

'A husband and wife should not have secrets from each other. Miss Blackwell should know before you are married. Indeed, any woman you marry should know. Secrets are very dangerous things.'

He banged his fists together, willing the guilt to be gone. Alice had gone into premature labour because of his driving. A thousand times in his memory he'd driven around that pothole that had jolted the carriage and sent Alice flying against the side. Everyone said that it wasn't his fault, but it didn't stop the guilt. He hadn't taken care of Alice properly.

He deserved a new life. Eleanor did not need to know every facet of his existence and shame.

'Aunt Violet, is it any of your business?' Viv asked. 'We do not need to quarrel. It won't bring Alice back.'

'I will stop when I have said my piece. You are obviously not ready to get married again, Benjamin, if you can't speak to your intended about your past. And neither is Miss Blackwell.' His mother tapped her shoe on the ground. 'All I am asking is for a slight delay. Surely Miss Blackwell will agree to that? I simply cannot understand the reason why you want to marry in such haste!'

The walls of the drawing room pressed down on Ben and he knew he had to leave. Or explode with rage. And it wasn't his mother he was angry with but his past. He could not undo his mistakes, but he could stop them from happening again. 'Enjoy your meal, Mother, Viv.'

'Where are you going?'

'Out.'

'Benjamin, I want to *help*.' His mother's voice floated after him.

'Not if I can prevent it,' he muttered under his breath.

Chapter Eight

Eleanor stretched slightly as she placed the last of her stepfather's horse brasses in a box for Algernon.

Sleep was an expensive luxury and one Eleanor knew she couldn't afford. Not if she wanted to get everything done before the wedding. Being organised and keeping to the task at hand was her key to not thinking about what had happened this afternoon.

Most of the house was now packed up. She wouldn't have anything that belonged to her stepfather when she moved to Broomhaugh. Goodbye to the misfit beanpole. Hello to the virtuous viscountess.

Packing made her heart easier. This marriage would happen, despite the humiliation of earlier. Everyone in the yard must have heard the remarks and then witnessed Ben and Lady Whittonstall's abrupt departure. It had only been by concentrating on replacing that grindstone and arranging for all the crucibles to be tested that she'd kept from sinking down into a heap. Before she'd even started to appear in society as Ben's wife she'd been deemed a failure by the one woman she'd hoped to impress.

She knew why she was doing this—for Moles. It should be enough that Ben was willing to marry and keep Moles from Algernon's greedy fingers. But somehow she'd secretly hoped that Ben's mother would take one look at her and see that she was not the misfit her stepfather and Algernon had proclaimed her to be but someone worthy, who would be an asset to the family rather than a hindrance.

A brief sigh escaped her lips as she put the lid on the crate. Was it too much to ask for Ben's mother to respect her and the work she did? To see her for who she truly was?

Eleanor rocked back on her heels, searching for another reason why she should stay up. To go to bed meant sleep and dreaming. The last thing she wanted to dream about was Ben kissing her. Passionately.

Her hand fingered her lips. Even hours later she

could still remember the taste of him. Then everything had seemed wonderful, but now she didn't know.

She began to wrap the shepherdess figurines that her mother had collected. One more job to cross off the list.

The steady crunch of gravel outside the window made her reach for a sword. Not an animal, but a human. No one visited at this hour. Mrs Nevin was as deaf as a post and had retired to bed, with a loud sniff about folks staying up too late and the necessity of beauty sleep for brides. Eleanor had told her to look after her own rest as she had things to attend to.

No one should be there. But it came again—the distinct sound of footsteps against the gravel path. Eleanor gripped the sword tighter, threw open the door and peered out into the not-quite-dark of a June night in Durham.

'Who's there?' she called out.

'I saw a light. Don't you ever sleep?' Ben's voice rolled over her.

Relief consumed her and she lowered the sword. Ben was here. Late at night. Her mouth went dry. Ben stood, resplendent in evening dress, partway down the path, as if he'd walked to the door and then turned around again. His stock was slightly askew and he didn't wear a top hat. Her hands itched to sink themselves into his mass of dark curly hair. Never before had she seen him anything less than immaculate.

'Ben?' she said, putting a hand on the doorframe. Her voice sound high-pitched and unnatural. She swallowed hard and tried again. 'What are you doing here? At this hour? Is something wrong?'

'May I come in?'

Eleanor's insides twisted. After the scene this afternoon at Moles he'd yielded to his mother's wishes and now wanted to delay the marriage. That was the only thing which could have brought him out this late. Otherwise why not wait until the morning? Everything had been going far too well. It had been far too easy. Oh, how her stepfather must be laughing.

'Yes, of course.' She retreated a few steps, hurriedly putting down the sword before retreating a few steps more. 'I'm in the drawing room packing. Mrs Nevin has retired for the night, but if you want refreshment I'm sure there is something in the kitchen.'

Eleanor clamped her mouth shut, aware that she was babbling.

He shook his head. 'I came to see *you*. If I wanted to eat and drink I could have stayed at Broomhaugh.'

'Is it something serious? The hour is awfully late.' Eleanor kept her back rigid. Whatever happened, she refused to make a scene. She'd absorb the blow and then go on. There would be a way out of this coil if she kept her head. She had to let him speak and not jump to conclusions. But with each passing heartbeat she knew that it was harder and harder not to consider the worst.

She struggled to breathe and wished she was wearing something more becoming. Not that it would make much difference. She couldn't change the way she looked, and Lady Whittonstall had made it very clear what a disappointment she was. But Ben was a man of his word, and he'd given *her* his word. It wasn't much, but it was something to hang on to.

He ran his hand through his hair. 'This afternoon's fiasco… My mother was insupportable. I fear you might have taken her ire the wrong way. It's been nagging and pulling at my conscience. It was the first time you had encountered my mother and her ways. She has certain views.'

'Your mother fears I will not make a good

Viscountess Whittonstall.' Eleanor wrapped her arms about her waist. Even acknowledging his mother's concerns made her stomach ache. Though it was no more than she'd already worried about. 'There is no other way to take it. She stated her opinion quite boldly. I might disagree, but there you have it.'

'I wanted to assure you that her opinion matters not a jot. She was wrong to criticise you.' His mouth twisted. 'Very wrong.'

Eleanor's heart leapt. He considered his mother to be in the wrong? A faint glimmer of hope shot through her. Was he going to give her a chance to prove Lady Whittonstall a false prophet?

Eleanor decided to be generous. 'She is entitled to her opinion…I suppose. Everything *was* in a mess. It was not the sort of meeting I would have desired. I was less than gracious. I stomped away.'

He caught her hand and raised it to his lips. The brief touch sent a distinct pulse throughout her body. A wild flare of hope arched within her. Maybe he felt this desire as well. She quashed it, not willing to believe in it yet. He was here because of his mother's behaviour, not because he desired her touch.

'As long as you realise that her view doesn't reflect mine. I intend to marry you and I consider you eminently suitable,' he said in a determined voice.

Eleanor withdrew her hand and tried to think sensibly rather than stare into his intense expression. What had his mother been saying? Had he been tempted to postpone? She noted he hadn't said a suitable viscountess, just that she was suitable.

'And you came over here to tell me this? At this time of night? Most people are in bed. It is hardly news.' Eleanor pressed her hands to her temples. There had to be more—something he wasn't telling her, something that had caused him to ride all the way from Broomhaugh.

The intensity of his black gaze faded. 'It seemed important. I wanted to let you know in case you were worried. I didn't want you to worry.'

'That is kind of you. More than kind. But my stepfather often said worse things.' Eleanor gave a light laugh, to protect herself against the hurt and to show clearly that the cruel words had not affected her—not in the least. 'I learnt not to pay attention.'

'Is your stepfather the reason why you carry swords with you?'

She tilted her head. 'Excuse me?'

'You always seem to have one within reach when you are at home. I can understand at the foundry, but this puzzled me for a long time. But now I see it was the threat of your stepfather.'

Eleanor kept her back rigid. Silently she cursed that she was that transparent.

'A precaution only.' She gave a careful shrug. 'He never tried anything. I suspect that he was a physical coward. But we had an uneasy truce and he had an uncertain temper.'

'I'm pleased not to have met him, then.'

'The swords served a useful purpose around Algernon. He had a fondness for chasing maids when he stayed with us one summer.'

Somewhere behind her Eleanor heard the clock strike the hour while around her the silence grew. Had she said too much about her stepfather?

'I wanted you to know that it is the future that is important and not the past. You don't have to prove yourself to me.' He inclined his head. 'You'll not need to carry a sword in my house. Leave them with your work at Moles.'

'I agree.' The tension rushed out of her. 'I promise not to carry a sword except if we are fencing. Past experience is best forgotten.'

His smile could have lit a thousand lanterns. A warm glow filled her. He understood what she was saying.

'You are very perceptive, Eleanor. A new start is precisely what I want.' He reached out and his cool hand touched her cheek. 'Don't allow anyone to tell you differently. Don't let anyone change you.'

'I won't.' Eleanor resisted the temptation to turn her face to his palm. She forced herself to step away from him. 'The hour is late.'

'Until the wedding, then.'

He lifted her hand to his lips and kissed her palm. A distinct tingle went through her.

'Go to sleep, Eleanor. I want my bride to be wide awake on our wedding night.'

Eleanor drew in her breath sharply as the heat on her cheeks flamed. She ducked her head and concentrated on the carpet's pattern rather than looking into his smouldering eyes. He was talking about them being together! The image of tangled limbs seemed to be seared on her brain.

'You do know what passes between a man and a woman?' he asked in a quiet voice.

'I grew up in the country,' Eleanor said, as evenly as she dared. 'You would have to be blind and deaf not to know.'

He gave a laugh. His face suddenly seemed far younger and more carefree. 'I should have guessed that you'd have an answer.'

With those words, he departed. Eleanor stared after him for a long time. He had never said precisely why he'd come over. *Had* he been worried about her? Was she reading too much into it?

The strange flatness she'd experienced ever since their fight vanished. Once again the world seemed full of possibilities.

Resolutely she packed the swords. The only place for them was at Moles, as display items. She'd given Ben her word. She would keep her work and her home life separate.

She hugged her arms about her waist. He wanted her wide awake on her wedding night! She did know what passed between a man and a woman. She'd heard the men talking when they considered her safely out of earshot. She knew the fundamentals, but had never had the opportunity to put it into practice. It should be enough. It had to be enough. He wanted them to spend their wedding night together.

A heady feeling swept through her, and she knew she was in serious danger of falling headlong in love with him. She caught her breath. Somewhere there had to be a flaw. But right now all she could think about was her future with Ben.

Eleanor paced the little vestibule of St Cuthbert's. In a few moments the organist would play the march and she'd begin to walk down the aisle. All the guests had arrived. More than she had considered would be there. But she hadn't seen Ben.

Since their late-night conversation he'd sent three notes about mundane subjects and she'd declined his invitation to tea. The installation of a new grindstone and the absence of Mr Swaddle at Moles meant she'd had more work than ever to be done.

Her nights had been plagued by dreams about the way Ben had kissed her. She'd woken filled with nameless longings, her body thrumming like a top. She knew she wanted more. She wanted to taste his mouth again. She wanted to feel his hands on her skin. And she wanted him to desire her. She wanted to be the sort of wife he could be proud of.

Eleanor straightened the lace on her gown before lifting her nosegay. She inhaled the rich scent of roses.

'Miss Blackwell.'

Eleanor turned and flushed before making a

quick curtsey. It was enough to knock the nose-gay she intended on carrying down the aisle to the ground. Eleanor rapidly picked it up. She pushed a few errant rose petals to one side and hoped.

'Lady Whittonstall,' she said, feeling distinctly clumsy and tall beside the woman in a dark green dress. It had been hard enough when Eleanor was young, trying to look less than beanpole-like beside her mother. Lady Whittonstall's petite form vibrated fashionability. Eleanor had no doubt that in a few months various magazines would declare that dark emerald-green turbans like the one Lady Whittonstall wore were *de rigueur*—even if Eleanor had never seen anyone wearing one before.

'Oh, how sweet. You are going to carry flowers. How lovely. If you will allow me, a few little touches will complete the picture. And you must call me Mother Whittonstall. It is fitting that my only child's wife should call me that.'

Before Eleanor could protest Lady Whittonstall had scooped up the nosegay and rearranged the flowers. Eleanor had to admit they did look far less bedraggled.

'That is very kind of you.'

'You know, I think Lady Acomb's daughter Honoria wore a dress very like that last season.

She wore the sleeves like this.' Lady Whittonstall darted forward and pulled the puffed sleeves down so Eleanor's shoulders were revealed. 'Much better. There—you look…charming on your wedding day.'

The pause before *charming* was not precisely the reaction she'd been looking for. Particularly not from Lady…no, *Mother* Whittonstall. There was nothing wrong with her wedding dress. The modiste had assured her it was the height of fashion in London. Mother Whittonstall's look implied that she was quaint and had completely misunderstood the current season's requirements.

Eleanor counted to ten very slowly. She couldn't change her dress now. She concentrated on Ben's late-night reassurances. *He* thought her suitable. He was the one marrying her, not his mother.

'Thank you. I tried,' Eleanor said as graciously as she could.

Lady Whittonstall looked at her with pity in her eyes. 'My dear, I fear we did not have a good start the other day. I do so want to have a good relationship with my son's wife.'

'Things were fraught.' Eleanor waved her nosegay. A few more rose petals drifted down. 'And things have been busy at the foundry. I regret I had to refuse your kind invitation to tea yesterday— and then there was the packing. I'm sure Ben explained.'

'He did.' Lady Whittonstall put her hand on Eleanor's shoulder. 'I do so want us to be friends. I know your mother is dead, and I want you to think of me as your new mother.'

'That is very kind of you.'

'I'm pleased you see it that way.'

Eleanor's heart leapt. Had she misjudged Lady Whittonstall? She'd been so intent on seeing her as an obstacle that she hadn't spied the deep love she had for her son. Wasn't it natural for a mother to be concerned? Particularly when she hadn't met the woman in question? Eleanor thought back to when she had met her stepfather. She'd been furious with her mother for marrying without consulting her. They hadn't spoken for weeks afterwards.

Eleanor breathed easier. Concern for her son drove Lady Whittonstall. They had simply got off on the wrong footing. And she knew from her business that there was no point in bearing grudges. She had to build bridges instead. She could forgive the words and show that she was a person worthy of being a viscountess.

'I look forward to receiving your advice,' she

said soothingly. 'Ben informs me you know everything about society.'

A tiny smile crossed Lady Whittonstall's features. 'Yes, that is very true. I have made it my business to learn.'

'Then there is no reason I can't. Knowledge can be acquired.'

Lady Whittonstall's gaze travelled down the length of Eleanor. 'Some remain in ignorance all their lives.'

Eleanor tightened her grip on her nosegay. What Lady Whittonstall was saying was no worse than what her stepfather had said on numerous occasions. What she had to hang on to was the fact Ben wanted her to be his wife. 'I don't intend to be one of those people. I intend to make Ben proud. I have always given everything to tasks I want to accomplish. Why should I stop now?'

'You sound very determined.'

'I am. Ben knows this as well. We have no secrets.'

Lady Whittonstall bit her bottom lip. Eleanor experienced a moment of triumph.

'I am so glad,' Lady Whittonstall said slowly. 'I was worried when I knew he hadn't confided in you about losing his child. Alice was pregnant, you see, when she died. Benjamin hates speaking about it. At the bottom of my heart, I knew he would. It shows that he is ready to marry and has closed the book on his past.'

Eleanor's throat closed tight and she wished Ben *had* confided in her about the child. After all their picnics and her confidences about Moles and her stepfather he hadn't confided this one simple fact. She swallowed hard. He had never spoken much of Alice. Nothing real or substantial.

Her soap bubble dream about Ben falling in love with her dissolved with a disconcerting pop and the world suddenly seemed a greyer place. 'Excuse me?'

'Surely he told you?' Lady Whittonstall's eyes opened wide and the colour drained from her face. She started to say something, choked it back and then blurted out, 'The other night I thought he must have done. I urged him to.'

'He said nothing.'

Lady Whittonstall grew more agitated, pleating her handkerchief between her fingers. 'You must forget that I said anything. Me and my big mouth. I am worse than a debutante. After all these years you'd think I'd learn. I most humbly beg your pardon. I had no intention for you to find out like this.

I simply surmised the other night…that he…he had done the correct thing.'

Eleanor knew the words Lady Whittonstall uttered were the truth. Lady Whittonstall had thought Ben had told her, and that was why she was willing to accept this marriage. Worst of all, Lady Whittonstall was correct. It was the sort of thing a wife *should* know.

'He did come to see me the night before last.' Eleanor looked up at the roof of the church. All the excitement went out of her, leaving her flat. Ben had not confided in her. Such a simple thing. Such an important thing. What other secrets from the past had he kept? 'We spoke of other things.'

'I adored Alice. Everyone did. She was that sort of person. Her death was a terrible blow.' Lady Whittonstall raised her handkerchief to her eyes. 'They had wanted children for ages. Alice's dearest wish was to provide an heir for Benjamin. Such a tragedy. But it was an important part of my son's life.'

'How did she die?' Eleanor asked, unable to stop her curiosity. Immediately she wished she hadn't asked. It should be Ben telling her this and not his mother.

'Benjamin must tell you. I have said far too

much.' Lady Whittonstall shook her head and seemed to recall her manners. 'He still needs an heir, Miss Blackwell. I hope you can provide it. It is your duty. He longs for one, but you are well past the first flush of youth.'

'He has an heir in Viv,' Eleanor said carefully. Ben had never said he hoped for a child of his own but it made sense that he'd want an heir. It was what marriage was for. 'Ben told me that when we agreed to marry.'

'It is not the same thing.' Lady Whittonstall laid her hand on Eleanor's arm. Her eyes became like Ben's and two bright spots appeared on her cheeks. 'I hope you will forgive me for unintentionally betraying my son. It was a mistake. We are all allowed mistakes, I hope?'

'I do understand.' Eleanor could see from the woman's agitation that she was unused to making *faux pas.*

'And I hope some day to hold my grandson in my arms. You will ensure that...'

Eleanor forced her shoulders back. She refused to allow this woman to intimidate her. She was sure she could get pregnant. Women did it all the time. And she did want a child. 'I shall do my best, but it is something God decides.'

'Benjamin has changed,' Lady Whittonstall continued. 'He used to take such joy from balls and other entertainments. Hopefully you and he will once again take part. You must. All of London will want to meet you as soon as possible. Benjamin appears to think you will be staying up here.'

'I have responsibilities towards my employees,' Eleanor said around the ash in her mouth. 'And I am in mourning.'

'You have a position to uphold, my dear. I want to assist you. I know it will mean a great deal to Benjamin.'

Eleanor kept her shoulders down and her head up. This conversation was the last thing she needed at the moment. To think that before Lady Whittonstall appeared she'd been worrying about her wedding night. She knew now that she was second best. 'I will remember that…should I ever need advice.'

'I am so pleased that we had this little conversation. May it be the first of many.' Lady Whittonstall patted Eleanor's arm. 'I'm sure Viv was right the other evening. Everything will be fine. You are an intelligent woman, Eleanor Blackwell. I can see that now. All it will take is a little effort on your part to follow my lead.'

Viv had defended her, not Ben. The knowledge hurt. Her stomach reeled from the blow and she concentrated on keeping her smile in place. 'Thank you for the compliment.'

'You are welcome, my dear.'

Before Eleanor could utter another word Lady Whittonstall left the vestibule, walking down the aisle as if she were the bride.

Eleanor stared after her, her mind whirling. Why hadn't Ben told her that Alice had been pregnant when she died? Why had he shunned society afterwards? And why had he come to see her the other night? To tell her that? She pressed her hand against her forehead, remembering how he'd smiled when she'd said that the past didn't matter. But this news mattered a great deal. There was no way she could tell him that she knew. He had to confide in her.

She wiped her eyes. There was no going back. She had to marry, but she knew she wanted their marriage to be more than a convenience.

'We are ready to begin, Miss Blackwell,' Mr Percy the curate said, giving a loud cough as he came into the vestibule. 'Everyone is waiting. The organist has played the opening chords three times.'

'Yes, I am coming now.' Eleanor pasted a smile on her face.

She stopped at the end of the aisle, looking down towards where Ben stood with Sir Vivian at his side. Resplendent. Self-confident. No different than he'd ever been. Except now she knew about his tragedy. What had she been hoping for? That he hadn't really loved his wife? That somehow he'd develop feelings for her? She knew what she was—an unattractive beanpole whose only assets were her brain and her business sense.

There was no one to give her away. Mrs Nevin had offered to act as her attendant and that was enough. Or should have been.

Eleanor took one look around the church as all heads turned towards her.

It gave her comfort that Mr Swaddle, with his arm in a sling, and his wife had made the trek over. Her mouth went dry and she wished that she hadn't been so quick to refuse Mr Swaddle's offer of escorting her down the aisle.

Her jaw began to ache from the smile.

Even Algernon would have been preferable to this lonely walk. Algernon was there, of course. With a face like thunder. He'd made the grudging offer this morning. She had refused.

She had to wonder if Miss Varney had reconsidered her acceptance of his suit.

Eleanor nodded to him as she progressed down the aisle. He glowered back.

A strange lightness settled on her shoulders. He couldn't do anything to her now. Today was her day. She should feel triumphant. So why did it seem so hard to manage those last few steps?

Her entire life was about to change. Her conversation with Lady Whittonstall had underlined that. She didn't really know Ben. She only thought she did. He hadn't bothered to confide in her about the way his wife had died or the fact that she'd been pregnant. What else had he kept from her?

She forced her foot forward and put it down too heavily. The sound ricocheted all around the nearly empty church.

Soon she would no longer be Eleanor Blackwell but instead Eleanor Grayson, Viscountess Whittonstall, with all that it entailed. What sort of wife did Ben want? Lady Whittonstall seemed to think he wanted someone like his late wife, and she knew she couldn't be. But she could try. She'd managed the foundry and she could manage society. She could do everything. She had defeated her stepfather after all.

Despite her legs trembling like jelly with every step she took, she made it to where Ben stood.

'Second thoughts?' he asked. His long fingers guided her to her place in front of the vicar.

'None at all,' she said brightly. 'I know why I am doing this.'

Except it had become about more than saving Moles. She wanted the marriage to be something more. She could not compete with Alice, and she couldn't give Ben what he'd lost, but she could try to give him his heart's desire—a son to inherit his title.

Eleanor very deliberately turned towards the vicar. 'Shall we begin?'

'I now pronounce you man and wife,' the vicar said.

The words sent a chill through Ben. This was the moment he'd dreaded. He'd spent the entire ceremony trying not to think about his wedding to Alice and compare it to this one. Today was the start of the rest of his life, a day when he no longer had to think about the past. Thus far he'd carefully kept his gaze on the vicar rather than looking down at Eleanor. Now he had to.

Ben glanced down at Eleanor's upturned face.

Her grey eyes were luminous but there was a faint hint of defiance to her chin. He knew in that instant he'd been wrong not to look at her. There was no need for comparisons. He was here and he was marrying Eleanor. He wanted to see if the passion she brought to her work and to the way she seemed to do everything would be brought to his bed. He wanted to taste her lips again and see if they were as sweet as his memory of them. His inclination was to draw her to him and drink, but he resisted the temptation. He remembered how Alice had protested at any displays of affection. And Eleanor appeared ill at ease enough.

His lips glanced over hers before he lifted his head.

'Moles is saved,' he said, trying to coax a smile from her. Later, he would discuss with her ways to decrease her involvement. He wanted to spend more time with her. To his immense surprise, he missed her when she wasn't there.

Her lips turned up briefly. 'I am grateful. It puts my mind at rest. Moles being safe is my sole concern.'

'But you are *my* concern now.' Ben gave Eleanor's hand a squeeze. Alice had always left all the important decisions to him.

'You needn't worry about me. I will be fine. I am used to looking after myself.'

'It will be my pleasure.' Ben smiled down at her. It had happened. He was free from his past. He never had to go there again. It was all behind him. All he needed to think about was his future with Eleanor.

Chapter Nine

'**W**here are you going on your wedding trip?' Mrs Swaddle asked Eleanor as the wedding breakfast progressed.

Eleanor froze. Thus far she had avoided thinking about the wedding trip. She hadn't even allowed herself to think about the wedding night, or the revelation that Ben hadn't even shared the smallest portion of knowledge about himself with her. Instead she'd concentrated on being gracious at the breakfast, demonstrating to Lady Whittonstall that she could easily take part in social events. The breakfast was far larger than she thought it would be, but Ben had explained his mother's determination.

'I suspect it will be somewhere fabulous.' Mrs Swaddle gave a long drawn-out sigh. 'I said to Mr Swaddle: Mark my words, Lord Whittonstall will have a lovely spot all picked out for our Mrs Blackwell.'

Ever since Ben had saved Mr Swaddle both he and Mrs Swaddle had been singing Ben's praises at every opportunity. He'd gone from being a pretty-boy aristocrat to the saviour of the foundry. At first Eleanor had found it amusing, but now she worried. What did Ben want from her? She knew very little about him and his life—a life she'd be expected to share. He hadn't even confided that there was to be this extensive wedding breakfast. And now she had to worry that he'd expect her to be his hostess at other glittering occasions when she must concentrate on running Moles.

'We haven't really discussed it,' Eleanor began. How could she explain that now, with Mr Swaddle injured, was not the time for her to depart any-where without seeming ungrateful? Or implying that she wanted Mr Swaddle to return before he was fully fit?

'A few nights away will be just the tonic for you, Mrs...I mean Lady Whittonstall.' Mrs Swaddle flushed scarlet. 'Our Mrs Blackwell is now a lady. Imagine. It is terribly exciting.'

Lady Whittonstall stopped her progress to give one of her social smiles. 'Benjamin will make sure it is somewhere wonderful. He knows the importance of a wedding trip.'

'Did you go somewhere pleasant, Mother Whittonstall?' Eleanor asked, seeking to move the conversation away from the trip that was not going to happen.

Lady Whittonstall's eyes turned dreamy. 'My late husband took me to Naples. That was where Benjamin was conceived. We were away for six months. My mother worried the entire time but I adored it. Of course Benjamin took Alice away for longer, but I think six months is the minimum one should spend on the trip of one's lifetime.'

Six months. Eleanor's jaw dropped. She couldn't imagine being away from her work for that long. Ben obviously moved in a different world from her, but in this he would have to give way. Her responsibilities came first. And she hated the little voice whispering that spending six months with just Ben would be wonderful.

'We are not going anywhere,' Eleanor said decisively. 'I don't have the time.'

'Not going anywhere?' Lady Whittonstall blinked rapidly. 'But you must. Sometimes I think if I didn't have those memories of Charles, I would go mad. Wedding trips are important. I insisted when Benjamin married—'

'My new wife is a busy lady, Mama. Remember that.' Ben placed his hand on Eleanor's shoulder. 'Now, if you will excuse us, my *wife* is required elsewhere.'

Without giving her a chance to ask him why, or question him about the wedding trip, he led her firmly away from his mother and Mrs Swaddle and out on to the terrace.

'That's better,' he said with a smile. 'Less crowded. Fewer questions. Fewer prying eyes.'

'Prying eyes?'

'This wedding breakfast is completely out of hand.' Ben gestured towards where a throng of people still huddled around the displays of food. 'Mama, with Viv's help, appears to have invited the entire region.'

'We had to meet them some time. It seems strange suddenly to be Lady Whittonstall.'

Ben made a face. 'I had asked for a quiet wedding breakfast. This is my mother's idea of quiet. You are handling it well.'

'It gives her pleasure,' Eleanor said diplomatically.

'Yes, she lives for playing the hostess. But you live for other things.'

Eleanor peeked at him from under her lashes. Did he mean that he thought she wouldn't be capable of organising something like this? She was not some shy wallflower, incapable of hosting a gathering. All it required was a modicum of attention to detail. Lady Whittonstall was correct. She could learn. 'Is there some reason you need me out here?'

'I have to do this. The need has grown in me until I can't think of anything else.' He reached forward and drew her into his arms. He lowered his mouth.

This kiss was very different from the perfunctory brush of his mouth earlier. This one lingered and lazily explored. Eleanor opened her lips as the warmth within her built. His arms tightened about her, pulling her close.

A discreet cough sounded behind her, making her recall where they were and what had nearly happened. He put her from him.

'Viv, you are not required here,' Ben said with fiercely burning eyes.

'One of Aunt Violet's Poms has escaped and I

have been roped into the search.' Viv gave an innocent whistle.

'Poms?' Eleanor asked, trying to get her heart-
rate back to normal. Being discovered locked in
Ben's arm by Lady...no *Mother* Whittonstall did
not bear thinking about.

'My mother breeds Pomeranians. She brought
three of them with her. Which one is it?'

'A little white one.' Viv gave a shrug. 'I think
the maid called him Romeo.'

'My mother always names her Pomeranians after
Shakespearian characters. Titania is the one who
nips.'

A small movement caught Eleanor's eye. She
bent down and saw a black nose and the tips of
two white bat-like ears hiding at the back of the
border. The escapee—Romeo. She held out her
hand and the little dog came snuffling forward.
She quickly reached out her other hand and captured the squirming body. The dog looked at her
with big eyes and then licked her nose.

'You've made a conquest, Eleanor,' Ben said with
a laugh.

She handed the dog to Viv, and then looked at the
smears of dirt on her gown. 'Do you think Mother

Whittonstall will forgive me? I am no longer the pristine bride.'

'It is easily brushed off.' Ben gave her his handkerchief. 'Think of the riot that dog could have caused if he had raided the wedding breakfast. You are the heroine of the hour!'

'I'll take care of this miscreant.' Viv adjusted his hold so that the dog was kept well away from his white dimity waistcoat. 'However, Aunt Violet is searching for you both. Something about the wedding cake? It was better that I discovered you. All things considered.'

'We are just married,' Ben said. 'My mother should know better.'

'A word to the wise. Discretion is better.' Viv gave a distinct wink.

'That is rich, coming from you!' Ben replied, rolling his eyes.

'But very true.' Viv's infectious laugh rang out, quickly echoed by Ben's. The dog joined in.

Viv stopped, readjusted his hold on the dog once more, and clapped Ben on the back. 'It is good to hear you laugh again, cousin.'

'I am rediscovering laughter's many pleasures.'

Eleanor stood facing Ben, trying to get her breath and knowing her face flamed as she heard Viv's footsteps retreat. How could she have given way to her passion in that fashion? She wanted to demonstrate what a good wife she could be and had simply shown that she had no sense.

'And this was…?' she asked, wrapping her arms about her waist.

'A rescue. I wanted to make sure you were fine with our not having a wedding trip.'

'With Mr Swaddle injured there is far too much for me to do,' Eleanor said, knowing it was her pride talking. 'And the kiss—was it supposed to be consolation for our not going away?'

He rubbed the back of his thumb along her aching lips. 'Because I wanted to. Because I could. To celebrate the start of our marriage. Do you object? Do you fear the physical side of marriage?'

Her heart did an odd little flip. She tried to push away Lady Whittonstall's earlier intelligence. But it niggled. She wanted to be more than a replacement wife, a wife who was needed to provide an heir. She wanted to be wanted for her own sake. She'd show him that she could play her part to perfection—even if her dress *was* now smudged with paw prints. 'We still have guests.'

'Yes, we do. My mother invited them.'

'I can't be rude.' She slipped her hand from his. 'You do understand?'

'Yes, I do.'

'I believe this will meet requirements,' Ben said, opening the door to the room he used when he visited Viv. He'd given in to Eleanor's pleas for more time for long enough. The last thing he wanted was for Eleanor to be caught up in a social whirl. When he'd married Alice she had insisted on staying at the wedding breakfast until the last guest had departed.

He noted with satisfaction that his valet Cartwright had followed his instructions. A decanter of port with two glasses and a chessboard sat on a small table in front of the fire. The bed was turned down, but that would come later if all went well. Right now he wanted to make Eleanor comfortable, ensure that she wanted to be with him.

'Your bedroom?'

'Privacy is best. I hardly want to spend my wedding night with my mother and cousin in attendance.' He ushered her in. 'When you are used to Broomhaugh you can decide on which suite you desire, but for now this one should meet requirements.'

Her neat white teeth worried her bottom lip, turning it a deep rose-red. It remained slightly swollen from the kiss they'd shared earlier. The memory of that kiss had his body thrumming. He had nearly undressed her on the terrace and his fingers itched to start now. He took a deep breath and controlled the urge. Slowly. Without rushing in like some callow youth. It had been so long since he'd made love to a woman that he worried about his ability to control his passion. And with each passing breath that desire to possess her fully grew.

He had no wish to have his passion frighten her. He wanted to get it right with Eleanor. He wanted to bury himself deep within her, but he also wanted her to enjoy the experience.

Eleanor stood in front him, her gloved hands clasped together. She had not moved a muscle since she'd walked into the room.

'I've not been in this sort of situation before. I am not sure what is expected of me.'

'Do you want a drink?' He gestured towards the port.

She shook her head. 'I'm fine. You have one if you like.'

'Take off your gloves. Make yourself at home. We have all the time in the world.'

She awkwardly removed her gloves, scrunched them in a ball, before she slid over to the chessboard and started to rearrange the pieces.

He watched her every move as she bent over the set, seemingly absorbed in placing each piece squarely on the board, wondering if he had acted too soon in bringing her up here. Perhaps they should have waited until after supper.

It had been such a long time since he'd even attempted to seduce a woman. Had he forgotten the knack? Where should he start with Eleanor?

He poured himself a glass of port, tasted it, and knew it was not something he desired at that moment. He wanted to taste her again and see if her mouth was as sweet as before.

Ever since the marriage ceremony she'd appeared nervous and on edge. Something had changed. He didn't want her to fear the physical side of marriage. He wanted her to embrace it.

'Do you play chess?' he asked in desperation.

'I have played a time or two.' Her hand paused on the black rook. With a hint of the bravado he remembered from their picnics, she continued, 'Do you intend on teaching me the finer points of the game?'

'I take it you are as good a chess-player as you are a fencer.'

'I like to think so.' She hurriedly dropped the piece and sent half a dozen other pieces skittering across the board. Her small cry of alarm filled the room and she dropped to her knees and started to pick them up. All the while she kept her face carefully from his.

'We both know where this is going to end, Eleanor,' he said. 'If it is something you don't want, then you can change your mind. We will leave this room and go back to the drawing room. But in order for a marriage to be unquestioned it needs to be consummated. You want to fulfil the terms of the will.'

'At any time?' She rocked back on her heels with the black rook still in her hand. Her eyes appeared troubled, and he was reminded how innocent she was, despite all her years of working in a man's world. And, despite her declaration the other night, he knew she knew little of what was about to happen.

His body ached with the need to bury himself deep within her, but that didn't matter. She needed to understand that she was safe with him. Nothing would happen without her consent. He wanted an eager bed partner for the rest of their lives—not someone who shrank from his touch simply because he'd been fumble-fingered on their first night. He wanted Eleanor to enjoy the physical side of marriage.

'Any time.' He cupped her face with his hands. Their breath intertwined. It took all his self-control not to cover her mouth with his. He could take her now. It was what his body wanted, what he thought she'd wanted out on the terrace, but he could sense her slight hesitation. She needed to give her consent. Seeing her great grey eyes, he knew how innocent she truly was and how much he wanted to demonstrate how good it could be. 'Is that what has been worrying you? Why you knocked the chessboard over?'

He picked up one of the knights and set it on the board. Waited for her surrender.

'Nothing is worrying me,' she said, scrambling up to face him with her chin jutting upwards. Defiant and proud. 'Nothing at all.'

'Trust me, Eleanor. Confide in me,' he said softly, as if he was coaxing a reluctant horse to take a jump. 'You enjoyed our kiss on the terrace. But something is bothering you. This is not the

Eleanor who was on the terrace with me. Neither is this the Eleanor who went on picnics with me.'

Eleanor gripped the black rook tighter. She could hardly confess about her conversation with Lady Whittonstall now. It seemed somehow wrong to bring up his tragic past. That was the last thing she wanted. But how could she *not* mention it?

'Your mother spoke to me...about your past.'

'She overstepped the mark.' His eyes became hard, but he reached out his hands towards her. 'The past doesn't concern you. Don't allow her to intimidate you into thinking it does, Eleanor.'

She longed to walk into his arms and lay her head against his chest. But equally she needed to think straight.

'Why didn't you tell me that your wife was pregnant when she died? That you lost two people that day?' The last words came out in a rush.

Instantly his hand fell to his side. He looked up at the ceiling for a long while. Eleanor knew that she had said precisely the wrong thing. He hadn't intended telling her ever.

'It is in the past, Eleanor,' he said slowly. 'She died and that is the end to it. That future never happened. There is no point in dwelling on that past.

Have I asked about how your father died? Or what drove you to devote your life to Moles?'

'If you must know, my father killed himself rather than face the debt he'd incurred. I couldn't allow the employees to suffer.'

'But that shame has nothing to do with the reason why you decided to marry me.'

'You know why I did it—the will.' Eleanor knew her words were too quick. The last thing she wanted to do was to start discussing those awful months. 'The manner of my father's death is not something I mention very often.'

'Nor is the manner of my wife's death.'

'Your mother thought it important enough to tell me,' she said in a faint tone.

'My mother had her own reasons.' He put his hands on her shoulders. His eyes turned blacker than midnight. 'I want to assure you, Eleanor, that this marriage is between us—no one else. What went before is in the past. It is the future I am spending with you that is important.'

'But—' She gripped the rook so tightly that her knuckles shone white. The effect of the rook pressing against her palm kept her focused. She was not going to make demands or show her hurt, but she wasn't going to be deterred. His past *was* important. It had made him who he was and she wanted to know everything about him.

'Eleanor, this is *our* wedding night. Why would I want to talk about anything but you?' He placed a kiss against her temple which did strange things to her insides. 'What is important for us is this, right now, between us. Nothing else matters. You must trust me on this.'

She made the mistake of glancing into his dark eyes. His gaze made her feel desirable and wanted. Her protestation died in her throat. She swallowed hard. She wanted to believe him.

His mouth slanted down and covered hers. Firmly, coaxing rather than demanding a response. Unhurried, but full of promise and expectation.

The feel of his lips moving over hers erased everything else from her mind. She forgot what she'd meant to say, how she'd planned to act, and to her amazement she discovered that she'd forgotten how to breathe properly. The world swung round and round and she had to grab onto his shoulders. The rook fell to the floor unheeded.

The intensity of the kiss deepened and the white heat urgency she'd experienced on the terrace swamped her. She wanted him.

His hands worked at the back of her gown and

she heard several of the buttons ping off. 'I'm sorry,' he murmured against her temple. 'I'm not a good ladies' maid.'

'Ben?' she said as she realised that the candles still burnt. He was going to see her naked. She had planned to have all the light doused and slip into the bed. She should have thought and asked for her maid. Between demanding to know about his late wife's death and neglecting to change she'd gone about this all wrong. 'I thought...'

'Hush, no more thinking. I have longed for this moment. Dreamt about it. I want to enjoy it.'

'You have?' Eleanor asked in wonder. 'Shouldn't we douse the lights?'

'There is no need for false modesty.' He put his finger under her chin and lifted it so that she stared directly into his eyes. 'You and I don't have to do the done thing.'

'The candles can stay lit,' she said, and hoped that he wouldn't prove disappointed.

He pushed the material of her dress down and it fell in a pool at her feet. She stepped out of it and stood only in her shift. Something flared in his eyes, making her feel desirable and even beautiful. His hand skimmed her shoulder.

'You are not wearing stays.'

'The dress was cleverly cut.' Eleanor's cheeks flamed. 'I am too thin. My curves are few.'

The dimple played in a corner of his mouth, giving him a devilish appearance. 'No one would mistake you for a man, Eleanor.'

He captured her hand and pulled her unresisting body to his. She crashed against his chest. A nervous excitement filled her.

His mouth rained tiny kisses down her face until he reached hers. Her lips instantly parted and she tasted the slight tang of the port he'd drunk earlier, as well as the clean taste of him. She looped her arms about his neck and pulled him closer.

His arms tightened, moulding her to him. Through the thin material of her shift she clearly felt his erection press into the apex of her thighs. She squirmed against him, enjoying the feeling—how the heat of his skin radiated through her shift, how his hands moved down her back to cup her bottom and hold her there. She'd thought this would be a duty, something that she'd want over quickly, but it was an absolute pleasure. She wanted it to last.

'This will be more enjoyable on the bed, Eleanor. Trust me,' he whispered against her ear, before his tongue swirled her earlobe, sending a fresh shower of sparks coursing through her body.

'I'm not sure I can make it.' She clung on to his shoulders for balance. 'My knees are like jelly.'

'That is a problem easily solved.' He bent and picked her up. 'Hang on tight.'

With a few strides he'd covered the distance to the bed. He placed her gently down and she sank into the feather tester's embrace. Above her the bed curtains loomed.

'I think we can remove the final article now,' he said.

Slowly he lifted the lawn shift over her head and then dropped it over the side of the bed. And she lay exposed, open to his view, in a way she'd never been exposed to anyone before. She started to cover herself but he caught her hands and held them above her head.

'Allow me to feast. The exact contours of your body have been playing on my mind.'

He bent his head and captured her nipple, swirling his tongue over the tightly furled bud.

Eleanor gasped as her body bucked. He then proceeded to do the same with the next nipple. A raging storm swept through her, exhilarating her, making her feel more alive than she had considered possible.

She glanced up and saw Ben looking at her with a very satisfied expression.

'I take it you approve?'

She nodded, but somehow, as good as his mouth had been, it had only served to inflame the hunger within her. She craved his touch. 'There must be more.'

He gave a very huge smile and she instantly knew she had said the right thing. Somehow that made everything seem possible. It didn't matter that she had no idea what she was doing. It only mattered that somehow her body seemed to get it right. All the taunts and dire predictions she'd suffered over the years made not a jot of difference, Ben made her feel beautiful and wanted.

'You are a demanding woman, but I am happy to oblige.'

He quickly undressed and she saw his skin gleam golden in the candlelight. She was pleased that she had agreed to leave the candles lit because otherwise she would not have seen the perfection of him. She tentatively reached out a hand and traced a line down his chest.

He drew his breath in sharply. She took it as an invitation to explore further and placed her other hand on his chest. His warm flesh moved under her fingers as he breathed in. Giving in to her impulse, she leant forward and flicked her tongue over his flat nipples. They hardened to points under her touch.

'Eleanor...' His voice sounded thick in her ear. 'Let me explore you.'

She nodded.

Slowly he stroked his hand down her body until his fingers reached her nest of curls. A single finger parted her and slid down her innermost folds. White-hot heat shot through her. If she'd thought his mouth on her breast was heaven this was total bliss. His finger probed, slipping inside her, playing. Her body tightened about him and he rubbed his palm against her mound.

'You like?' he asked, stilling his hand, leaving it hovering above the apex of her thighs.

She clawed at his shoulders, knowing that she needed more. As wonderful as this was, something was building inside her and urging her on. She wanted to explore this new heady world.

'Please,' she whispered, hardly knowing how to ask. 'I need you. I want to have more. I want it all.'

Her voice trailed away and she knew she couldn't begin to describe the pleasure that coursed through her.

'You shall have me.' He rubbed his thumb along her bottom lip and sent a fresh tremor coursing through her. 'It will hurt, Eleanor, I can't deny it. But I will be as gentle as possible. Try to relax. It will get better, but first there will be a little pain.'

She didn't look down at where he loomed, large and ready. All she knew was that she needed him. She needed this reaffirmation of life. So far it showed that everything she had thought about herself was wrong. Right now she felt utterly feminine. Maybe he was correct and the past didn't matter. Maybe all that mattered was right here and right now.

'I trust you,' she whispered.

He positioned himself between her thighs and slowly moved forward. She felt him nudge her, and then a burning sensation as he sheathed himself. She stiffened and tried not to move a muscle. She had to trust that it would become wonderful.

Ben regarded his new wife. Her passionate response to his kisses surprised and delighted him. What she lacked in experience she more than made up for in enthusiasm. He had thought he might have to coax more.

He'd been able to feast on the hollows and curves of her body with all his senses engaged. Eleanor might be willowy, but very inch of her was feminine.

He had felt her barrier break with that final thrust forward. She belonged to him now. His responsibility. He had already brought her to the brink earlier, but he wanted her first time to be memorable. Concentrating on controlling his breathing, he started to withdraw.

'It feels so right,' she breathed, tightening her arms about him. 'Nobody ever told me that this joining could feel wonderful. It is as if I've been reborn.'

He smoothed a tendril of hair from her forehead. 'I don't want to hurt you.'

'You did for a moment but it is gone now.'

Her hand stroked his back to the base of his spine and nearly destroyed his control. It amazed him how someone who was so demonstrably innocent seemed to know instinctively what he wanted. She shifted her hips, drawing him in deeper.

'Is that all or is there more?' she murmured.

'Much more.'

Her lips curved upwards in a sultry smile. 'Good.'

He drove into her, slowly, but as she lifted her hips and urged him he increased the pace. He watched her face until she hovered on the brink. Then and only then he allowed himself full release, joined her in the climax. Wave after wave washed over him.

He gave a satisfied smile. His life was about Eleanor now.

When Eleanor woke, the room was bathed in grey light. The candles had guttered down to nothing. Beside her, the bed was cold and empty. She drew the sheets up to her chin and tried to ignore the knot in her stomach. It didn't seem right for him to leave after what they had experienced together. Or maybe it was just her. All the doubts she had had about her femininity came rushing back. How could she truly have thought that she could satisfy a man like Ben?

Ben had done as he had said he would—made sure their marriage was legal. Nothing more. Nothing less. Moles was safe. It should be enough, but she knew it wasn't. She wanted to…

A faint noise made her turn her head. He stood

naked, peering out into the moonlight. His hand gripped the window seal and his shoulders shook. She thought at first that it must be grief, but then she realised he was laughing.

Eleanor put her hand over her mouth. She desperately wanted to know what he was thinking.

Had she disappointed him? Did he regret their marriage? She attempted to see his expression in the shadowy light.

'Ben?' The single word escaped her throat.

'Did I disturb you?' He turned from the window, but all she could make out was the outline of his body. 'It is very early. Is something wrong?'

'No, no. I wanted to make sure you were all right.' She held out her arms. 'Come back to bed, Ben.'

'I'm more than all right.' He walked over to the bed and gathered her in his arms. His lips touched her hair. 'Our marriage has properly begun, Eleanor. No one can gainsay it now.'

The questions she'd longed to ask died in her throat.

Did it really matter about his past? How did she compare with his late wife? Was he thinking about *her* at all? Had he only returned to her arms because she'd begged?

She hated that she wanted to know. She was competing with a ghost. He was here, with her, and she would make certain that everything was going to be fine. That he never had to think about his late wife again. The past was going to stay firmly where it belonged.

She would learn how to do everything. Mother Whittonstall would help her. She would become the sort of wife Ben deserved.

'I thank you for that from the bottom of my heart,' she said, giving her mouth up to his.

She knew then that she was in danger of falling in love with him—and that was something he had not asked for and she hadn't bargained for.

Chapter Ten

After breakfasting with Ben, Eleanor wandered out on to the terrace. Later she planned to go over to Moles and take care of the daily crises, but right now she was content to explore her new home. Her entire body ached after last night. She had sore muscles where she'd never dreamt she could have sore muscles. It was even worse than after a bout of prolonged fencing.

She put her hands in the middle of her back and stretched. Her light blue gown fluttered in the breeze. This marriage had turned out far better than she'd had the right to expect.

A small snuffling noise made her freeze. She glanced over her shoulder and saw Romeo, peeking out from the border. She crouched down and held out her hand.

'I'm sure you are not supposed to be there. Have you escaped again?'

Romeo tilted his head and stared back at her. If he'd been a person she'd have sworn he'd tell her to hush.

'Romeo! Romeo! Come here!' Ben's mother came out on to the terrace. Romeo covered his head with his muddy paws and flattened his body.

'He's here, Mother Whittonstall. In the flower-bed.'

Romeo gave her a look that said *traitor*.

She knelt down and held out her hand. 'Your owner is looking for you. Playtime is over.'

The dog shook his head and retreated further into the flowerbed.

'If you won't come out I will pick you up.'

He planted four paws in the muddy earth and dared her. Eleanor reached forward and swiftly captured the miscreant. Romeo gave a contented sigh, leaning his dirty head back against her.

Lady Whittonstall came around the corner and stopped. Her gaze seemed to take in every flaw. The frown between her eyebrows increased. 'Romeo is with *you*. I've been so worried. If you are going to take the dogs, please can you inform someone next time, Eleanor? It will save so much worry and bother. Poor Marie has been distraught.'

Eleanor winced. Why, when she met Lady

Whittonstall, did she always feel at a disadvantage? She straightened her backbone and met the woman's gaze. 'I heard you calling for him. He was in the flowerbed, intent on digging up the borders. I was the finder, not the taker.'

'He needs to get ready to go rather than play.' Lady Whittonstall gave a long sigh. 'I want to depart as soon as Vivian returns. His mother and sister are well behaved. Why can't *he* be?'

'You are returning to London?' Eleanor set Romeo down and saw the dog had put muddy paw prints on her muslin dress and one particularly large one over her bosom. Romeo did not look in the least repentant, and neither did he trot over to his mistress as Eleanor had expected. He sat down next to Eleanor and began to lick his paw.

'Of course, my dear Eleanor.' Lady Whittonstall looked at her as if she'd grown two heads. 'My work is done here. And neither Vivian nor I desire to play gooseberry. You and my son are properly married. Although it was hasty, everyone could see that I welcomed my son's bride into the bosom of the family. It is the right thing to do. One doesn't want gossip.'

'I thank you for that.' Eleanor inclined her head and wondered where this conversation was going.

Did Lady Whittonstall expect her to go down on her knees in gratitude?

Lady Whittonstall reached into her reticule. 'I'm sorry we haven't time for a little chat, but I've written a list of useful things in case you should need them. It is a harsh world out there, and I have no wish for my new daughter to be unprepared. You will have get rid of your white muslin. *Ackermann's Repository* was quite clear on the subject—muslin is quite exploded and should be confined to the less distinguished order of attire. My dear, as *my* daughter-in-law, your attire must always be of the highest order.'

'I thought the gown pretty.'

'Pretty doesn't come into it.' Lady Whittonstall gave a long sigh. 'Undoubtedly you consider me a harpy of the worst sort and that people should see the real you. But believe me, my dear, people in society…well…they operate on a different plane. They prefer style to substance.'

Eleanor suddenly understood this speech was one Lady Whittonstall had given many times. She was grateful for it, but she didn't need it. She knew all about society and the need to impress. Moles made its fortune on that very fact.

'Thank you.' Eleanor slipped the envelope unopened into her pocket. There would be time enough to feel inadequate later. She might even destroy it before she read it. Right now, she was savouring the news that she would be alone with Ben. 'Shall I carry Romeo in for you? I think he may have rolled in something nasty.'

'That dog!' Lady Whittonstall gave a long-suffering sigh. 'He has no sense of timing. He had a huge fight with his sister Juliet this morning. I don't know how I will cope with the two of them in the carriage. Dear Vivian is sweet, but he has no idea about dog management. That dog is a severe disappointment to me.'

'Perhaps he would like to stay here?' Eleanor said on impulse. Romeo raised his nose and stared directly at her, his bat ears quivering. She knew what it was like to be a disappointment. 'We could bring him when we come to London...if it will make it easier?'

She waited for Lady Whittonstall to decline the offer. Instead Lady Whittonstall turned quite pink with pleasure. In that instant Eleanor realised that Lady Whittonstall was not invincible. That she, too, wanted to be judged on more than style. The knowledge brought Eleanor comfort.

'You like Pomeranians?' Lady Whittonstall

asked eagerly. 'Why didn't Benjamin say? He never tells me anything of importance.'

'I've only met Romeo,' Eleanor confessed. 'But he seems lovely. I prefer to judge dogs on their personalities rather than their breed. But then I am not in society. Is there a fashion for dogs?'

Lady Whittonstall had the grace to blush.

'I personally prefer the smaller Pomeranians, but the Queen has an affinity for larger ones. I'm not sure what the old Empress Josephine prefers, but she is supposed to be fond of the breed.'

Eleanor's shoulders relaxed. She knew she did the same thing when she was nervous—mentioned people that she considered to have good taste as having had the good sense to buy her swords. Perhaps Lady Whittonstall was not that fearsome? It was time to build bridges rather than to take offence. She refused to allow anyone to spoil the day.

'Is Ben fond of the breed?'

'Ben grew up with them, but Alice was not an animal person,' Lady Whittonstall said with crushing dignity. 'It was the one place where her view and mine did not coincide.'

Eleanor stored that little chunk of information. Alice hadn't been perfection.

'I don't know many, but Romeo is a scamp. He

very nearly ruined my wedding dress with his paw prints. I like to think we have a certain rapport. It would be good to have a dog. My stepfather wasn't fond of dogs and I went with his wishes.' Eleanor stroked Romeo's head and the small dog instantly licked her hand.

Lady Whittonstall looked amazed. 'He has never done that to a stranger before. He has obviously decided you are his person. Pomeranians are very choosy about whom they like, but once they decide they like you they are loyal.'

Eleanor decided to be truthful. She didn't want to claim some sort of prowess with the dog who was now looking up at her with adoring eyes. 'He probably smells the bacon from my breakfast.'

'Do you enjoy belittling yourself, Eleanor?'

Eleanor bit her lip. 'I hardly know how to answer that.'

'The dog likes you. He is yours to keep. You may have him as a wedding present from me.' Lady Whittonstall gave a huge smile. 'You are family now, after all, and you are going to provide me with a grandchild. That is the reason why Benjamin married you. Who could be more fitting to have Romeo?'

Eleanor forced herself to smile back and not to

hear the unspoken words—*as much as I may dis-approve*. She concentrated instead on the little face that gazed up at her. The dog appeared to want her. 'I'm happy to help out.'

'Did you offer to keep the dog just to please my mother?' Ben asked as they stood waving good-bye to the carriage.

Romeo had not left Eleanor's side since she'd agreed to have him. Eleanor bent down and stroked his ears. His pink tongue gave her hand a little lick. 'No, I offered because I like the dog, and could understand his reluctance to be cooped up with your mother and Vivian for days on end.'

'As long as you know that you didn't have to do it to please me.'

'I wasn't thinking about you.' Eleanor held back from asking about Alice and whether *she* had done things just to please him. 'I haven't had a dog since my father died. It is time I had one.'

Ben raised his eyebrow. 'How did you lose your dog?'

Eleanor gulped in a lungful of air. She had to tell him so he'd understand why she wanted Romeo.

'My father suffered from a fit of the blue devils and shot him just before he shot himself. They were found together.'

'Could it have been an accident?'

Eleanor shook her head. 'There was a note.'

'Which you found?' His eyes turned troubled.

'There wasn't time afterwards for me to get a dog,' Eleanor said, not bothering to deny it. She simply didn't want to relive the trauma of those days—not when her future stood in front of her. Ben had been right. It was better to go beyond the past and make a new start. There were some things that were better left unsaid. 'It wouldn't have suited. Perhaps you are right. Perhaps I should have thought. I will be awfully busy...'

She avoided looking at Romeo's little face. If Ben didn't want the dog she'd find a good home for it. It would be better that way. Next time she'd remember to consult him. A lesson learnt. She wouldn't make that mistake again. She didn't want anything to jeopardise the new-found closeness she had with him.

'You didn't want to give your stepfather any opportunity to abuse a dog,' Ben said, before she had a chance to make her offer. 'That's why you decided not to have one. Not because you were too busy. I was wrong to question you and I am delighted you have now found a dog.'

She glanced into his eyes and his dark gaze seared her soul. He knew without her saying. He'd remembered the swords in the house.

Eleanor buried her face in Romeo's fur. Why did Ben have this habit of so accurately guessing? It would be easy to start to care for him and to hope that their marriage could become more than just a convenience.

'We shall keep him?'

Ben put his hand on her shoulder. 'I think that little dog has landed on his paws.'

She stood up and brushed her skirt down. 'It is not the only thing that his paws have landed on. This is the second dress he has ruined today.'

'What are you planning for the rest of the day?' A seductive gleam in his eye deepened.

'I need to get back to Moles.' Eleanor strove for a natural tone as her breath came quicker. What did *he* plan? She had spent the morning trying to forget her desire for him.

'Tomorrow. No one is expecting you today.' He turned her towards him. His eyes were heavy with sensual promise. 'You can't leave Romeo alone. He'd miss you too much.'

'You are quite right. Romeo would hate that.' Her voice caught slightly. Was he asking her to stay? Did he want her with the same ache with which she wanted him? This was all so new to her.

'I can see the dog will have his uses,' he murmured, pulling her against his body.

'I'm glad you approve.' She gave her lips up to his.

Eleanor walked into the library at Broomhaugh. The French doors leading out to the terrace were open to allow in the heat of the late-August afternoon. Romeo trotted at her heels.

The little dog had taken to going to the foundry with her and sleeping in the office as she worked. She'd been pleasantly surprised at how well behaved Romeo was. True, he occasionally barked at Mrs Nevin, and dug holes in the borders, but she'd come to appreciate him.

Ben looked up from his pile of correspondence. His curly hair was slightly mussed and he had an ink smudge on his cheek. Eleanor's heart did a funny flip. She liked him best, she decided, when he wasn't perfect and pristine but had been absorbed in something.

Romeo gave a sharp little bark and bounded over to demand that his undercarriage be tickled.

'You are early,' Ben said, bending down to adore Romeo, who made little snuffling noises of appreciation at the attention.

'Is that a problem? I can go away.'

'I am surprised, but pleased.' Ben rose and enfolded her in his arms. She rested her head against his chest, listening to the sound of his heartbeat. 'Is there some reason? Or did Romeo miss me too much?'

'Can't you tell from the way Romeo greeted you? He was desperate to see you.'

She leant back against his arms. Somehow it was easier to talk about Romeo missing him rather than admitting that she had been the one. She'd found it nearly impossible to keep her mind on the meeting with Mr Swaddle's son and Mr Johnson about the new sword range. She'd spent the entire meeting wondering what Ben was doing and if he could be persuaded to make love to her. She enjoyed their lovemaking, but it seemed right to let him make the first move.

'And I wanted to put our new lady's sword to the test and desired an excellent opponent—someone who will test my skills to the utmost.'

'And that someone would be me?' He pushed the hair from her face.

She smiled back at him. It seemed incredible that in a few weeks he'd become the centre of her existence. She knew the sword and Romeo were transparent excuses to see him, but it didn't matter. It was better than admitting her true feelings. He had made it clear at the outset that the best she could hope for was companionship. It wasn't his fault that she longed for something much less tepid. She wanted fire and passion.

'I need a worthy opponent.'

'May I see the sword?' he asked, moving away from her. 'A few more visitors left their cards while you were out. They are over there.'

Eleanor wrinkled her nose. More cards. She knew she needed to make visits, but her work took precedence. And if they had been normal they would have still been on their honeymoon. 'I will write short notes later. Who knew that there were so many people to visit in the area?'

'My mother would be appalled. She always answers them straight away. Whenever she returns to the house, the first thing she does is collect up any cards that have been left in her absence and answer them.'

And what would Alice have done? Eleanor bit back the words before they spilled from her mouth. She hated the little curl of jealousy. It happened at the oddest times. Ben never mentioned his late wife, never confided about his first marriage or the child he'd lost. Other than when he'd decided to keep Romeo he'd never mentioned her past troubles, either. The past was behind her. Behind them both.

'Lucky your mother is not here, then,' she said, keeping her chin up and pushing away the feeling. The list his mother left remained sealed and pushed under a pile of handkerchiefs. She kept finding reasons why she couldn't possibly open it.

'I certainly have no plans to tell her.' He gave a half-smile. 'It is refreshing that you put other things ahead of your social obligations.'

Eleanor took a deep breath. It was impossible to tell if that was a compliment or not. And if it wasn't she didn't want to know. She quickly went and retrieved the sword. She held it out to him.

'You see there is a slight difference in the balance? Ladies prefer a lighter sword, but it still has to be firm. This is not a toy. You need to adjust your grip accordingly. Getting the hilt right took dedication. Davy Swaddle had to recast it three times, but I think this time it works. Romeo agrees.'

The dog gave a little snuffle of approval before wandering out of the room and into the garden.

Ben turned the sword over. His long fingers curved around the hilt and his lips became a thin white line. '*You* managed to make the correct hilt? Are you making steel again?'

'Steel is far too expensive for a hilt. It needs to be saved for the blade,' Eleanor said lightly. The last thing she wanted was an argument about her being near the furnace. She knew he wasn't happy about the accident before the wedding, but she hoped he'd trust her to be sensible. She trusted Davy to know what he was doing, yet his father's accident still gave her nightmares. There would be time enough to work on the super-flexible sword when Mr Swaddle returned. 'We used silver plate with brass highlights.'

'You didn't answer the question.' There was a definite edge to his voice. 'Has Mr Swaddle come back?'

Eleanor's heart sank. She really didn't want to quarrel about this. Not today. And particularly not when she was innocent.

'Mr Swaddle will return in a week or two. His arm is healing nicely, but the burn was deep and takes a long time. Why?'

'I was curious.' He turned the sword over. 'No engraving?'

'This is a prototype. I want to see if it is light enough and yet not easy to dislodge.' She struggled to keep her voice even. 'That is if I can find a willing partner?'

His eyes developed a slight twinkle. 'You are suggesting fencing in the library?'

'Best place for it now that Viv has taken his vases away and his pictures have gone into storage.'

'Do you have many customers who are ladies?'

'You'd be surprised. We have them from all walks of life.' Eleanor gestured with the sword. 'The reputable, the demi-rep, and some distinctly disreputable who pay cash. I prefer those who pay cash.'

'Are you trying to be shocking?'

'Not particularly.'

He shook his head. 'My mother would have a fit if you voiced such a sentiment in public. She likes to pretend such women don't exist.'

'That would be folly for Moles.'

'And Moles comes first?'

'In matters of business, yes,' Eleanor said firmly. 'I do know how to behave in public, Ben. And your mother left a long list of instructions just in case I should encounter something unfamiliar.'

His gaze narrowed. 'Where is the list now?'

'I put it under my handkerchiefs,' Eleanor admitted. 'I haven't had time to look at it.'

His eyes sobered. 'You would do well to tear it into little pieces. My mother is notoriously overbearing in her instructions. She has reduced people to tears in the past.'

Eleanor tilted her head. 'What are you saying?'

He reached out and touched her shoulder. 'I like you as you are, Eleanor.'

Eleanor ducked her head. *Like,* not love. She amused him. She had to wonder if Alice had amused him. 'Are we going to fence?'

'I'd be delighted. Shall you fence like a reputable client or a disreputable one?'

'What would your mother say?'

'It is most definitely not any of her business.'

A tiny bubble of laughter welled up in her. Ever since their wedding night Ben seemed happier and more relaxed. That had to be a good thing. But she couldn't help feeling that this contentment wouldn't last. And she certainly didn't want to be the one to destroy it. Despite giving him opportunities, he never spoke about his late wife or what he'd done in London. He never mentioned going to London to see his mother.

She was conscious of feeling that it was all too good to last. And every day she wanted it to last a little longer. Every day she was pleased when he kissed her or brushed her hand. It meant he still desired her. That this fire she felt for him wasn't one-sided.

'Will you fence in a gown or in breeches?'

'Does it matter?'

His slow gaze travelled down her, caressing her curves. She grew hot from his glance. Physically he took her to places she'd never dreamt possible. He made her feel beautiful and wanted. But how long would it last? How long until he wanted to rejoin society? Before the little endearing things became massive annoyances? Until he started to judge her by her appearance and discovered her lacking?

Eleanor thought about the list. She might have placed it under her handkerchiefs but she wasn't going to get rid of it. Before she entered society she would know each and every item on it. She did intend to do it. It was simply that Moles had to come first.

'I like you in both.' The dimple in his cheek deepened. 'It depends on how vigorous your intended clients will be.'

'Shall we place a wager?'

'You lost the last time,' he reminded her, and a slow curl of desire wound its way around her insides. She knew precisely how delicious losing had been.

'And *you* lost the time before,' she retorted. 'And I only lost because you distracted me with a kiss.'

'That was because you had the most delightful frown. And we both benefited.'

'I will fence in my gown.' Eleanor kept her mind away from how he'd undressed her last night, using the tip of his sword to cut the buttons off her gown. If she thought about what might happen afterwards she'd never stand a chance. And, although it was pleasant to lose to Ben, it was much more fun to win. She wanted to cut the buttons off his shirt. 'I always assume my clients to be reputable.'

'And the wager?'

'The winner gets to decide what we do for the rest of the afternoon,' Eleanor proclaimed.

'Then I had best play to win,' Ben said with a distinct gleam in his eye.

She wet her lips. The faint feeling of being un-settled was back—as if she'd been riding back-wards in a carriage for a long time. It had been there yesterday morning and this morning, but had gone after she'd eaten a square of toast. Romeo had had the remainder. It annoyed her that it had returned. She wanted to fence, not to eat. She'd shunned lunch at the foundry because she'd wanted to return to Broomhaugh early, and the smell of chicken soup always made her stomach feel upset.

She willed the wave of whatever it was to go. The last thing she wanted Ben to think was that she was somehow delicate and in need of cosset-ing. She'd been looking forward to fencing all day.

'You appear a bit pale, Eleanor.'

'I'm fine,' Eleanor snapped, and immediately regretted it. 'Truly I am. The thought of fencing with you has kept me going all morning.'

'Was it that bad?'

'Mr Johnson wanted to discuss our latest order from the Bow Street Runners for cutlasses. Why does that man have the ability to turn the simplest thing into a great drama? It was all straightforward until he started muttering about the type of hilt.'

She looped a tendril of hair behind her ear. 'You had best be ready. I have some excess energy to work off.'

Ben did not smile at her feeble attempt at a joke. If anything, his face became sterner. 'Are you sure you are not overdoing it? Surely Mr Johnson can make some of the decisions? Or even Mr Swaddle's son. He seems to be sound.'

'Things will be less frantic when Mr Swaddle returns.' She put her hands behind her back and tried to ease it. She knew she was working harder than ever before, but she wanted to spend time with Ben. It wasn't his fault that this was one of the busiest times of the year. 'I suspect lack of sleep is not helping either.'

'And whose fault would that be?'

'Both of ours,' she admitted.

'Once Mr Swaddle returns I want to reclaim my wife. We are supposed to be on honeymoon. Sometimes I feel I see Romeo more than I see you.'

'Romeo goes where I go, so that is impossible.'

'You know what I mean, Eleanor. You can delegate.'

'I am here now—ready to fence. I want you to give me a good match, but I am particularly interested in the parry and counter-attack.'

'You take the swords very seriously.'

'Someone has to. Someone has to care.'

Eleanor lifted the sword and had to readjust her stance to take account of the sword's lightness. It had nothing to do with the light-headed feeling that suddenly swamped her.

The sword was far too light for her preference, but many of the ladies, particularly in London, desired a lightweight sword. Fencing with it with a skilled opponent was necessary, and she'd promised to report back on it. If only she could clear the muddle from her brain. She felt as if she was on a packet bound for London rather than being in Broomhaugh's library. She brought her foot down far too heavily.

Ben cupped her cheek and his thumb lightly stroked her skin. The gentle touch did much to dispel her queasiness. It took all her strength not to rest her head against his chest.

'Are you sure you want to pursue this? We could have a quieter pursuit? Perhaps a game of chess? Or we could go for a stroll with Romeo. A bit of air?'

'I came home specifically to fence.'

It still amazed Eleanor how quickly this place had become home and how easily the word tripped off her tongue. How familiar the walls were. She still had not chosen her rooms, preferring to stay with Ben. That would come in time. Right now she enjoyed the pleasure of waking up in his arms. Other than on that first night, he'd never slipped away to look out of the window.

'You can always change your mind.'

'I came home to fence...with you. No other opponent would do.' Her voice came out high and tight. Ben had to realise that she needed to do this. She wanted to win and to demand her reward.

'That's what I like about you, Eleanor.'

'What's that?' she asked suspiciously.

'Your determination. Once you set your course there is no dissuading you.'

Eleanor tilted her head. How bad did she look? Had he guessed that she wasn't feeling well? She'd hated it when her mother had used feeling weak as an excuse. Weakness like that was for other people. Not her!

'Of course if you don't feel up to it I'll understand. After all we have been having a few late nights, and you have been working hard to get the estate in order. And you *are* older than me.'

'You make it sound like I'm in my dotage.' He reached for his sword. 'I wanted to give you the option in case *you* preferred a more sedate occupation.'

Eleanor squared her shoulders. A little thing like feeling sick was not going to stand in her way. She'd looked forward to this all day. To how she was going to undress him and suggest they make love in the library rather than in their bedroom. 'Shall we have at it?'

Their swords clashed and Eleanor allowed the now familiar rhythm of fencing with Ben to fill her. The exertion allowed a faint breeze to wash over her, cooling her. It felt good to be active rather than sitting behind a desk. Yes, this was the right thing to be doing.

Ben parried, pivoting to the right—a simple manoeuvre, one which he had made a hundred times before. She was ready for it and proud that she had anticipated it. She pivoted to the left to block his move. Too fast. The world spun slightly. Becoming unbalanced, she put her foot down a bit too heavily and stumbled. She gripped the sword but the hilt was suddenly slippery in her hand.

'You can do better than that!'

Ben's laughing voice came from a long way away. She dropped the sword and put her hands on her knees. She attempted to focus on Romeo, who had come back into the library completely covered in dirt. The world turned black at its edges. 'Give me a moment.'

'Eleanor?'

'I will be fine. All I need is time.' Even saying the words was an effort. Her lungs refused to fill with air. She wanted to breathe. 'Air! I. Want. Air.'

Chapter Eleven

'Eleanor!'

Ben dropped his sword as his wife went very pale and crumpled before his eyes. She pitched forward on the library's Turkish carpet, missing the edge of the oak table by a hair's breadth.

He reached her side in a single stride, turned her over and lifted her shoulders up. Eleanor's lips were tinged blue and her skin was a clammy white. Her head lolled to one side.

Panic clawed at his stomach. He concentrated on checking that she was fine rather than running nightmare scenarios through his head that somehow the blade had cut her. No blood. Nothing. Simply Eleanor in a faint.

Deliberate?

Ben rejected the notion instantly. Not Eleanor. Eleanor didn't do things like fainting for effect. His mother's protégées might. One of his mother's proud boasts was that she taught her girls how to faint with elegance and grace, rather than falling to the floor in a crumpled heap. That was not Eleanor's style. She was bigger than that. His heart clenched.

When had he started to care for her? Beyond as a friend? When had this started? If he cared for her he could lose her, and he wasn't prepared to lose her. He hadn't planned on that.

He pushed the thought away. His feelings for Eleanor were too new to be examined. The one thing that thrummed through him was the fact that he had to protect Eleanor and prevent this from ever happening again. He should have stopped the bout earlier. He should have seen that she was in trouble. He knew about her recklessness and inclination to ignore her own safety.

Romeo came over and licked her hand, as if he knew something was wrong and was trying to wake her.

'Leave off, Romeo,' Ben growled. 'Sit.'

The dog looked at him quizzically, gave a sharp bark, but obeyed the command.

Ben gathered Eleanor more firmly to him and

the faintest whisper of a breath hit his cheek. She moaned softly.

He whispered a silent prayer as relief rushed through him. There would be a second chance for him to get it right. History would not repeat itself.

Her lashes fluttered slightly and her grey eyes stared up into his. She lifted a hand and touched his cheek.

'Ben? What is wrong? You appear to have seen a ghost.'

'Eleanor! What are you playing at?' Concerned anger filled him. How dared she frighten him like that?

She gave a wry smile. 'Never pivot on an empty stomach. Particularly when your stays are tight.'

Ben didn't smile back. He refused to allow her to make light of what had just happened. Laughing it off was the wrong thing to do. Eleanor had to understand that as her husband he had a duty to protect her. The muscles in his neck eased. Duty and responsibility were far easier than examining why he felt this way. 'When did you last eat?'

A crease developed between her brows. 'This morning. I had a little toast. Romeo had the rest.' She ruffled Romeo's fur. 'Romeo loves toast.'

Romeo looked up at her with adoring eyes. Ben

pressed his lips together. He'd seen her do this be-fore—particularly after Mr Swaddle's accident. Seeking to deflect his concern by concentrating on other people—or the dog. It stopped now. If Eleanor couldn't look after herself he'd do it for her. He was her husband.

'Stop feeding the dog at the table. When did you last eat properly? Something beyond buttered toast?'

She bit her lip. 'Last night.'

Even then she hadn't eaten much, he recalled. He should have seen it before. She was sickening for something. Or, worse, she'd become worried about her figure. He'd had that with Alice and it wasn't going to start with Eleanor. He wanted his woman healthy, not fashionable. His stomach clenched. She had become his responsibility whether he liked it or not. Whether he'd sworn it wouldn't happen again after Alice or not. He *had* to look after her.

'It is three o'clock in the afternoon. You drove the governess cart to Moles early this morning and worked straight through—all on a small meal last night and a square of toast this morning. You thought you could fence on that amount of food?'

'I wasn't hungry.' She struggled against the

bounds of his arms. 'A momentary weakness. Stop making it into something else.'

Ben didn't even try to keep the sarcasm from his voice. 'What are you trying to tell me? You are worried that your figure might not be fashionable?'

'I gave up on following fashion a long time ago. I settle for fitting into my clothes.' She screwed up her nose. 'Not that it matters, but I'm gaining weight. My stays are a bit tighter recently. Mrs Nevin had to let the lacing out this morning.'

'Are you given to suddenly collapsing, then?'

'Hardly. Imagine if I gave way to vapours at the foundry. How could I command the men's respect then?' There was a proud tilt to her chin but her eyes slid away from his. 'I pivoted too quickly. End of story.'

'Were you going to tell me about this feeling un-well if you hadn't collapsed?'

'Why?' She gave a maddening shrug of her shoulders. 'You are making an enormous fuss over nothing, Ben. I locked my knees on an empty stomach. It won't happen again. A unique combi-nation of circumstances conspired against me. But I ended up in the right place. In your arms.'

She wriggled so that she was more firmly planted in his lap. Ben's body responded instantly to her nearness. He hated his lack of control where Eleanor was concerned. He should be thinking about her welfare rather than wanting to kiss her, taste her skin, or worse still sink deep within her and forget the blind panic that had accompanied the knowledge that he cared for her. It was precisely the wrong approach.

He carefully removed her from his lap and fixed her with his gaze. 'And what do you propose to do?'

She stood up, swaying slightly as she reached for her sword. Her hair curled in damp tendrils about her face and there was a determined set to her jaw. 'The match remains unfinished. I never quit the field first.'

Ben plucked the sword from her hand and set it down on the ground. 'The first thing you are going to do is eat properly. Never fence on an empty stomach again.'

She made a face. 'And if I am far from hungry?'

'You lost the match,' Ben reminded her. Next time he would be more cautious and remember that Eleanor disliked paying attention to her body's demands. He refused to make the same mistake twice. He would be a better husband from now on. He refused to repeat his past mistakes. 'It is up to the winner to decide what happens next. Our wager.'

'The match was abandoned.' She lifted her chin and gave a pale imitation of her usual bravado. 'The wager no longer signifies.'

'Due to your fainting—which you claim is because you failed to eat properly.'

'Fine. I will eat.' She crossed her arms and her face took on a mulish expression. 'You are making far too much of it. It was quite simple—a pivot on an empty stomach and too much spinning about like some whirligig top. I feel much better now.'

'After you eat we'll see…'

'See what?'

'See how you are.' He put his hand on her shoulder. He searched her face. He hated the nagging sense that something else was wrong—something more serious. He hated the sense that he was going to lose her and step back into the shadow world of grief. He'd chosen Eleanor because she was strong, but now she needed to be looked after as she refused to do it herself. 'If you are no better you will go to bed.'

Her eyes widened. 'You are thinking of getting the doctor out over a little thing like this?'

'What a tremendously good idea.' Ben placed a

kiss against her forehead. Her skin was cool, not feverish. A good sign. 'We can have tea and toast while we wait.'

She gave a weak smile and squeezed his hand in a most un-Eleanor-like manner before sinking down on to the chaise-longue. She clasped her hands about her middle. 'That will be good. I'm feeling not quite the thing.'

Something in the way she looked stirred a long-suppressed memory. Ben frowned. It was far too soon. He wasn't ready for something like that. It had to be weeks before anything happened. It had taken Alice *years* to fall pregnant. Alice's desire to become pregnant had gradually pervaded every corner of their relationship until Ben felt all the joy and sparkle had vanished.

'How long since you last had your monthly visitor?' he asked, using his mother's expression. The number of times he'd seen her quiz Alice over it, and how upset Alice had been. Then, when she'd finally been able to tell for definite, she'd run out to greet his mother, telling her before she told him. It assaulted his memory. Silently he prayed he was wrong. 'Does it come regularly?'

Eleanor looked perplexed, and then her brow cleared. 'Two weeks before we married. I'm usually very regular.' She put her hand over her mouth. 'But it's been nearly three months since we married. With everything that was happening I forgot about it. It never occurred to me. Ben, you don't think…?'

Her face became an expression of delight as she put her hand to her stomach. When Alice had been pregnant it had been all about the child and what was going to happen once she had produced The Heir. It had become a sort of madness with her. Why did women desire babies so much? He wanted a wife more than he wanted to procreate.

'It is a possibility. You *do* know how babies are made?'

'I simply hadn't thought about the possibility,' she said, stuffing her hand in her mouth. 'That sort of thing happens to other people, not me. I accepted that years ago, when all my friends married and had babies. I walked a different pathway. But, yes, it would be a pleasant occurrence. A very pleasant one.'

'You do want children?' he asked carefully.

'What woman doesn't?' she answered far too quickly. 'Your mother will be so pleased. When she gave me Romeo she mentioned how important it was that I produce an heir.'

Ben silently cursed. His mother and her precious dynasty. All he could see was the shadow of a coffin behind Eleanor if she didn't change her ways. She'd worked too hard and ignored her body's demands. 'I have warned you against listening to her. She is the one fixated on a dynasty. Not me.'

'I do want children, Ben. It will be wonderful to pass my heritage along. I plan to be an excellent mother.'

'I'm sure you will be.'

Ben could easily picture a little girl with Eleanor's eyes and the way she tilted her chin. But just as quickly he could also see that coffin, with Eleanor ghostly pale. A deep chill invaded his being.

Ben pinched the bridge of his nose and banished the image. This time he wouldn't take any chances. Eleanor needed to be kept safe. He was not going to make the same mistakes twice. He was not going to live with the guilt of having failed her as well. And he had seen that she refused to admit any weakness just now. This time he would cheat death.

'Are you ready to go to bed? I think it is best if you use the rose bedroom,' he said, naming the room his mother had used. It was supposed to have been Eleanor's but she had not spent any time in it. Having her there rather than in his bed would make it easier for him to keep his distance.

'I'm not sure it is necessary. We're going to have tea and toast while we wait for the doctor.'

She wrapped her arms about her legs, bringing her knees up to her chest. She peeked up at him from under her lashes and he saw a pale imitation of the woman who had been making his nights so enjoyable. His heart twisted. He should have noticed the changes before now.

'Bed, Eleanor.'

'If you are asking if I want to spend the afternoon in bed with you…' She stretched slightly, highlighting the curve of her breasts. 'I might be open to suggestions. But if the doctor is to be called he might think it odd that we are not here to greet him.'

'That wasn't a question, Eleanor.' He smoothed the hair from her forehead, ignoring the sudden rush of blood throbbing through him. Eleanor never made suggestions like that. She normally allowed him to make a suggestion. A cold fear clawed at his insides. She wanted to distract him. 'Fainting is not your usual way, and you remain pale.'

She gave a weak smile. 'If it will make you happy. But I feel so much better now that I know what it must be. Sometimes you know. It is bound to be a boy. A strong boy. We can teach him to fence and...'

'I am thinking about it.' He put a hand on her shoulder and her flesh quivered under his fingers. 'You will need to take care of yourself, whatever happens. I refuse to have you fainting again. Let me carry you upstairs.'

'I am hardly made of spun glass. I have a backbone of pure steel.' She stood up, but immediately put her hands behind her back as if it pained her. A frown crossed her face but rapidly cleared. 'I'll give in gracefully this time, as you won the match. You may carry me upstairs if it will make you happy.'

Ben picked her up. Her soft scent filled his nostrils as her breasts crushed into his chest. He struggled to dampen down his desire for her. Her face remained too pale and her eyes far too large.

'We shall see what the doctor says.' Ben pressed his lips against her hair and mounted the stairs with grim determination. This time he was not taking any chances. This time he would keep his wife safe.

* * *

Eleanor lay staring up at the white dimity bed curtains. She hated being in bed alone while the sun shone. The dull ache in her middle had become an insistent cramping. There would be no baby.

The doctor moved about the rose bedroom, putting his various instruments back in his black bag. Ben hovered like an avenging angel, insisting that the doctor check everything from her heart to her lungs, peering into her eyes and ears.

'There is no reason why you won't have children, Lady Whittonstall...in time,' the doctor said with infuriating cheeriness. 'Despite losing this pregnancy you appear fit and well. A few days' rest and then you may resume your regular activities. Many of my ladies suffer a miscarriage, particularly in the early days. In next to no time you will hear the patter of tiny feet.'

Eleanor forced a sickly smile at the easy platitudes spilling out from Dr Fairchild's lips. Her entire world had collapsed and the doctor was making it sound like an everyday occurrence—something that she'd forget once she had another child in her arms. The heartiness in his tone made her want to hit something. Hard.

Didn't he realise that this had been more than

a pregnancy? Those few brief shining moments when she had thought herself pregnant she had known what it was. It had been all her hopes and dreams for the future, her legacy. The person whom she would love unconditionally until the day she died.

'Listen to the doctor, Eleanor,' Ben said from where he stood at the foot of the bed. She'd thought that Ben would leave the room when the doctor arrived, but he'd stayed, listening with his arms crossed and his face inscrutable.

'Yes,' she said, around the lump in her throat.

'I'm pleased you are taking this so well, Lady Whittonstall.' The doctor gave another of his hearty smiles. Eleanor hated him for it. 'Within a year I predict you will be holding a wee bairn in your arms and all this bother will be a distant memory.'

'If you say so.' Eleanor forced the words from her throat.

She willed him to finish and go, taking all his wise sayings and ill-thought-out messages of hope with him. Her entire body felt like a limp dishrag, wrung out and sore, and he dared speak of future children and other trite things.

'I do, indeed. The future may seem bleak today,

Lady Whittonstall, but once you have a baby this will be no more than a minor hiccup. I've seen it happen more times than I would like to count.'

'I will bear that in mind,' she said, and tried to stop her body from shaking. But she couldn't even do that. She bit her hand to stop the tears from falling. Today would be forever scarred on her conscience.

'My wife needs her rest, Doctor. We will contact you if we need anything else.' Ben's tone allowed for no refusal.

Eleanor gave Ben a grateful glance. She owed him so much. For what he'd done for her and how Moles was now safe. And yet she'd lost the one thing he wanted. She'd blithely assured him that all would be well, basically laughing in his face when he'd counselled caution and told her that she was working too hard. He'd been right all along.

'You do that.' The doctor gave her shoulder a perfunctory pat. 'And drink that laudanum. It will help ease the pain.'

The pain of her body. But her heart? Eleanor knew nothing could ever ease that. Her very soul seemed to be torn in pieces. She'd failed in something so basic and important. She had not even really considered the possibility until it was too

late. And now she didn't know what was worse—
not knowing or knowing about her body's failure
to nurture this baby. She picked up the glass with
the laudanum, tilted it and put it back down again.
Untouched. 'Later. The pain is manageable.'

A great enveloping silence descended. Ben continued to stand there, looking at her with sombre
eyes.

'The doctor is right, Eleanor.' He held out his
hand. 'Take your medicine and the pain won't be
so bad. You can stop being brave. Everything will
be better tomorrow.'

'You can't promise something like that.' Eleanor
ignored his outstretched fingers and turned her
face towards the wall. 'No one can. I don't want
to think about the future.'

'You will soon. Trust me on this.'

All she knew was that she couldn't go through
it again—the pretence that Ben desired her and
wanted her when all he'd wanted was a child. And
yet her arms ached to hold a baby. Was it wrong
to want more when the wanting made her heart
ache so?

She glanced back over her shoulder. 'Leave me
now, Ben. My eyes grow tired.'

He looked as if he were going to say something

else. 'Take your medicine first. It will help to ease the pain. Help you to sleep. You need to sleep. It cures most things.'

'Sleep won't cure this.'

'Do it as a favour to me. Let me rest easier, knowing you have had the medicine.'

'If it means you will leave me alone, I will.'

'If that is your desire, I will let you rest after you've taken your medicine. It is your choice.'

Defiantly she downed it in a single gulp. The medicine coursed hot and bitter down her throat. 'Are you satisfied?'

He took the glass from her fingers, being careful not to touch her. 'For now.'

She waited until his footsteps died away. She turned her head and even the bright sunshine mocked her. By rights it should be pouring down, or at least be misty.

Everywhere people were going about their business, but she was in this dimity-hung bed in a lawn nightgown as her hopes and dreams flowed out of her. She felt far too numb to cry. She simply stared at her hands. The engagement ring and the wedding band stood out. Gold against the white of her hands.

That was a mockery as well. Their marriage was

not some great romance but an alliance. He'd ensured that Moles and its employees would survive, but she'd failed to provide him with the one thing he craved.

The door creaked open and she instantly sat up, plastering a smile on her face and wiping her eyes with the back of her hand. Ben had returned. But a dark wet nose appeared at the side of bed.

'Oh, Romeo.' She leant down and gathered the dog to her, even though she knew strictly speaking Romeo should not be on the bed. Sometimes comfort was more important than rules. Romeo snuggled against her, his solid body warming her increasingly cold one. She was grateful for the dog, but wished it was Ben.

She dug her hands into Romeo's fur and stared at the dimity curtains.

The memory of Ben's stricken look when the doctor had announced she had lost the baby haunted her. It had been gone in an instant, but she'd known then that she had lost something precious. She hadn't even considered the possibility and had gone on in her heedless way. He hadn't said, but she had known what he was thinking. If she had done things differently, concentrated on her duty towards producing an heir rather than her duty to Moles, the outcome would have been different.

The doctor's words thrummed through her. One day she would have a baby. She had to give it time. Once she'd done it then she'd prove herself lovable.

'Thank you for coming so promptly, Doctor,' Ben said, cutting short Dr Fairchild's homily about problems of disease and overcrowding. Normally he would have listened and argued with the doctor, as he had his own ideas about what the solution might be, but today he needed time to think.

Eleanor meant something to him. He wasn't in love with her in the heady way he'd been with Alice in the early days but he felt something—a green shoot of something that had begun to grow within his heart. Possibility. Hope. Entirely unexpected and in its own way troubling. The sense of responsibility and duty gnawed at his insides. Eleanor was not as strong as she pretended. Was she as fragile as Alice? Would her mind go? Would he be sucked into that living hell again? The one where he'd prayed for release only to find the future was far worse than he could have dreamt? He didn't want to imagine a future without Eleanor, his strong Eleanor.

'You do realise that Lady Whittonstall is older than many women when they have their first child?' Dr Fairchild said.

'She is thirty. Many women of her age safely have children.' Ben held up his hand, forestalling any more from the doctor. Alice's doctor had taken him to one side a few weeks after Alice had discovered that she was finally pregnant and had explained about women and their need to be left alone during pregnancy. He had refused to believe it, but Alice had cringed from his touch, accusing him of being a selfish monster. A few weeks later he'd proved what a monster he was. What would Eleanor do if she knew the full truth?

His feelings for her were too new and too deep. He didn't want to lose her when he had so recently found her.

Could he trust Eleanor to look after herself properly? To tell him if she was ill? Or worse?

'I refuse to allow her to take any unnecessary chances.'

'Just so.' The doctor made a deep bow. 'Thank you for being sensible. I am sure all will be well with your wife if you are cautious.'

Ben permitted a small smile. This time he would succeed. He would keep his wife safe. He would protect his own. He'd prove that he was far from being a monster. This time the angel of death would not win. 'I will try.'

A soft woof as Romeo jumped down from the bed alerted Eleanor that someone had come into the darkened bedroom.

'Mrs Nevin?'

'I can get her.'

Eleanor's heart flipped over. Ben had returned. She longed to ask him to hold her but the words stuck in her throat. 'Are you coming to bed?'

She winced, hating the plaintive note in her voice. She refused to beg.

'I wanted to make sure you were comfortable. Do you have everything you require?'

'Yes, thank you,' she managed to choke out around the lump in her throat.

'You will let me or one of the staff know if you require something?'

'I will.'

He stood in the doorway with his candle. Eleanor willed him to do something rather than just stand there. 'It is one of those things that just happen, Eleanor.'

She pleated the linen sheet between her fingers. 'I know what the doctor said.'

'And you believe it?'

'I'm not sure what I believe any more,' she confessed. She wanted to demand his opinion but knew she was a coward.

'It is the shock.'

'Some day we will have a baby. I want a baby, Ben. You mustn't doubt that.'

'Shall we allow God to decide?'

'I'm…' Her throat worked up and down and she found it impossible to continue.

'You mustn't apologise. Please not that. Promise me that you won't. Ever.'

Eleanor tightened her grip on the sheet. She knew Ben was attempting to help but he was making it harder. She wanted to take the blame. It had been her body. Her insistence on fencing when she wasn't feeling quite the thing. 'I want to.'

'You must listen to what the doctor said. Don't think about what could have been. Think about what will be.'

'You should try it some time.'

'It is how I live my life.' He raised the candle so it hid his expression. 'Things will be better in the morning. You are being awfully brave, Eleanor.'

Eleanor hated the way her stomach knotted. She was tired of being brave. 'I always try.'

'It is all anyone can ask.' He went out of the room, closing it with a distinct and terrible click.

The shaking started again. Eleanor choked back a sob. With furious fingers she brushed away her tears. Why hadn't Ben seen that she wanted to be cradled? Why hadn't he touched her? Why had he left? Was she truly that unlovable?

She clenched her fists. From here on she'd change. She flopped back against the pillows and started to make plans.

Chapter Twelve

The clock in the drawing room at Broomhaugh was the slowest clock on the planet, Eleanor decided. Even five minutes seemed to take an age. She'd spent the morning reading Lady Whittonstall's list but it had not provided any great revelation. Instead it was mostly common sense and manners. Conquering society could happen, but she needed to speak with Ben about her plans to go to London.

'Where are you, Ben?' she muttered for the fortieth time. The clock stubbornly refused to move again.

Exasperated, she threw off the light blanket and walked over to the window. Romeo looked up from his border excavations around the delphiniums, more a dirty dog than a pristine one. At least she could spend time combing and brushing him to perfection. She wondered if he would look good with a little blue bow. *The state of your dog reflects on its owner.* Romeo ignored her tap on the window and went back to his pursuit.

What harm would there be in sitting outside?

Reaching for the bell, she felt a wave of dizziness pass over her. She grabbed on to the ledge. Perhaps she should have stayed in the bed. She knew she should go to the foundry—particularly with the potential problems of the Bow Street Runners order—but the last thing she desired was to collapse in front of the men. She could imagine the sarcastic remarks and how much respect she'd lose. She'd fought too long and hard, and now her body was refusing to co-operate.

'You need to eat more than toast, my girl,' she said aloud. Food had never seemed so unappealing.

Ben's footsteps resounded in the hallway. Eleanor rapidly sat down on the covered bench by the window and knew her heart beat a little faster. She bit her lips to give them colour. If she looked well she might be able to convince him to take her out for a drive and she could try to put Lady Whittonstall's words of wisdom into action.

He strode into the room and gave her a hooded look. 'Are you sure you should be up?'

'I'm feeling better,' Eleanor replied cautiously.

It was far from a lie. She *was* feeling better now that she was seated and had someone to talk to.

'Most people would stay in bed for a week after the ordeal you have experienced.' He came over and gathered her hands between his. A warm tingle flooded through her. 'Your cheeks are pale and your eyes seem bruised.'

Eleanor withdrew her hands and forced a smile. The last thing she wanted to think about was how dreadful she must look. She didn't want to think about what had happened to her. She wished Ben were more pleased that she was up and trying to put the episode behind her.

'I've been planning a new scheme for the drawing room and wanted to get a different aspect. My mind is positively brimming with ideas,' she said brightly, keeping the hurt from her voice. 'What do you think about spring green with an accent of pink? Something more classical? I'd like to get the decorating started as soon as possible.'

'The decorating is not as important as your health.' He held out his hands with a placating smile. 'There is no need to rush. The walls will still be here when you have rested.'

'It is time I took charge and started to make decisions. We will have to entertain at some point. It is expected.'

If anything, Ben's gaze became colder. Eleanor hurriedly recalled specific points from Lady Whittonstall's list. According to his mother, Ben lived for entertaining. He knew everyone and was welcomed everywhere. So why did he object to her scheme?

'It is a larger concern than you are used to,' he said. 'Mrs Perkins seems to be doing well as housekeeper. I am disposed to keep her on now that Mrs Nevin has decided to retire.'

She tilted her chin upwards. It gnawed at her insides that he thought her incapable of running his house efficiently. 'I believe I am doing it admirably under the circumstances.'

'There is Moles as well.'

White-hot anger swept through Eleanor. Did he think she couldn't do both? Or that she would neglect her duty to her company? 'Do you wish me to stop working?'

He drew his brows together. A muscle jumped in his cheek as if he were struggling to control his temper.

'If I had forbidden you working why did I drive over to Moles this morning and bring back the papers?' he asked finally in an overly reasonable voice.

'You have brought the papers home for me? You did that for me?' Eleanor stared at him. She put a hand to her face. She'd had it all wrong. All the anger and hurt flooded from her, leaving her feeling flat and more than a little foolish. 'You should have said you were going.'

'It would have been irresponsible. You would have begged to accompany me and I have no wish for you to collapse twice in two days.' A smile tugged at the corner of his mouth. 'I take my responsibilities seriously.'

He withdrew a sheaf of paper and handed it to her. She quickly flicked through the statement from her London bank, Childs and Co, several orders from various London merchants, and correspondence from her solicitor as well as other less important pieces of paper. She saw that Ben had made notes in the margins. She closed her eyes. From the notations, she knew who had asked questions and why.

A great lump in her throat developed. Ben had taken the time and the trouble to make it easy for her. What was worse was that the figures failed to excite her. All they did was remind her how blind she'd been—how wrapped up in everything but what was happening to her body. A lump came into her throat. Her decision to change was the correct one. She wanted her life to be more than figures on a ledger.

'I thought we could go through them if you are feeling up to it. Mr Johnson has asked me to highlight several concerns, and Davy Swaddle asked about getting more coal.'

He stood next to her, and she was more aware of how his coat fitted his form, the way his stock was tied and the way his hands moved than the information he was pointing out.

Eleanor took a deep breath. He hadn't kissed her. That was what was wrong. She wanted him to kiss her. Once he'd kissed her properly everything would be fine. She would be able to concentrate properly again. She raised her mouth in expectation.

He very deliberately turned a page over, ignoring her blatant invitation. Eleanor slumped back against the chair.

'You're supposed to look at the rate of spoilt iron. Mr Johnson thinks it is too much and advises caution. He also wants to be sure that the Bow Street

Runners require this design as it has significant differences from their last order.'

'He always worries—but then he is a cutler rather than a steel-maker.' Eleanor fought to keep the disappointment from her voice. Ben had shown he cared by getting the papers. It wasn't his fault that she felt flat. She had to stop wanting more. She forced a smile. 'I will attend to these things immediately. You are right. In the face of these, decorating schemes can wait. Thank you.'

'It was my pleasure. I found it very interesting. My first chance to poke around and ask questions without fearing that you were looking over my shoulder. Fascinating, and a real credit to you and your organisational ability. The men are looking forward to your return.' He gave a pleased smile. 'Don't work too hard.'

'I won't. I know my limitations. I am looking after myself properly, Ben.'

'You barely touched your breakfast.' His smile became a frown.

'I dislike porridge, even at the best of times, and Romeo begged politely for a piece of toast.' She regarded him with narrowed eyes. 'How do you know?'

'You looked green when I came in,' he continued relentlessly. 'Are you sure you should be out of bed? Being a martyr impresses no one—least of all me. You can take the papers with you.'

'Yesterday I had a miscarriage. An unfortunate occurrence but one which happens to many women, according to Dr Fairchild. Staying in bed is for people like my mother.' She clasped her hands together and hoped she'd convinced him. The thought of quarrelling was beyond her. It required too much energy.

He raised his eyebrow. 'I know you feel rotten. It will pass. I promise.'

'How can you know anything about it?' The words erupted from a place deep within her. 'How can you know anything I feel?'

A muscle jumped in his cheek. He paused for a long while. 'I've been married before. I have intimate experience with such things. Unfortunately.'

Eleanor closed her eyes and cursed her quick tongue. Of course he knew. Alice and the baby he'd lost. The thing that they'd never discussed except on their wedding night and the last thing she wanted to talk about now.

'I'm not Alice. I'm me.'

'Do you think I can't tell the difference?'

He patted her shoulder. The touch felt more like

that of a brother or an uncle rather than a lover. A shiver went down her spine. Suddenly the papers he'd brought seemed less than appealing. Lady Whittonstall's admonition to *keep Benjamin's interest; remember he is highly competitive and likes to win* leapt into her brain.

'Shall we have a game of chess?' she asked, pushing the papers away.

'You look exhausted, Eleanor. There are dark smudges under your eyes.'

'With wagering?' she continued. A warm glow filled her as she remembered their last game. It had ended in a draw before Ben had taken her to bed and made passionate love to her. Though right now she'd settle for being held all night.

'We shall have to see.' He squeezed her hand but his eyes didn't meet hers. 'It depends. You need to conserve your strength. In next to no time you will be back to your old self. We will fence again to celebrate.'

She toyed with her pen. 'I'm not ready for that.'

'Some day you will be. Give it time.'

His words hurt. As if what had happened to her was something trifling. She didn't want to go back to who she had been. She didn't see how she could. She'd learnt a long time ago not to allow hurt to show, not to be weak, but it didn't stop her throat tightening or her longing to be held. She could remember clearly how she'd wanted her mother to hold her after her father had committed suicide, and to stay with her. Instead her mother had fled to the relative safety of Gilsland Spa, leaving Eleanor to cope with the mess and save Moles.

'Yes, of course,' she said around the growing lump in her throat. 'Time is a great healer.'

'Now, are you going to look at these papers or shall I keep them for later, when you have rested? You look all washed out.'

All washed out. The words stung. Did that mean she'd lost whatever little bit of beauty she'd possessed? Eleanor thought about the picture of Alice she'd found buried in his handkerchiefs. All blonde, dimples and curls. She'd be willing to wager that he'd never called his late wife washed out.

'I suppose you are right. It is best not to make any plans,' she said when she trusted her voice.

'Sense at last.' His hand touched her cheek. 'You are too impatient sometimes.'

'I dislike wasting time,' she said, tilting her chin upwards. She wanted her new life to begin. 'Right now I need to get on with these papers. I promise not to work too hard.'

* * *

'Eleanor, have you finished with those papers?' Ben stopped on the threshold to the library. The past few days had gone well. Better than he had anticipated. But an aura of sadness clung to her.

Each morning he went to Moles and returned with papers, hoping to interest her in them. He had never dreamt that the foundry could be so interesting. The more he learnt, the more his admiration for her business sense and the way she delegated the work grew. Every time he brought papers home he hoped that they would trigger that spark within her.

She looked at them, but her conversation revolved much more around redecorating, or other un-Eleanor activities like visiting. Her excuse was that she didn't want to return to the foundry until she knew she was completely well. She did not want to appear less in the men's eyes. Given her stature within the company, he doubted that would be the case.

'Eleanor!' he cried again when she failed to respond.

Eleanor lay asleep, her head resting on a stack of papers, fountain pen clenched in her right hand. At her feet, Romeo dozed. Her blue gown had slipped slightly, revealing the cream of her shoulder. Her dark hair tumbled about in disarray. Utterly appealing. Most definitely off-limits. He had to give it time.

Ben's body disagreed. His nights had been tormented by the memory of their lovemaking. Even her lavender scent clung to the bed. And now it was clear, despite her promises, Eleanor was working too hard. His stomach clenched. Despite all his own promises about keeping his distance he knew it was impossible. Someone needed to look after her before she harmed herself.

'Eleanor…Ellie?' he called. 'Time for you to go to bed and rest properly.'

She stretched slightly and blinked her sleep-filled eyes. Her breast jutted out and his groin tightened. He wanted to strip her bare. Ben struggled to keep hold of his libido.

'I only rested my eyes for a moment, and it isn't late.' She absentmindedly rubbed at an ink blotch. 'I wanted to get my ideas for redesigning the lower terrace written down.'

'The lower terrace can be redesigned in the winter. What did you think about Mr Johnson's suggestion for the type of iron for the Bow Street Runners order?'

Her brow furrowed. 'It is one solution. I shall have to think on it. There is no hurry.'

Ben raised a brow. 'And the new lady's rapier? Mr Johnson wants to know if it should be included in the autumn catalogue.'

She winced. 'I can't even begin to think about that now. It is far too hard a decision. In the morning, perhaps.'

He held out his hand and willed her to take it. Things had to change. Day by day the strong woman who had challenged him to a duel was slipping away and this person who professed interest in the domestic scene was replacing her. If he didn't know that his mother was in London he'd have accused her of meddling. But as it was it was a mystery. Something had to be done to reignite Eleanor's interest in her business.

'Redesigning the terrace has to be done when I think on it.' She put her hands behind her back. 'Sometimes it feels like my brain is made of porridge.'

'Let me take you back to your bedroom.'

He'd take her and leave her. She needed to rest rather than to be distracted. Or worse. And his body singularly failed to realise that being with her was bad for her. He forced steadying breaths.

'Be sensible, Ellie. You will be more wide awake in the morning.'

'Nobody calls me Ellie. Ever.' Her teeth worried at her bottom lip, turning it a deep pink. 'Not since my grandfather died.'

'It is about time someone did.' He gave in to temptation and put his hand on her shoulder. Her flesh quivered under his fingertips. It took all of his will-power not to crush her to him.

'Why should I have a pet name?'

She ducked her head. A single dark curl caressed his hand. His body became physically painful. He abruptly released his hand.

'You most certainly don't look like the fearsome harridan who is reputed to run Moles with an iron fist. Neither do you look like the Eleanor who challenged me to a duel and took unholy delight in crushing my hubris. I think the name Ellie suits you when you are all sleepy-eyed like this. Is there something wrong with that?'

She peeked back over her shoulder. Her grey eyes glowed. 'Should I *like* being Ellie? I am determined to change.'

'Yes, most definitely.' He forced a smile but a vague disquiet came over him. Why was Eleanor trying to change? 'There is no need for you to change. I meant I'm enjoying discovering the woman behind the various masks you wear. The true you.'

'And you do like what you see?'

'Yes.'

'I will keep that under consideration.'

'Please do.'

Ben clenched his jaw. He might like the woman behind the various masks, but would she like *him* if she knew the truth? Perhaps he should have told her before now, but he could not bear to think that he'd look less in her eyes.

Something had to be done fast to stop her from twisting herself into knots. The need to confess grew within him, but he knew if he did he'd lose her. At least this way she was here with him. He could protect her.

'And what should I do now?'

'You should go to bed. Alone. You need your sleep.' Letting her go was one of the hardest things he'd ever done.

'Am I an Ellie, Romeo?' Eleanor gazed at the small silver-backed mirror and wrinkled her nose. 'What sort of person am I? Does Ben find me attractive or is he wishing he could leave? Do you think if I continue to pretend an interest in the domestic scene he will become interested in me?'

Romeo made a non-committal grunt and went back to pursuing a bit of fluff around her bedroom.

She wrapped her paisley shawl tighter about her body and concentrated on the mirror. The last thing she wanted him to know about was her concern for his well-being—particularly after he'd rejected her so emphatically last night. The last thing she wanted to seem was pathetic, but she had hoped that he'd understand she wanted affection and forgiveness for losing the baby.

She reached for the well-thumbed list and started to read Lady Whittonstall's rules again, to see if she'd missed any insight.

'Ah, there you are, Ellie,' Ben said, coming into the room. 'I thought you would have been downstairs, writing out an answer for Mr Johnson. Are you feeling quite the thing?'

Eleanor shoved Lady Whittonstall's list under her handkerchiefs. She glanced at the small clock. It was far later than she had considered. At the open door, Romeo gave a smart swish of his tail and disappeared.

'Is there some reason you are here?' she asked, keeping her voice carefully neutral.

'I've come up with a solution to your problem.' Ben rocked back on his heels. A wide smile cut across his face. 'It has been perplexing me for ages, and I finally figured it out when Cartwright was shaving me. Someone needs to go to London and speak to the Bow Street Runners about this order.'

'Someone?' The word tasted like ash in her mouth. She knew what *someone* was code for— him. 'You want to go to London?'

'It is the perfect solution. All these letters going back and forth by packet. Mr Johnson is beside himself with guessing. If someone goes and speaks to them the perfect cutlass can be designed and executed in next to no time.'

Her stomach ached but she refused to give way to tears. How could she demonstrate that she'd changed if he went away?

Dignity in all things. She knew what his words were code for and now that he said them she found she had been expecting them for ages.

'You want to go without me. There is no need to be polite, Ben. I completely understand. You have duties and obligations that call you away from here. It is to be expected.'

He stopped and gave her a curious look. 'What nonsensical tale are you spinning, Ellie? Why on earth would anyone with half a brain think any-body but you could go?'

Her heart thudded in her ears. 'You want *me* to go to London? On my own?'

'I was rather hoping we could travel together.' His brow lowered. 'Why would you think I wanted to be away from you? Do you think I am a mon-ster?'

Eleanor drew a deep breath and knew she had to say it. 'Because it was my fault that I lost the baby. There is so much I regret, but my thoughts keep circling back to the same thing—I should have taken better care of myself. You said last night you thought I had changed, and I am determined I shall. You are *not* a monster. I am the one who was so ignorant that I didn't even guess I was pregnant until it was too late. I could have done so many things.'

'You feel guilty over that?'

'Yes.'

'Guilt can eat at your soul. I know. Trust me on this. Forget it. Let it go.'

'I can't. I've tried. I keep thinking about our fencing match and wondering. If I was more lady-like, if I had behaved correctly, would things have been different? I'm determined not to make the same mistake.'

He gave her a terrible stare that chilled her to the bone. 'You did nothing, Eleanor. But perhaps you are right. Perhaps it would be better for both of us if I left. There were two people in that match and we both should have known about the possibility. Me more than you.'

'What are you saying, Ben?'

'You were happy before. You will be again. You have saved Moles. That is what you wanted.'

'That is what I wanted *then*.'

He cocked his head to one side. 'Your desires have changed?'

He put his hand on the door and Eleanor knew if she allowed him to go her marriage would be truly over. And she was the one who had put the idea in his head.

'Why have you lived with guilt? Why is it destroying you even now?' she cried, holding out her hands. 'Why should I think you are a monster? Give me a reason, Ben. Why do you think we should part? If you told me maybe I could understand—because right now I have a hard time understanding.'

Ben looked at her for a long time. The time had

come. She could hardly think any worse of him than she already did. She needed to know the full, ugly truth. He braced himself. 'I was driving Alice in my carriage when it hit a pothole. Alice was thrown against the side. The jolt sent her into early labour and neither she nor the baby survived.'

He waited for the repulsion. She folded her hands on her lap and looked up at him.

'Did you mean to hit the pothole?' she asked finally. 'London is full of potholes.'

'I was driving too fast. That was half the fun of it—hearing her mock shrieks of horror as we bounced. She'd cling to my arm.' He closed his eyes and saw Alice's features as she pleaded to stay. 'Alice was not the bravest of souls, but she did enjoy things once she started them. I always had to coax her.'

'What was Alice like?'

'She was perfection. We were young and very much in love. A golden couple who were touched by the gods. In my youth and arrogance I thought I was the happiest anyone could be. I was wrong.' He bowed his head and admitted the truth. 'There were so many things that I didn't understand about her. Things I could have helped her with if she had let me know or if I had opened my eyes. But she kept her fears to herself and pretended that everything was glorious. She worked very hard to make everything seem effortless. And she felt that having a baby and preserving the Grayson dynasty was her most important task. It consumed her when she failed to fall pregnant. And then when she did finally become pregnant worry overrode her joy. She shrank from me and it made me angry. I told her that I was tired of her, that she exhausted me with her emotional needs.'

'What happened on that ride, Ben? Before you hit the pothole?'

'We were laughing. I'd had the idea that I needed to bring her out of herself—I suggested the ride. Alice seemed happier than she had in ages. We were going to repeat the drive every day.'

'For the baby's sake rather than for hers?'

'Yes.' Ben winced at her gentle tone. He didn't deserve her understanding. 'Everyone was very kind. Sometimes these things happen. My driving wasn't to blame. Those were the most common expressions of sympathy. Everyone kept telling me that it was a terrible tragedy. But I *knew*. I knew what my last words to her were. The last thing I said to her. The last thing she said to me.'

'No, that is wrong,' she said in a fierce tone.

'She would have heard you when you struggled to save her.'

Ben stared at her in astonishment. She hadn't recoiled. Or, worse, made sympathetic noises about the awfulness of the thing. 'How do you know I did that?'

'Because I know *you*.' Her chin lifted and there was a flash of the old spirit in her eyes. 'Because you never give in. You would have urged her to fight. You would have done everything possible. You are no coward, Benjamin Grayson. I saw that the day you saved Mr Swaddle. Was the baby a boy or a girl? I like to think the baby we lost was a girl.'

'A boy,' he said slowly. It was the first time anyone had asked him that. Mostly they spoke about Alice, not the baby. And Eleanor giving the baby they had lost a sex made it more real to him. 'A perfect little boy, whose only fault was that he was born too soon.'

'Did you give him a name?'

'Alice had wanted to call him after my father— Charles. The gravestone has both names.'

'I would like to see it some day. Will you take me there?'

The bed sagged under his weight. He buried his

face in his hands. She had seen something in him that he'd refused to see and had tried to keep out of his life. She hadn't recoiled. She had understood. 'When we go to London. When the time is right.'

'You are right. The Bow Street Runners order should be seen to. We can go by packet. It is the quickest way.'

He gave a half-smile. *'Now* she tells me. The post coach up here nearly shook my teeth from my mouth.'

'You only had to ask. Travelling by boat is easier. It is how I send the swords. We can leave as soon as practicable. Mr Johnson can be in charge until we return.'

'I bow to your superior wisdom.'

'Tell me more about Alice,' she said. 'I want to know.'

The story spilled out of him. How he'd always protected Alice because she'd seemed to worship the ground he walked on. How they'd fallen in love. How she'd put him first and given in to his wishes even when she hadn't wanted to. How he'd found her diary and realised far too late that he could have done more in the marriage. Things he'd never confided in anyone. But once he'd started he found it impossible to stop. And all the while

Eleanor remained silent and inscrutable. He told her about everything except his growing feelings for her.

'There you have it. I have lived with the guilt ever since. You can call me a monster now.' He waited for her to order him out of her life.

'You should have told me before,' she said slowly. 'I deserved to know but was too scared to ask.'

'I didn't want you to think less of me.'

A crease appeared between her brows. 'And now? Why tell me now?'

'Because it means more to me that you think well of yourself. Never doubt that our baby was real. It simply wasn't her time to be born. I find it is the only thing that helps me.'

A single tear trickled down her cheek. Ben reached out and captured it. Her lips turned up into a trembling smile.

'You were wrong. I don't think less of you. I wish you had told me before. It would have helped me to understand.' She put her hand to his face. Her mind whirled. She had not expected that Ben carried that sort of guilt, and yet the clues had been there. She had been wilfully blind. Lady Whittonstall was correct about one thing. Until she knew the full story their marriage was doomed to repeat his past mistakes. And she did have to learn about the world Ben inhabited. She didn't deserve Ben. Not yet. But some day she would ensure he regained some of the happiness of his youth.

His hand covered hers. Strong and warm. Her entire being tingled at his nearness. She took a deep breath and tried to control it. She needed to do something to show him that he wasn't a monster. Mouthing words was not enough.

He's going to kiss me. The knowledge thrummed into her, making that curl of desire flare even higher, and she knew what she had to do. Her lips parted. 'Kiss me, Ben. Please.'

With a soft sigh he lowered his mouth and captured hers, demanding a response. Fierce and hot.

A tremor went through her and she knew this was why she'd had the restless feeling earlier. She wanted to kiss him back. She opened her mouth and slid her tongue under his top lip, teasing his teeth. His arms convulsed about her, pulling her against his body.

She sucked in her breath as her body hit his arousal—evidence, if she wanted it, that he wanted her. She longed to melt against him and give herself to his ministrations. She wanted to go to that place that only he could send her. But…

She tried to cling to her sanity and ignore this rushing feeling of heat. When she'd thought about making love to him it had always been like before—in the comfort of their bedroom at night. Not in the middle of the morning. Somehow it seemed unbelievably wicked and wanton. And precisely what she wanted.

'Ben, you need to think about what time of day it is,' she said, trying to be sensible.

His face took on a wicked glint. He traced a finger down her throat, causing butterfly sensations in her stomach. 'No one will disturb us.'

Eleanor took a deep breath as his words reverberated through her. No one was here. She couldn't use convention as a shield. She must live in this moment. Nothing else mattered except that he was here. With her. But she knew the invitation had to come from her. She had to be the one to take charge.

She wound her arms about his neck. 'As long as we don't make a habit of it, I suppose there is no harm…in sharing another kiss.'

'You suppose?' His hands worked at the back of her dress, undoing the tiny pearl buttons as his mouth made an open-mouthed trail down her neck. He nuzzled the point where her throat reached her shoulder, sending fresh waves of desire coursing through her body. 'Care to wager on that?'

Tiny flames licked at her insides, enveloping her in their primitive warmth. He wanted to wager with her. Her heart sang. It was time to trust her instincts. She wanted this. Here. Now.

'We both win with a kiss.'

Eleanor brushed his mouth with hers, slowly exploring the contours of his lips. She allowed her body to say all the things that she had not dared to say before.

With a swoosh, he pushed her gown to the floor. His hand traced her collarbone and then skimmed the outline of her curves. 'You have lost weight.'

The words made her pause. She could allow this to go back to the way it had been before, when he had always taken charge. It would be easy to allow it to happen but she'd hate herself afterwards. She wanted this on *her* terms, not his. She needed to be in charge for once and to set the pace. She wanted to give him solace. She wanted to be different. Her limbs trembled at the thought.

Did she dare?

All she knew was that she couldn't go back to where she'd been before, waiting for him to tire of her. Neither did she want to keep living encased in ice, pretending that she had no need of such things. The longing to be with him reverberated through her but she wanted it on her terms. As an equal. This might be her sole chance of changing things and starting afresh.

His hand moved down her body, cupping her breasts and encircling her nipples. The cloth of her chemise was rough against the increasing tenderness of her breasts. Eleanor knew she had to do it. Now. Or she'd lose herself in the pleasure of his touch.

Ignoring the growing heat inside her body, she let her hands work feverishly at his stock. 'You are overdressed.'

'Do you think so?'

'I'm certain of it.'

He shed his coat, his shirt, and his skin gleamed in the sunlight. She put out a hand and touched his golden skin, felt the muscles ripple under her fingertips.

'I want you, Ellie.'

She smiled at his endearment. Somehow it felt right when he called her that now. She pushed him back on the carpet. 'My bedroom. My rules.'

'You have a fine bed.'

'I don't want to wait for a bed or for darkness

to fall or for a thousand other things to happen. I want you *now*.'

'What do you mean?' He looked slightly surprised.

She smiled, enjoying her new-found power. Before, even when they had wagered, it had been about him doing things to her—now she wanted to do things to him. She wanted to be an equal partner. 'Always before you took the lead. I want to do things to you.'

His eyes blazed. 'I am in your hands.'

She lowered her mouth and tasted his skin, moving slowly down his body. She took his nipple into her mouth and suckled. She heard him groan.

She slid her hand down his body, cupped his arousal. The power within him sent a hot spark arching through her. Giving in to impulse, she lowered her head and tasted the tip of him, slowly circling her tongue about him.

'Please...' he murmured with half-closed eyes.

She positioned herself above him and drove herself downwards, impaling her body on him. His hands grasped her hips. Slowly they began to move together. And she knew that this was much better than before. This time she was participating, calling the rhythm, and he was responding to her.

She knew that he was using her to forget, but that didn't matter. She could accept that for now.

She ran her hands along his back, feeling the muscles tighten and release.

This time she wouldn't fail. This time she'd find a way to make herself indispensable to him and would demonstrate that she could be the woman he needed. She would restore his world to him and he would love her for it.

'I can do it,' she whispered. 'I have to.'

Chapter Thirteen

A low murmur of voices assaulted Eleanor's ears as she and Ben entered Ben's London townhouse after their packet journey from Newcastle. The cutter had been quick, but Eleanor had learnt there were plans to start a steam-powered line with one of Fulton's new-fangled boats, which would make the journey to London even quicker still. The news had made her nerves tingle. It would make it much easier to carry out her plans for taking an active part in London society as well as retaining some direct control of her business.

'Does my mother have visitors, John?' Ben asked, arching his brow. 'I was under the impression her At Homes were always Monday morning.'

The footman looked apologetic. 'It is Wednesday, My Lord. Her Ladyship...'

Ben held up his hand, stopping the footman. 'I know.'

'Wednesday?' Eleanor cocked her head to one side and tightened her grip on Romeo. 'Does that present a problem? Should we return later?'

'Tonight is the night to be seen at Almack's. My mother will be in the throes of getting her protégées ready with final instructions. Normally I retire to the peace and tranquillity of Whites. I had hoped to spare you the trauma, but it can't be helped. Ships will arrive on schedule and I refuse to take to lodgings.' He paused, cocking his head to one side. 'It sounds worse than usual—or is it that my memory is faulty?'

'It is nearing the end of the season, sir. Expectations run high. Her Ladyship always feels it keenly, but particularly so this year. Miss Martyn is a charming girl.'

'Quite so, John. I had blocked the full horror from my mind. Shall I surprise her, or do you wish to announce us?'

The footman looked stoically at Ben. 'Her Ladyship specifically requested not to be disturbed for any reason.'

Eleanor tightened her grip on Romeo's squirming body. All during the journey she had attempted not to think over much about society and the ton, or the part she intended to play and how it would ensure that Ben would fall in love with her. She had counted on being able to beg Lady Whittonstall's assistance. Now it would seem that Lady Whittonstall was in the throes of some crisis. The last thing she wanted was to antagonise her mother-in-law when she needed her help the most.

'Perhaps we could return later,' she said, shifting Romeo to her other hip. 'I've no wish to cause upset. Lodgings will not be too bad for one night. There is a hotel near Hyde Park where I have stayed in the past. The rooms are airy and light.'

'Ellie, it is *my* house. My mother will have to yield.' Ben gave a sudden smile. 'Mama would be even more horrified if we went away. It is the sort of interruption she adores. To say otherwise would be to wrong my mother. She may seem formidable but she loves her family.'

Despite Ben's easy words, Eleanor had to wonder if Ben fully grasped the essence of the problem. It was not about whether or not Lady Whittonstall would be pleased to see them, but about their arriving at the best time. For once she wanted everything to be perfect. Her future happiness depended on it.

'I wish you had warned me.'

'I had blocked the dreaded Wednesday afternoon ritual from my mind.' He gave a half-smile. 'Forgive me.'

'There is nothing to forgive.' Eleanor reached out her hand towards him. She would find a way. 'We can get settled in our room and greet your mother when she has finished.'

Romeo chose that moment to wriggle free from her grasp. He bolted through the footman's legs and headed straight for the drawing room door.

'Romeo, come back here!'

Romeo gave a sharp bark and started to scratch the door.

'John, what is going on out there? I thought the dogs were supposed to be in the breakfast room,' his mother called. 'Hero's nerves are shredded as it is. Now, practise with your fan again, Hero dear. The way I taught you. You do *not* want to put someone's eye out with your elbow, and you want them to notice your eyes rather than your lace. Concentrate and all will be well. Think about what you want to happen rather than what is happening about you.'

'A thousand apologies, Mother Whittonstall.' Eleanor hurriedly scooped up Romeo. Romeo gave her an unrepentant lick on the nose. 'I am afraid Romeo heard your voice and refused to wait.

Everything is under control now. We will wait until you are free.'

'Eleanor? What in the name of heaven—? Is Benjamin with you?'

'We have travelled a long way today, Mama,' Ben said with a wide smile on his face. 'The least you can do is be civil and open the door...if it is not too much trouble to greet your only son and his wife?'

'You talk a lot of utter nonsense, Benjamin. You are always welcome.'

Ben gave Eleanor a significant look.

The drawing room doors were flung open and Lady Whittonstall rushed out and immediately enfolded Ben in a hug. Romeo again escaped from Eleanor's grasp and started to jump up at Lady Whittonstall, trying to lick her hand. Although she was immaculately groomed, in an afternoon gown of light rose silk, Lady Whittonstall bent down and made a fuss of the dog.

Eleanor wondered that she had ever been scared of this woman. Underneath the fashion and the poise she was Ben's mother and a woman who adored animals.

Finally, when she had finished greeting Ben and Romeo, Lady Whittonstall turned towards Eleanor.

Her eyes shone with unshed tears. 'You brought him to me. I thought I wouldn't see you both until Christmastime. You were quite wrong not to send word, but I instantly forgive you both. You are here now and you must stay for a long time. I want my family with me. I have such plans. We must consider how best to launch Eleanor in society.'

'Eleanor has business in London. We shall stay only until that is concluded. Your plans will have to give way.'

'Of course she does.' Lady Whittonstall enveloped Eleanor in a hug. A cloud of jasmine scent threatened to overwhelm her. 'It is a bit late in the season but there is enough time. Eleanor shall have a taster, and then next year she can fully play her part.'

'Time for what?' Ben's eyes narrowed. 'Mother, what are you planning? Eleanor is not here to amuse you but to work.'

'The intricacies of getting a wardrobe will be far too much,' Eleanor said, disentangling herself from Lady Whittonstall's embrace as Romeo gave several more excited barks and started to paw Lady Whittonstall's gown. 'Be quiet, Romeo. We can speak about what will happen later.'

At Lady Whittonstall's signal, the footman cap-

tured Romeo and bundled him away. From somewhere in the bowels of the house Eleanor heard
other equally excited barks of Pomeranians and
knew he'd been reunited with his family.

'At this time of year all the dressmakers and
milliners have a surplus,' Lady Whittonstall said
when the noise had died down. 'You must not use
lack of a proper wardrobe as an excuse.'

'Surplus?'

'A death here, an unexpected pregnancy there.'
Lady Whittonstall waved a vague hand. 'You know
how it is. Life happens. There are a thousand and
one reasons why a wardrobe might suddenly not
be required. One woman's loss shall be our gain.
With the correct incentive you can have the right
sort of wardrobe in a week's time. Ten days at the
most. I guarantee it.'

'Impossible.'

Ben's mouth quirked upwards. 'Never underes-
timate my mother, Ellie. Her ability to organise is
second to none.'

'I witnessed the wonders of her wedding breakfast,' Eleanor replied carefully. She might submit
to a new wardrobe, but she absolutely refused to
wear ruffles, boas and swathes of lace, even if it

was fashionable. 'It was truly astonishing what was accomplished in such a short span of time.'

Lady Whittonstall linked her arm with Eleanor's. 'That, my dear, was veritable child's play. You are too generous in your praise. We must discuss which colours would suit you best, and if you look through *La Belle Assemblée* or *Ackermann's Repository* you will get an idea about the different dressmakers and their styles. It is all about developing your personal flair while staying strictly fashionable.'

'I am not generous enough in my praise. Both Mrs Peters and Mrs Nevin have remarked about your receipts for raised pie and salamagundy. They hadn't expected you to share them so readily.'

Lady Whittonstall's cheeks flushed and Eleanor smiled inwardly. She was halfway there already. It was one thing to read Lady Whittonstall's list and quite another to get specific advice from her in person.

Lady Whittonstall would help develop her personal flair, and once she'd proved a triumph Ben's regard for her would increase. She hoped that she knew enough to follow advice without being a slave to it.

She was under no illusions now about what she

was to him. He used their lovemaking as an escape from his memories. Eleanor knew she wanted it to be more. She wanted to take an active part in his life, and to do that she had to be a success.

'There will not be time to arrange for Ellie to be presented,' Ben said, in a tone that allowed for no dissent. 'We are here on business, Mama. For a short time only. This is to give Ellie a sampling of London and no more. The true assault, if it needs to happen, can happen next season.'

Lady Whittonstall raised an eyebrow. 'I believe I know what I am about, Benjamin. How many years have I done such a thing? How many miracles have I engineered? Now that she is here, Eleanor will shine. Your marriage has been one of the *on-dits* of the season. People wish to meet her. Perish the thought that anyone should think you are cutting them.'

'Perish that thought indeed. I wonder who could have put it in my head?'

Lady Whittonstall's cheeks flushed. 'That was before I knew dear Eleanor properly. Our first meeting was fraught. I have come to appreciate her many qualities. Romeo appears to be very happy.'

'I would like to partake of *some* society while I am here—if it is not too much trouble and the correct wardrobe can be found.' Eleanor made a little curtsey and watched Lady Whittonstall glow.

'I would not worry about being presented at Court.' Lady Whittonstall gave Ben a significant look. 'It is frightfully dull, given the King's health. Almack's commands the premier position. It is far too late for this week, but the Lady Patronesses always meet on a Monday afternoon to decide the list. The question is which one of them should we approach for dear Eleanor? It is awfully late in the season...'

Ben tapped his fingers against his lips. 'I would have thought that *you* would yield, Mama. Mothers can give daughters their vouchers. I will take Eleanor next week, provided you are right about the dressmakers. Why there should be this much fuss over lemonade, thinly sliced bread and dry cake, I have no idea. The dances tend to be the same tedious reels year after year.'

'I can't, my dear boy. Not this time. Not in the next few weeks.' Lady Whittonstall glanced over her shoulder towards the drawing room. She lowered her voice. 'There is Miss Martyn to think of. It would be wrong of me to put family interests first. I have given my word to her mother.'

Eleanor kept her chin up. Lady Whittonstall did not mean to be insulting, but she could see that Ben was far from happy with his mother's response.

His smile became deadly. 'Then Ellie will simply have to get a voucher on her own. That process should be relatively simple. After all, Ellie is *your* daughter-in-law. Which one of the Lady Patronesses is currently your pet source? Whom shall you demand the voucher from?'

'You make it sound like I have some power, Benjamin, when in fact nothing could be further from the truth. One may only suggest and advise. One may never demand.'

'Which one, Mama?'

'Lady Sefton provided our vouchers,' a well-bred voice called from the drawing room. 'Isn't that right, Mama? Lady Sefton has the reputation as being the most amiable of the Lady Patronesses. She always seems to have a kind word for everyone.'

'Hero, you should mind your tongue. It is most impolite to reveal that you are eavesdropping.'

'It is terribly thrilling to see the new Lady Whittonstall. Everyone will want to meet you, and I am to be one of the lucky first.'

A petite blonde came into the hall. Eleanor realised with a start that she looked very like Ben's miniature of Alice. She had to wonder if it was a deliberate ploy by his mother to nurture similar types of women or if the majority of women in the ton looked like that. All the petite blondeness did was highlight her own feelings of inadequacy.

Miss Martyn's face broke into a wide smile. 'You are *so* lucky to have black hair, Lady Whittonstall, and to be tall.'

'Hero, you are being vulgar,' her mother warned.

Miss Martyn quickly bobbed a curtsey as her cheeks reddened. Lady Whittonstall gave Ben a significant look, as if to emphasise why she had to go to Almack's. Eleanor understood completely, and only hoped that Lady Whittonstall's efforts would be rewarded.

'Lady Sefton it is, then,' Eleanor said positively, turning to her. 'Miss Martyn has made an excellent suggestion.'

The young lady gave an infectious giggle. As she and her mother took their leave Lady Whittonstall imparted some last-minute advice about how Miss Martyn must refrain from giggling too loudly during the reel.

'I trust you to do the honours, Mama,' Ben said as the door closed behind the Martyns. 'It should be merely a matter of contacting Lady Sefton and requesting Eleanor's name be added to the list for next week.'

'I will do what I can, Benjamin. With the rise of Mr Brummell things have altered slightly. There are only two Wednesdays left and then London empties for the winter. You should have come sooner.'

'The delay was unavoidable.' Ben's voice might have been chipped from ice.

Lady Whittonstall's gaze narrowed and she seemed to take everything in. Eleanor had to wonder if there was a big sign about her miscarriage stamped on her forehead. 'I was unwell, Mother Whittonstall.'

'But you have improved?'

'Considerably.' Eleanor tilted her chin upwards. 'Sometimes things are not meant to be.'

Lady Whittonstall patted Eleanor's shoulder and it provided Eleanor with comfort. 'It will happen, my dear. You mustn't doubt that. It will happen. I understand entirely.'

Eleanor bit her lip and blinked rapidly. She hadn't expected her mother-in-law to be so perceptive. 'I look forward to a successful visit.'

'We both do.'

* * *

'Are you coming to bed, Eleanor? Or has my mother given you something to memorise?' Ben called from where he lay in the large four-poster bed. He had moved in here after Alice's death. The room did not have as good an aspect, but it had the advantage of not being infused with memories. He had planned on making some more memories with Ellie, but she seemed preoccupied with his mother's list.

'Mother Whittonstall has kindly written out a programme for me. I am amazed that your mother took the time before she went off to Almack's.'

'My mother is an amazing woman. And she is determined to mould you. If you are not careful she will have you dripping with fripperies in the name of fashion.'

He waited for Eleanor to bristle at the suggestion.

'We are going for a drive in Hyde Park tomorrow morning, before visiting several milliners, modistes and mantua-makers. We want to find a woman who can accentuate my assets.'

She gave a little laugh, inviting him to join in the joke. Ben frowned as his disquiet increased. He wanted Ellie to return to the strong woman she'd been before the miscarriage, rather than be reduced to a quivering lump of jelly by a succession of tyrants. His mother meant well, but she had certain ideas and was unafraid to express them in forthright terms. He had seen it happen before with Alice and had ignored it. It remained one of his deepest regrets. He had learnt from his mistakes. He intended to protect Eleanor—if she'd allow him to. He wanted to demonstrate to her that he was no longer a monster.

'Your assets look fine to me.' Ben patted the empty pillow.

'You are a man.' Ellie waved her hand. 'Hopefully the experience will be more pleasant than shopping with my mother. We always quarrelled. She had a love of jonquil-yellow which makes me look bilious.'

'I like you in aquamarine. The dress you had on at dinner tonight was pretty.'

'Mother Whittonstall did not like the neckline. It fails to reflect the current thinking in fashion and is strictly for dining *en famille*.'

'My mother is not the person wearing the clothes.' He gave a small smile. 'Or the person paying for them. Trust your judgement, Ellie. You don't have to go along with my mother's wishes if they clash with your own. My mother doesn't mean to be forceful. She just is. She respects people who know their own mind.'

Eleanor slammed the paper down on the dressing table, picked up a brush and started brushing her hair with fierce strokes.

'I shall,' she said with crushing dignity. 'I have done so for more than fifteen years. Your mother seeks to help me. She wants me to be a success… as your wife.'

'Funny—I thought you already were.'

'You know what I mean. In society.'

'Did my mother include your appointment with the Bow Street Runners? You shall need to speak to them as soon as practicable. Johnson is keen to know the verdict.'

'I can work around that. I shall send a note in the morning and arrange a time.' Eleanor brushed her hair with a few more strokes. 'Apparently your mother has a new carriage.'

Ben frowned inwardly. Eleanor had decided to shift the subject away from her schedule. His unease grew. What was she trying to hide?

'I knew it was threatened,' he carefully. 'It is a landau. She wants to cut a dash as she is driven along the Rotten Row. My mother enjoys being seen. My own personal feelings on the trim count for nothing.'

Eleanor's hand paused in mid-brush. Her eyes met his through the mirror. 'What quarrel do you have with your mother?'

'What quarrel? Not a quarrel, merely an observation. She swore she needed my advice before she purchased the landau. I declined and now she has shown what I suspected—my mother will do as she wishes. Her request for advice was a feint. Remember that.'

'When was this?'

'Is it important?'

'I had the distinct feeling that there was a strained air between you two when she left after the wedding.'

Ben ran his hand through his hair. With Eleanor in this mood he hardly wanted to go over the past. He wished he hadn't mentioned the point. 'It is in the past.'

'But it matters. What did your mother do? Does it have to do with Alice?'

'You have had a long day.'

She put the brush down with a trembling hand and reached for her beribboned nightcap. 'You think I am going to fail. You are ashamed of me.

You should have said earlier. It is hardly as if I have two heads, and I know not to be forward. I won't need your mother hovering at my elbow like she has to with Miss Martyn.'

'Did I say that?' Ben stared at Eleanor in astonishment. Her words cut through him. 'Did I *ever* say that? Would I ever be so cruel?'

'But you thought it. You don't think I shall conquer London. You are trying to be kind but you don't think I can do it. Mother Whittonstall will get me the required voucher and I will show you.'

'I don't think you *need* to. There is a subtle difference, Ellie, which I am sure you can appreciate.'

'I have no plans to fail. I have plans to conquer.'

'I thought we were here for Moles.'

'We are here for a number of reasons.' She came over and knelt on the bed. Her dark hair was under her nightcap and he could see the delicate hollow at the base of her throat. An air of vulnerability remained in her eyes.

'I wanted to remind you of the important one.'

'You needn't have bothered. I know where my duty lies. I've known that since I was fifteen.' Her voice held a wistful note.

'I'm glad to hear it.'

He ran a hand down her delicate skin and wondered if he'd done the right thing in bringing her to this place. He wanted the woman he thought he'd married back, and he couldn't bear the thought of her struggling in society. He wanted to protect her, but he also wanted her to experience the magical world that she'd glimpsed as a young girl. He could remember how her eyes had shone as she'd described it during their first picnic. He'd made a vow then and he intended to keep it.

'Just remember where home is.' He straightened her nightcap so it sat squarely on her head.

She moved away from him, turning her back to him. 'I won't forget. I could never forget.'

Chapter Fourteen

The morning sunlight streamed into Lady Whittonstall's new landau. Two footmen were perched behind, while the driver rode one of the lead horses, thus giving Eleanor and Lady Whittonstall a clear view of the proceedings. Ben had declined a place in the carriage, preferring to ride alongside.

Eleanor watched all the great and the good mingle along Rotten Row while Lady Whittonstall kept up a running commentary about who was who and how they fitted into the wider world of London society. She explained about what had happened at Almack's, and how poor sweet Hero still had a chance to bring the Earl of Rothbury up to snuff before the season finished, despite her *faux-pas* in the second reel.

Ben, looking splendid in chestnut-brown

breeches and riding coat, snorted. He seemed less convinced than Lady Whittonstall about Miss Martyn's chances, but it was the ease with which he discussed everything that impressed Eleanor. She was painfully aware that these people were known to Ben but not to her, and some of them, like the Earl of Rothbury, appeared to be intimate acquaintances. These were the people he had been afraid of judging him a monster.

More and more carriages entered Rotten Row, and Eleanor realised, as she saw the various fashionables, that her dress was hopelessly out of date and quaint.

'Do you sing, Eleanor?' Lady Whittonstall asked, having exhausted the topic of Miss Martyn's matrimonial prospects.

'I find it difficult to keep a tune, and I stopped playing the spinet after my father died.' Eleanor felt her cheeks begin to burn. 'But I do like hearing music. It is inflicting my voice on others that troubles me.'

Lady Whittonstall frowned.

'Is something wrong?'

'Nothing, dear. I am merely attempting to figure out how we shall introduce you to Lady Sefton. What accomplishments we should highlight. Lady

Sefton prefers the ladies on her list to be ladies of true accomplishment.'

'As your son's wife?' Ben called down from his horse. 'Surely that will be recommendation enough?'

'I want something more—something that shows Lady Sefton what an asset you are. I overheard her complaining recently that far too many of the younger set lack a distinguishing feature and will have to be ruthlessly culled next season.'

'You are trying to over-complicate matters, Mother. Eleanor is more than able to hold her own in any conversation. She is far from dull, and she most definitely does not chatter like some of your protégées have had a tendency to do.'

'It is not that simple, Ben. I dare say that viscountesses are two a penny at Almack's.' Eleanor gave him a hard look. Didn't he understand that she was doing this for *him?* She wanted to do it right. She wanted to demonstrate that she was worthy of taking her place at his side. 'Even I know the potential problems of getting vouchers at Almack's. It is what gives it its cachet.'

'You are making a mountain out of a molehill,' Ben said with a twist to his mouth. 'Relax, Ellie.

It will happen. No one would dare be that insulting. This family has a certain standing.'

'A few years ago it might have been that simple, but Brummell does stalk the corridors,' Lady Whittonstall said in a musing tone. 'How is your dancing, my dear? A pretty dancer always impresses.'

'I occasionally dance, but generally there has not been time. I do run a business.' A heavy weight settled on Eleanor's shoulders. Back in Shotley Bridge it had seemed straightforward. All she needed was a new wardrobe and perhaps a different hairstyle. But Lady Whittonstall seemed to imply that it took much more.

'We shall get you to a dancing master—someone who knows what he is about. We might introduce you at a few gaieties, or perhaps at Gunnersbury, Cremorne, or even Vauxhall. I hear there is an old gypsy who tells fortunes in the grotto.' Lady Whittonstall's smile increased. 'That might be the best way to do it. Introduce you gently to society and save Almack's for next season. I do so hate a full-frontal assault. These things should evolve naturally, when the girl is ready. At least a full season is required.'

Ben's mouth twisted. 'Eleanor is my wife, not a

naive debutante, Mother. She runs a business and does not have a full season to devote to the dubious pleasures of Almack's and society.'

'Who said anything about pleasure?' Lady Whittonstall exclaimed. 'Almack's has nothing to do with pleasure and everything to do with being seen. You matter to the people who matter. Should dear Eleanor be blackballed for some trivial and preventable reason the word will get out and all the lovely invitations will dry up.'

'Precisely,' Eleanor agreed. Ben surely had to understand what was at stake? He might have been born with an entrée to society clasped in his infant fist but she was an outsider. The last thing she wanted was to be blamed for his exclusion from the world where he belonged. 'If it takes longer than first anticipated, then so be it. Mr Johnson is quite able to look after Moles.'

Ben gave her a look of utter disgust, spurred his horse and rode off. Eleanor's insides twisted. Between last night's quarrel and today's contretemps her relationship with Ben did not appear to improving. If anything, it was rapidly unravelling. He refused to understand how important this was.

Eleanor raised her chin and glared at his disapproving back as he rode away. Everything would change once she had acquired the voucher, made her entrance and proved beyond a shadow of a doubt that she could compete with the best. She would demonstrate that she was worthy of being loved.

Lady Whittonstall put a hand on Eleanor's knee. 'Follow my lead, dear girl. We are in luck. Mrs Branson, who is one of Lady Sefton's dearest friends, rides out today. With her backing Lady Sefton is certain to approve your request for a voucher.'

Eleanor sat up straighter as Lady Whittonstall effusively greeted Mrs Branson.

'And this must be your new daughter-in-law.' Mrs Branson's gaze travelled over Eleanor, making Eleanor more aware than ever of the deficiencies of her dress. 'She is quite the country mouse. No doubt you will soon have her in hand. The wonders you have done with the Martyn girl this year are more than astonishing. And last year it was the Shaw chit, and the year before...'

'Thankfully Benjamin has shown the good sense to finally marry.'

'I and the rest of the ton shall be agog to see what you accomplish.' Mrs Branson lent forward and said, *sotto voce,* 'Her hair is very old-fashioned. It needs more curls, and it should be shorter.'

Eleanor could not decide if it would be better to sink down upon the cushions in embarrassment or cut the woman dead. Mrs Branson might hold the key to her getting a voucher, but she was also incredibly rude.

'This is one of Eleanor's first visits to London. It is hard to find a decent dressmaker north of London, and Eleanor requires the very best. And I have plans for her hair. Eleanor will emerge from the cocoon of Whittonstall House a veritable butterfly.'

'Take your mother-in-law's advice to heart.' Mrs Branson gave a tremendous sigh. 'Lady Whittonstall is known to all as a transformer. I still remember what she did for sweet Alice.'

'I have found her advice invaluable thus far.' Eleanor made sure that she lowered her head modestly. 'I have much to learn, and I have been told that Lady Whittonstall is an excellent teacher.'

Mrs Branson's gaze sharpened. 'Then you were not a debutante?'

'I didn't have time. I was far too busy running the family business.' Eleanor practised deep breaths. She could get through this.

'You are in *commerce?*'

Lady Whittonstall covered her hand with her mouth and shook her head vigorously. Eleanor ignored her. There was nothing wrong or immoral in what she did.

'My company manufactures swords.' Eleanor tilted her chin in the air. 'We are, I am happy to say, the best sword manufacturer in England. Moles enjoys an unparalleled reputation for its excellence and I am proud to play my part.'

Lady Whittonstall gave a faint moan.

'You make *swords?* You are a *businesswoman?*' Mrs Branson's lip curled. 'How on earth do you manage?'

'Manage? It is quite simple. I use my brain, rather than saving it for tittle-tattle and other bits of gossip,' Eleanor retorted. She curled her fists. 'Thanks to me, over a hundred men and their families have food in their bellies and a roof over their head.'

'Do they?'

'It is hard but honest work.'

'So I understand. Thankfully I have never had to sully my hands.' Mrs Branson gave a nod to Lady Whittonstall. 'Good day to you both.'

'We must return home.' Lady Whittonstall gestured towards the driver, who turned the carriage around, and they quickly started back towards the house.

'Is something wrong?' Eleanor asked when they had left Hyde Park and the Rotten Row behind. Lady Whittonstall had gone pale and a faint sheen of sweat shone on her forehead.

Lady Whittonstall turned and clutched Eleanor's hand. 'I'm sorry. I couldn't risk another incident. Putting food into the bellies of men, indeed. How do you think that remark will play with the Lady Patronesses?'

'Incident?'

'I shall have to find another Lady Patroness for you. Mrs Branson is sure to fill Lady Sefton's ears with this tale. They are bosom friends and Lady Sefton will do as she suggests. I know this in my bones. I fail to see how you can recover from this *faux pas.*'

'Are you certain of this?' Eleanor looked up at the blue sky and struggled to control her temper. 'I merely sought to explain why I wasn't a debutante. I am not ashamed of how I have lived my life, Mother Whittonstall. Far from it.'

'But is Benjamin?'

'He did marry me.'

'You should have let me speak. You should have

allowed her to assume, rather than being forthright. Subtlety is all. Nuance.'

'I don't understand.'

'Mrs Branson is a snob of the highest water. She can't abide anyone in commerce. And you manufacture swords.'

'Which a great many people purchase.'

'I don't see them lining up to get you vouchers to Almack's.' Lady Whittonstall put her hand over her eyes. 'Forgive me. It has been a trying season with one thing and another. I had such hopes, Eleanor, and despite everything those hopes remain. It will happen. But you must follow my lead rather than going off on your own tangent and causing a scandal.'

Eleanor's stomach knotted. She should have kept her mouth shut—but the woman had baited her. And she wasn't ashamed of what she did. 'If I have to lie to get a voucher where is the pleasure in that?'

Lady Whittonstall gave her an agonised look.

Eleanor bit her lip. She'd have to find another way to return Ben to that state of perfect happiness and make him love her. She pressed her hands against her eyes and tried to think.

'It will be fine, Eleanor. Something will come to me.'

'Is there a problem?' Ben said as he strode out of the stables.

'Mrs Branson exchanged greetings. I failed to hold my tongue,' Eleanor confessed, before Lady Whittonstall had a chance to say anything. 'Mrs Branson fears I'm tainted with commerce and therefore beyond redemption. I merely sought to defend Moles. Your mother believes I may have ruined my chances.'

She waited for Ben to look disapproving, but his eyes danced with hidden mischief. 'A pity—and more than shocking. How does Mrs Branson think this country makes its money? The ignorance of some people never ceases to amaze me.'

Eleanor kept her face blank until she saw the corner of Lady Whittonstall's mouth twitch. Then she was unable to smother the giggles that bubbled up in her. 'You should have seen her face.'

Ben sobered. 'I only wish I had been there. I feared something like this would happen, Mama.'

'Perhaps it might be fine,' Eleanor said. 'Perhaps she won't say anything.'

'Gertrude Branson will be pouring the tale into Lady Sefton's ears.' Lady Whittonstall wrung her hands. 'She has waited a long time for this. She has never forgiven me for when her daughter lost out to Susan Craven in the marriage stakes of 1808.'

'Mrs Branson may be many things, but she is not one of the Lady Patronesses. And she is a snob of the first order. Alice could not stand her. Why did you even approach her?'

Eleanor ignored Lady Whittonstall's swiftly indrawn breath. 'Although I am loath to make a judgement on such a short acquaintance, I trust your late wife's view to be the correct one.'

'Sensible—very sensible. I would expect no less from you. It is my mother who is being less sensible.' Ben nodded his approval. 'Have you decided on your next move? There are bound to be any number of gaieties, from balls to breakfasts. Once people get to know Ellie, people like the odious Mrs Branson will not stand a chance.'

Eleanor's heart soared. Ben didn't want her to slink away in shame. He was on her side rather than on his mother's. He wanted her to fight and he was willing to stand beside her. A great warmth flooded through her. Ben believed in her and he cared for her.

'What I'd really like to do is fence.'

His face broke into a wide smile. 'Shall we return to Hyde Park and fence there?'

'Benjamin! You will scandalise everyone! Think of your reputation! You will ruin everything!'

'On the contrary, Mother, I intend to show everyone what fine swords my wife makes and how proud I am of her industry.' He held out his hand and helped Eleanor down from the carriage. 'Are you willing, Ellie? If they cannot accept what you do then it is their loss, not yours.'

'I would like that very much.' Eleanor put her hand against her stomach. For the first time since the miscarriage she felt like her old self. She might not have what she wanted yet, but Ben had stood up for her. It showed that she was following the correct strategy. 'It would be my absolute pleasure to fence in Hyde Park.'

'We have an audience,' Ben murmured as their swords clashed in Hyde Park. He had chosen a relatively secluded knoll, well away from the Rotten Row, and they had managed two bouts without attracting much interest. But the deciding bout had caused a small crowd of ladies, bucks and assorted people to gather.

If he allowed the bout to continue Ben knew one

or two of the younger gentlemen would be unable to resist placing bets. It was one thing to show his approval of his wife's profession but quite another for her to become a common fixture in Whites' betting book.

'I know. I recognise several of them.'

'Shall we end this?' He parried and managed to deflect her blow. 'I believe the point is proved for today. We are well-matched.'

He lunged forward and twisted his hand. Eleanor dropped her sword instantly. It fell to the ground with a thud.

'You are right, and it is your match. I concede defeat.'

He reached out and touched her cheek. Her eyes were troubled. His heart squeezed. This morning's mishap had done much to dent her confidence. He silently damned all society. They would return north as soon as practicable. He'd seen his mother behave in this fashion before. She pointed out faults until the woman in question began to accept her word for everything. He wanted his wife back. Not some idealised version perfected by his mother.

'I didn't mean let me win.'

'I assure you *that* wasn't the case.' She shook her

head. 'How could you even think it? The sword slipped from my grip.'

'When does your sword ever slip?'

She tilted her chin upwards. 'When I haven't practised enough.'

Ben pursed his lips together but decided to let her evasion go. The last thing he wanted was for Eleanor to start losing deliberately. He'd had enough of that before. When he won, he wanted it always to be on his own merit.

'Then we shall have to practise more often,' he said lightly, but all the while he watched her like a hawk, waiting for the smallest sign that she understood what he was asking. 'I require a certain standard in my fencing partners.'

Eleanor rewarded him with a heart-stopping smile. 'I would like that. I have missed it more than I thought.'

Ben clasped her hand and her fingers curled tight around his. He started to pull her towards him.

'Impressive,' an autocratic woman's voice called out from the onlookers. 'Very impressive, indeed.'

Eleanor jumped back from him and hurriedly ducked her head.

Ben forced his breathing to stay even as he recognised the voice's owner. He'd expected to encounter several members of the ton, but not one of the Lady Patronesses. Silently he prayed nothing untoward would happen before he could get Eleanor away. After this morning, the last thing she needed was another failure.

'We should go,' he murmured in an undertone.

'Shortly.' Eleanor glanced up. Her smile widened and she waved enthusiastically to Lady Jersey.

Ben flinched, seeing her dream of going to Almack's vanish before his eyes. In that instant he knew he wanted it for her. He wanted her to once again be the wide-eyed girl who had thought the Newcastle Assembly Rooms were magical. Somehow he'd find a way of making it happen.

'Very impressive,' Lady Jersey said again, coming over. 'You are to be congratulated.'

'Not really,' Eleanor said, picking up her sword, seemingly unconcerned about the personage in front of her. 'My grip needs work. It has become rusty. I should have made a better fist of it.'

'I meant your sword rather than the bout, Mrs Blackwell,' Lady Jersey said, inclining her head. 'I know your expertise in fencing to my cost.'

Ben stared. Eleanor was *known* to Lady Jersey? How? And why hadn't she said before now? This morning's unpleasantness could have been avoided.

'It is a new design, Lady Jersey,' Eleanor said with a faint smile. 'Would you like to try it? It should be perfect for you and the way you hold a rapier.'

Eleanor held the sword out and Lady Jersey took it with a practised hand. She gave an experimental flourish. Her smile became genuine.

'The balance is excellent. It puzzles me why you are fencing in Hyde Park, Mrs Blackwell...with a gentleman. I have never seen you here before. You are normally more discreet.'

Eleanor tucked her hand in Ben's arm. He fought against the temptation to crush her to him and tell her not to worry.

'I am Lady Whittonstall now,' Eleanor said, tilting her chin upwards. 'I believe you are acquainted with my husband?'

'Our paths have crossed, but not recently. Your reputation as a swordsman is excellent, Lord Whittonstall,' said Lady Jersey after pleasantries were exchanged. 'I can see why Mrs Blackwell chose you. You are well matched.'

'I shall take that as a compliment,' Ben said.

Lady Jersey ran her hand along the blade of the sword. 'What price do you put on this sword?'

'A voucher for Almack's?' Ben said, before

Eleanor had a chance to open her mouth. 'My wife has expressed a wish to attend. If Mrs Branson is to be believed it is the only way my wife will be able to set her foot inside the hallowed portals. There again, perhaps you have another solution.'

Lady Jersey's tinkling laugh rang out. 'That would be a small price to pay to possess such a sword. Fortunately Mrs Branson is not a Lady Patroness. Nor is she ever likely to become one. Such things are settled in different ways—as you well know, Lord Whittonstall.'

Eleanor wanted to sink to the ground. Did he think that she possessed no sense? Lady Jersey could not help with her current difficulty with Almack's. She was well aware of Lady Jersey's own mother-in-law problem. It must be her mother-in-law who was a Lady Patroness as she could not see how Lady Jersey would have the time, given her obligations at Childs and Co.

If Ben wasn't careful, the news that Lady Whittonstall had her begging bowl out would be all around London. She could imagine what the wags would say about that one. Vouchers to Almack's being *sold,* indeed!

'Ben, will you stop teasing Lady Jersey?' she

said, putting her hands on her hips. 'The rapier is not for sale.'

Lady Jersey's face fell. 'That is a pity. Is there no way I can persuade you to part with it? It fits my hand very pleasantly.'

'I will give it to you as a gift.'

'I can't allow you to do that,' Lady Jersey exclaimed.

'If I can use your endorsement of it in our advertising then,' Eleanor said, thinking out loud.

'It is a truly exceptional sword,' Lady Jersey said. 'And the endorsement would be discreet?'

'Yes, of course.'

'Eleanor!' Ben roared beside her, but she ignored him.

'Goodness knows, we have done enough business together in the past,' Eleanor continued.

'We have, indeed. Moles is one of my more reliable clients.' Lady Jersey tucked the sword under her arm. 'I look forward to using my sword, and to telling everyone who has made it. Just as you shall tell everyone where you bank.'

'Business? What business have you done together?' Ben asked.

'Your lady wife uses my bank as her principle place of banking in London,' Lady Jersey explained. 'She is one of our most valued customers. We always share a cup of tea when she makes one of her infrequent visits to London. I treasure them very much. Her witticisms roll around in my brain for days afterwards.'

'Taking tea with you is always a pleasure,' Eleanor said, bowing her head. She wished she had thought of consulting Lady Jersey earlier. She should have remembered that in addition to being one of London's leading bankers Lady Jersey was very well-connected socially.

'Hopefully, now that she is married to you, you will be able to convince her to come to London more often.'

'I will do my best,' Ben said.

'But I must confess, Lord Whittonstall, this is the first time I have heard of your wife's desire to attend Almack's. Is this your doing? Nothing would give me greater pleasure than to see her there. There are times when I long for intelligent conversation.'

'A recent development,' Eleanor said, stepping away from Ben. The last thing she wanted to do was explain the exact nature of her marriage and her current scheme to make Ben love her. 'I believe your mother-in-law might have some influence…'

'You are at cross-purposes, Lady Whittonstall. My mother-in-law has nothing to do with Almack's, and thankfully has no say upon who might be admitted. I shudder to think the havoc she might wreak.'

'I do apologise.'

'I, however, have some small influence.' Lady Jersey's lips curved upwards. 'I have become one of the Lady Patronesses, for my sins. Someone had to take charge—and I am privy to certain intelligence about finance.'

Eleanor's mind reeled. Lady Jersey was a Lady Patroness and Ben had known it. It was possible that she could still recover from her mistake. She could easily imagine Mrs Branson's face if she knew. She had to wonder as well what Mrs Branson would say about Lady Jersey's connection to commerce—or did she not dare criticise a Lady Patroness in that way?

'Should I apply to you for a voucher?' Eleanor forced the words from her throat. It was far harder to ask Lady Jersey for this than to ask her for a loan, or any of the other business transactions they had had over the years.

'Should you happen to do so I will look on it

with great sympathy—great sympathy and great pleasure.'

'Because of my husband and his family?' Eleanor hated the way her stomach knotted as she waited for confirmation.

'Because of you and who you are.' Lady Jersey's brow knotted. 'We who inherit businesses have a duty towards them and their employees. It is impossible to turn our back on them. I know you feel that as keenly as I do. You have accomplished wonders with Moles and serve as an inspiration.'

'One does have a duty to one's employees. I could never give Moles up.'

'And furthermore—' Lady Jersey held up her hand, forestalling any more comments '—I know your intelligence and quick wit. I always enjoy it when you come to London. You must do so more often. Lord Whittonstall, I *order* you to bring your wife to London more often. She should not be hidden away. My husband and I shall be giving a dinner party next Thursday. You will both attend.'

Ben made a bow. 'We should be honoured.'

'It depends on whether my business permits as to when we will be in London,' Eleanor said carefully, keeping her gaze from Ben's. Her spirits soared. She had never guessed Lady Jersey's

opinion. And Ben had agreed to take part in society life again. The day which had started so badly
suddenly sparkled with possibilities.

'You will not mix the two spheres in your life?'

'I had no plans to do so,' Eleanor said hurriedly,
before Ben had a chance to intervene again. Her
mind reeled. She was going to get vouchers. She
would be invited to places. All her worry had been
for nothing. She wasn't solely dependent on Lady
Whittonstall after all. She could compete, and once
Ben saw her success he would love her. For the
first time since she had started this quest she felt
as if it was going to happen. The knowledge gave
her a surge of confidence.

'And how is your dancing? We do set great store
by dancing. Mr Brummell is especially useful in
discovering those people who merely pay it lip
service.'

'I promise to dance beautifully.'

'I will ensure she does,' Ben said. His fingers
tightened on her elbow.

'I would never have expected less. Should you
require some extra lessons I have recently started
a small dancing school at Almack's, to assist
debutantes and those unused to our ways. The
Frenchwoman who runs it accomplishes miracles.

Your mother-in-law will know about the times. I believe she plans on sending her latest protégée there.'

'I will ask her,' Eleanor promised.

Lady Jersey raised her chin. 'One further piece of advice, dear Lady Whittonstall. You should follow my example. Allow your husband into the bedroom but not the boardroom. I find it makes for a more congenial relationship.'

'I will take that advice under consideration.' Eleanor watched Ben simmer next to her and silently prayed he would keep quiet.

'Do, Lady Whittonstall, do.' Lady Jersey swept away, leaving a trail of expensive scent. Her ringing voice could be heard exclaiming about the balance of her new sword and what a perceptive person the new Lady Whittonstall was to know that it was precisely the sort of sword she'd longed for.

'I knew you banked with Childs!' Ben said, when Lady Jersey's voice finally faded and the crowd which had gathered had dispersed. 'But why didn't you say that you were friends with Lady Jersey?'

Eleanor tilted her head to one side, trying to assess his mood. He seemed to be taking the news with a great deal of consternation.

'We first met when Lady Jersey became senior partner five years ago, but Childs has been Moles' London banker since my grandfather's day. Her father is one of our most valued customers. It is only natural that we are friends after a fashion.'

'You might have said! It would have saved the agony of this morning.'

'Lady Jersey had not confided about her position at Almack's in our recent correspondence.' She gave a smile. 'On consideration, though, I don't approve of Lady Jersey's suggestion to keep you in the bedroom. You are far too good a fencer...'

Ben's lips quirked upwards. 'My mother will not believe this. It will do her good. She thought you and I would create a scandal when in fact we have performed a minor miracle in her eyes.'

'Your mother *will* be pleased, won't she?' Eleanor asked, tilting her head to one side, trying to discern the cause of Ben's joy. There was something more than the fact that she would be able to go to Almack's.

'My mother will be relieved you have obtained the correct vouchers. I am sure she filled your ears with dire predictions—none of which came true.' His eyes sobered and his face was deadly serious. 'Remember this lesson, Ellie. You obtained those vouchers on your own. You will succeed on your own. My mother and her ways aren't always correct.'

She might have obtained the vouchers, but Eleanor was under no illusion. The hard work started now. Everything had become horribly real. And she wasn't naive enough to think she could do it without help.

'Your mother possesses quite a store of knowledge,' she said. 'I'd be foolish not to take advantage of it.'

'As do you. Do not allow anyone to say differently.' He tucked her hand in his. 'And now, my dear, we shall have to visit a dressmaker. I hope to God that my mother is correct about her ability to obtain an appropriate ballgown in time, as I believe your attendance at Almack's has become compulsory.'

Chapter Fifteen

Eleanor smoothed the folds of her new ballgown. The gown was a cream silk round gown, with an embroidered gauze overskirt, and fell to exactly an inch above her ankle as the current dictate from *Ackermann's Repository* commanded. When she pirouetted in her pointed kid slippers the skirt swirled agreeably. It was the sort of gown that made her want to dance.

'Tonight,' she whispered to her reflection in the mirror, barely recognising the starry-eyed woman who looked back at her. 'Tonight I will triumph and Ben will fall in love with me. He will see that I belong in his life.'

Thankfully Lady Whittonstall's prediction had proved correct. A dressmaker which Ben's late wife had used did indeed have a complete wardrobe which could easily be restyled for her. Rather than dressing in her old practical style of muslin Eleanor now had gowns of every hue, and in a variety of fabrics. Her dressing room positively dripped with boas, sashes and lace shawls. All of which had to be worn negligently. And she had discovered that, given the right cut, ruffles did improve her assets.

In the privacy of her room she had practised for hours the art of seeming negligent and careless, as well as taking lessons at Lady Jersey's dancing school so that she had mastered the steps of the various reels.

The only trouble was that she wasn't entirely sure she enjoyed it. And she'd had barely time to attend to Moles business, let alone fence with Ben. Rather than growing closer together, as she'd hoped, they seemed to be drifting apart as Ben had started to spend more time at his club.

Eleanor raised her chin. After tonight's triumph that would stop. Everything would become wonderful once Ben had seen how well she did.

'Ellie? May I finally see you in all your finery?' Ben came into the room and stopped. 'You look divine. The sort of creature who is more likely to inhabit a fairy glen than be on earth with us mortals.'

The heat burnt on her cheeks. Did Ben really think that? Ben's black silk breeches and cutaway coat perfectly complemented his figure. 'I could say the same for you.'

'My tailor has done a good job, and thankfully—unlike some—I do not have to pad my calves.' He pointed his foot. 'You see—all real.'

'I never doubted it.'

A tiny frown appeared between his brows. 'It was a joke to make you relax. Tonight should be pleasant and memorable, Ellie, but it will not change the course of your life.'

'Do you really like my gown?' Eleanor gave another twirl. Her heart pounded fast as she waited for his verdict.

During one of their intensive practice sessions Lady Whittonstall had confided that Ben had fallen for Alice just before her first visit to Almack's. She hated that she'd pinned her hopes on it happening again. It should not matter a jot, but it did. She wanted Ben to be proud of her and what she could accomplish in his circle.

Tonight was when she would clearly demonstrate that she belonged there, rather than being some abomination as her stepfather had claimed. Tonight she wanted him to be proud of her.

He tilted his head to one side and his eyes slowly assessed her. Eleanor kept her chin up and her shoulders back, making sure the ostrich feathers in her blue silk turban didn't tremble.

'What have you done to your hair?' he finally asked. 'You have had it cut.'

'Grecian curls are the thing to wear at the moment. I think they rather suit me—particularly with this turban.' Eleanor resisted the urge to pat her hair. She had nearly cried when her hair was cut, but afterwards she'd had to admit the style suited her. It made her look younger, and her eyes appeared more in proportion with her mouth.

'They certainly make you look different.' His smile did not quite reach his eyes. 'I have a hard time thinking of you as a fearsome business-woman. There is definitely not the whiff of commerce about you tonight. One would think you spent your days devoted to pleasure rather than getting the Bow Street Runners order sorted.'

'I'm very grateful to Lady Jersey for suggesting the combination. She has been more than kind.' Eleanor struggled to keep from crying. She had built this moment up. She had remade her life to be the sort of woman he would appreciate. And he didn't appear to appreciate her new look at all.

His mouth twisted. 'Between Lady Jersey and my mother I have barely had a chance to speak two words to you over the last week.'

'After tonight it will end. Life will return to normal. Our business is nearly finished here.'

His eyes filled with pity and remorse. She wanted to reach out and wipe that sadness away, but instead she clasped her hands together and silently willed him to tell her what was wrong.

'After tonight it will *begin*,' he said. 'You will be the toast of London. Invitations will arrive. A breakfast here, an invitation to Vauxhall there. Another soirée or dinner party. A reason to stay in London. Before you know it, it will be Christmas.'

'I doubt that.'

'The invitations are already flooding in.' He caught her hand and raised it to his lips. The touch was cool and impersonal. 'You only have to decide which ones you want to attend and which ones you'd rather not. You have spent a long time practising. You need to be able to show off your dancing slippers. Moles will be able to spare you for a few weeks, if that is what you decide.'

'I do hope I get the reels right.' Eleanor focused on a spot beyond his shoulder. This interview was not going the way she had planned. 'Miss Martyn told me several horror stories when we were in our dancing class together. My mind positively whirls with all the different steps I am supposed to know. And if I get them wrong everyone will see.'

'I'm sure you will be fine. You are taking this far too seriously.' Ben held out his arm. 'Your carriage to your new life awaits, my lady.'

She concentrated on gathering her fan and reticule. All the time she'd spent in happy anticipation of these last few moments before Almack's—how he'd suddenly see what an asset she was—and they'd been awful. Worse than awful. She felt as if she were a player in a play rather than someone on the brink of a marvellous evening.

Eleanor swallowed hard and tried to regain her initiative.

'Is something wrong? Have I done something wrong? Is it my hair or my dress?'

'They are up to the minute. Why do you think something is wrong?'

'You seem so reserved.'

A muscle twitched beside his eye. 'Nothing at all is wrong. Everything is how I hoped it would be when I first suggested coming down to London. Stop seeing shadows where there are none and concentrate on enjoying tonight.'

'I love you.'

The words slipped out before she could stop them. Eleanor froze, and in the ensuing silence desperately wished she could unsay them. She willed Ben to do something—anything rather than look at her with a numbed expression of disbelief.

'Why now? Why are you telling me this now?' The finality of his tone underlined her error.

'I wanted to tell you before…before tonight…in case anything untoward happened.' She winced, hating the way she stumbled over the explanation. It sounded pathetic and false.

He regarded her, and if anything his manner became more glacial. 'What am I supposed to do? What do you want from me, Eleanor?'

Eleanor bit her lip. This was not the way she'd dreamt it. He was supposed to enfold her in his arms and whisper how much he loved *her,* how love had sneaked up unawares on him, and seeing her like this had made it all crystal-clear.

Eleanor shrugged a shoulder. 'Only you can say.'

'I dislike playing these sorts of games, Eleanor. We are about to go out to Almack's and you make this bold statement. You must know what you require from me.'

If anything, Eleanor's heart sank lower. She

raised her chin and met his ice-cold gaze. She tried to reach the man she knew was inside him—the one who had held her when she'd lost the baby, who had shared his guilt and who had forced her to fence again and rediscover her joy in life.

'I know you didn't ask for it, but I wanted to tell you anyway.' Eleanor strove for a natural tone. 'It just happened. I appreciate all you have done for me and it seemed the best way to express it. Tonight is the start of a new chapter in my life and I wanted to thank you for giving that to me. That's why I said it. I don't expect anything from it, nor will I repeat it.'

He watched her with inscrutable eyes and an expression of sorrow crossed his face.

He felt *sorry* for her! Eleanor tightened her hand about the delicate fan.

'You will be fine, Ellie. I did what any husband would do for his bride. You mustn't build me up to be something I'm not.'

'I hope so.' Inside her heart was dying. Ben didn't seem to understand. She could hardly explain that she wanted reassurance. She had taken a chance and lost. She had wanted to explain while she knew who she was. She'd also wanted an answer and knew she had had it. He had not fallen instantly in love with her. He was only doing his duty towards her as he saw it.

She'd survive. She wasn't sure her heart would, though.

'Shall we go and get this over with?' she said around the thick lump in her throat.

Ben knew the instant he had said the words that he had made a mistake. He felt it even more keenly here in Almack's crowded ballroom, where Eleanor was such an obvious success. Men queued to claim her hand in the dance and he let her go, despite his inclination to throw her over his shoulder and take her far away from this place. Tonight was her moment. He knew he couldn't begrudge her an instant. But each time she took to the dance floor with someone else he felt her slipping away. He was losing her. He loved her and he'd driven her away.

Worse still, he knew why he'd made light of Ellie's declaration and why he'd wanted to run. Why he'd been callous and unfeeling when his natural instinct had been to gather her in his arms. *Fear.*

When Eleanor had stood in front of him holding out her hands she had reminded him of the night of Alice's debut at Almack's. She too had held out her hands and given her declaration. Then, every night before a ball or other gaiety, she'd said the same thing, until it had become a ritual saying of words rather than an expression of deep meaning.

He did not want history to repeat itself. He had no desire to lose Eleanor as he'd lost Alice. The knowledge had clogged his throat and he'd given in to his fear.

He'd tried to rationalise his behaviour but he knew he'd hurt her. If she didn't know that he loved her and demanded proof then she didn't want to see. And he didn't want only to say the words to an elegantly coiffured woman just before they went out. He wanted to whisper the words when they made love, or at breakfast time, or any time that he pleased. But he'd handled it badly. Now he had to recover—*if* he could recover. Otherwise he'd lose her for ever. And that would be the worst punishment of all.

The orchestra finished its latest reel and Viv led Eleanor back to Ben.

'Is it as magical as you remember?' he asked in an undertone. He put his hand under her elbow and felt her start to pull away.

'Magical?' Eleanor stared at him in astonishment

and tried to think. She'd spent the entire evening wishing she was some place other than here. All her plans had backfired. She might be a success, but she felt as if she had lost. She wished she had never made her declaration out loud.

'On the first picnic we shared you told me about your memory.' He gave her hand a squeeze. 'I wanted this to be special. I wanted it to bring joy back to your life.'

A warm pulse went through her. He remembered that? She couldn't confess how much she was hating this. Or rather, not hating—but compared to making swords it seemed trivial and false. She could dance the reels, smile and make small polite talk, but it was never going be the centre of her existence as it was for Lady Whittonstall.

'I...I suppose so,' she stammered. 'Yes, definitely unlike anything I have experienced before.'

He nodded, seemingly satisfied. 'I want it to be.'

'Because you want me to like balls? Do you want to spend the season in London? This is the sort of thing you love.'

His gaze darkened. 'Do not confuse my taste with my mother's.'

'Then why have you pushed me?'

'Because I want you to enjoy yourself in the way

you should have done if your life had been different. Everyone is impressed with you. I overhead
Mr Brummell making one of his remarks, and it
was far more complimentary than is his normal
fare.'

'You are seeking to distract me.' Eleanor crossed
her arms. 'I thought you enjoyed this sort of life.'

'You are dismissing a compliment, Ellie. Why
do you do that?'

Her face grew hot with humiliation. Hadn't he
seen her mistakes in the last reel with Viv? Or had
he not even bothered watching? She was never
going to achieve perfection. Tonight was an un-
mitigated disaster. 'Because it is a lie.'

'You are overreacting. Nobody expected perfection.'

Nobody but her. She had wanted it and had
dreamt about it. Tonight was supposed to be her
chance to be triumphant and for Ben to fall madly
in love with her. She'd planned everything and it
hadn't worked. 'Shall we forget it, Ben?'

'No. You always do this. You look gorgeous. You
dance beautifully. You should be proud of what
you have achieved. But you shouldn't be doing it
because you have some misguided notion that it
will make *me* happy.'

She stared at him. Her stomach hit her knees. He didn't understand. He wanted to give her this because he didn't want to give of himself. The knowledge made her insides shrivel. 'I'm sorry. I can't do this. I'd like to go now. The evening is starting to overwhelm me.'

'Yes, we can depart.'

Ben put his hand under her elbow and led her through the throng and out to where their carriage waited. The coachman came up instantly and lit the lamps. Eleanor tried to keep her gaze straight ahead.

'Ellie?' Ben said once the carriage started. 'Before we go home there is somewhere I want to take you. It might explain why I reacted the way I did tonight.'

'You were right. It was nerves. I am over it now. A lapse of manners.' Eleanor hated how the words tasted like ash. 'Why I was so afraid I don't know. It was the sort of place that Algernon would enjoy. I would like to go home—back to where I belong.' She bit back the words *without you*.

'Even still, I want to take you there. I believe I hurt you earlier, and that was the last thing I intended.'

They travelled in silence for a little way, and then

the carriage stopped before a church gate. Ben took one of the lamps from the coachman and beckoned to Eleanor. 'It is just down this path.'

Eleanor drew her shawl tighter about her shoulders and followed after him. He stopped before a simple headstone. The names on the headstone stood out. A small shiver went down her spine. Of all the places in the world, this was the last place she wanted to be.

'Why do we need to come to Alice's grave?'

'Because I want you to understand about this evening and why I reacted the way I did. This is the only way I can think of to do it. The only way in which I can convince you.' The lantern highlighted the intentness of his face. 'Please hear me out before you decide.'

'It doesn't matter. I won't make that particular mistake again.' Eleanor forced her back to be straight. Whatever happened, she refused to be pathetic again. She might love him, but she knew she'd asked too much to want his love in return. She'd been wrong to believe that she could make him love her. From here on she'd behave as she wanted to.

'I hurt you earlier. Don't deny it. I saw it in your

face. I see it in your face now. It was unforgivable of me—particularly on your debut at Almack's.'

Eleanor put her hand on her stomach and willed herself not to cry. He'd noticed her hurt. It shouldn't matter, but it did. He cared for her—just not in the way she'd hoped. 'Say what you have to say. But I understand your heart is for ever buried. I was over the hurt by the time we arrived, and I was a triumph—in case you hadn't noticed.'

He placed the lantern on the ground and turned to face her. His face was incredibly intent as he gestured towards the grave.

'Alice and the baby lie in that grave, and I thought that included my entire life. But I was wrong. Like the green grass that grows after a hard winter, I discovered my heart still has the capacity to love and live.'

Eleanor forgot how to breathe. All she could do was stare at him.

'However, I don't want my old life back. That one has ended. I am not the same person. I want to live my new one as the person I am now.'

'I don't understand.'

He ran his hand through his hair. 'Alice had a little ritual of saying she loved me every time she went to a ball. It started with that first ball at

Almack's. It was the only time she ever said it. In the end they became meaningless words—a talisman that meant I knew any flirting on her part was just that: light-hearted flirting. I feared you were seeking to copy her—or worse still trying to give me my old life back when I want my new life. It unnerved me and I became frightened. I'm sorry, but I have no desire to return there. I want you only to want me in your life, rather than needing a string of men to hang on your every word.'

Eleanor looked at the carved names on the headstone. Her heart soared and for the first time she felt sorry for the lady who lay there. Superficially she might have had everything, but she'd been unable truly to love.

'I didn't mean to frighten you,' she whispered.

'It wasn't you but my feelings for you. They sneaked up on me and I became scared. The more I knew you, the more I wanted you in my life. I became afraid of losing you, having my heart break all over again.' He put his arms about her. 'I need you, Ellie. You give my life meaning. I thought if I didn't say it then I wouldn't tempt fate. But I refuse to stand by and let you slip away from me. You are far too important to me, and if you need words then you shall have them.'

She rested her head on his chest and listened to the steady thump of his heart.

'We have been at cross-purposes,' she said, looking up at him. 'All I wanted to do tonight was demonstrate that I could take my place at your side whatever the circumstance. I had hoped you would fall instantly in love with me because of how I looked and my accomplishments. I thought if I became perfect then maybe...'

He put two fingers over her mouth, stilling her.

'You may be very intelligent and single-minded, Ellie, but sometimes you display no more sense than a goose.' His arm tightened about her. 'Your imperfections are what I love about you. And how could I fall instantly in love with you tonight when I already am and have been for weeks?'

Eleanor froze. She had to have heard wrong. Ben might care about her but he didn't *love* her. He loved his late wife. She'd accepted that. That was why they were standing beside her grave—so he could explain it clearly. 'Love? You are in love with me?'

'I love you, Eleanor Blackwell Grayson, because of who you are—not who you might be or who anyone else, including yourself, thinks you ought to be. You are the light and essence of my new life.'

'But…but…I will never be as socially adept and graceful as your mother, or indeed your late wife. Although it is fun for a little while, I find it hard to be excited about the trim on the bottom of my skirt.'

'Alice?' There was genuine puzzlement in his voice. 'Why on earth would I want you to be like her?'

'Because you loved her and you will always love her.' Eleanor gestured towards the grave. 'You brought me here to tell me that.'

'The boy I was will always love her. But I have never sought a replacement for her. Her death changed me. The boy I was died and I became a man. I require different things from my life.' Ben put his arm about her and led her from the grave-yard. 'We have spent enough time here, Ellie. We need to get back to living our lives.'

When they had settled in the carriage and it had started towards the townhouse, Ben continued. 'If I had wanted to marry someone just like Alice there were a hundred other women with her accomplishments. My mother made a hobby of training them. I married *you*.'

'Because you felt sorry for me and played the errant knight,' Eleanor protested, not quite ready to believe him.

'No, to save my soul. You were wrong that day when you said that I suffer from complacency. It was far worse. My life was becoming narrower and narrower. Slowly and steadily I had cut myself off from everything. I was existing, waiting to die. Then you happened.'

Eleanor stared at his profile in the darkened carriage and tried to digest what he was saying. He loved her because she had brought him back to life. 'What did I do?'

'You didn't let me win. Worse than that, you clearly demonstrated how my arrogance and complacency had led to my downfall. You forced me to re-examine my life.'

'I beat you in a fencing match. Your grip was appalling. You thoroughly deserved to lose. But I don't understand—why did that make you want to marry me?'

He brought her hand to his lips. 'Alice always let me win.'

'And that was bad?'

'Nobody wants to win all the time, Ellie.' He gave a soft laugh that made a warm curl circle about her insides. 'Just sometimes—when they deserve it. It makes the winning all the sweeter. And they want to think the other person will fight back.'

'But you said—love.'

'I started falling in love with you when my sword destroyed your hat.' He shook his head. 'Your face was priceless. It was the first time I had truly laughed in years. In that instant I stopped existing and started living again.'

'I never liked that hat. It met a just end.' Her heart did a little flip. All these weeks she'd been so blind, so wrapped in trying to win Ben's love, that she'd failed to see Ben already loved her. It had been there in the way he'd taken an interest in Moles, how he'd insisted that she fence, and most especially when they'd made love. Like him, she'd been too scared to admit it. 'You came awfully close to winning.'

'I could have killed Viv when he arrived. A few more heartbeats and I would have kissed you. I wanted to. It was the first time I had desired something like that since…since Alice died.'

'Out of all the women in the world, I was the one you wanted to kiss?'

'You were the only one. You *are* the only one. You complete my life.' He gestured towards the bright lights. 'All that means nothing without you.'

Eleanor trembled. He had desired her even then. The thought amazed her. She had been so wrong and misguided, so intent on her misery that she'd failed to understand how special she was to him.

'Was that the only reason you married me?' she breathed. 'Because I made you laugh?'

'That made me want to pursue you. That is why I showed up at Moles. There I saw how much heart you had and how strong you were. How much you gave of yourself to keep that forge going, and how much you were willing to give without asking for anything in return. I knew I wanted a piece of your heart.' His hand cupped the back of her head. '*Do I have a piece of your heart? Are the words you said before the ball true? Or did I kill them?*'

'I love you, Ben. I have loved you since I first met you.' Eleanor stopped. 'No, that's wrong. I desired your touch, and then my love grew gradually as I learnt about the worthiness of the man I married. You may have hurt me earlier because I didn't understand, but now I do. And I am in wonder that I was so blind.'

'No, we both were.' He rubbed his thumb along her mouth, sent fresh tingles thrumming through her. 'But now we know the truth. Actions prove far more than words.'

'However, I plan on whispering my love to you whenever I wish, and I hope you will consider it as well. Something like love shouldn't be saved for special occasions. It should be celebrated every day.'

His rich laughter rang out. 'There are so many reasons why I love you.'

She pulled his face down to hers. 'And I you. Shall we go home?'

'I can't think of any place I'd rather be, as long as we are together.'

Epilogue

Eighteen months later

She enjoyed this moment of the day best of all, Eleanor decided, looking down at the cradle where her four-month-old baby son slept with a small milk bubble on his lips. The house was hushed and all was right with her world. She was able to lavish love on those who loved her back equally fiercely.

'It took an age to get him to sleep. I don't think we will have time for a game of chess tonight.'

'You should let the nurse do it,' Ben said softly.

'I enjoy it far too much. And I know it is far from fashionable, but I refuse to have a wet nurse.'

'This has to be better for him. Luckily Johnson is proving an able manager for Moles. It goes from strength to strength—particularly as this blasted war with Napoleon seems to be never-ending. I can't see a time when England won't need swords.'

'Mr Johnson swears he is only following the path that I set out, but I know he and Mr Swaddle have plans to expand and find new markets for the steel just in case.'

She found it hard to believe how much easier it was now that she'd stopped trying to do everything and had allowed other people to pursue their dreams and innovations.

'So you are planning on having our son run an empire?'

'I want him to be able to follow his dreams.'

James made a little sucking noise and flung out his arms.

'I suspect, whatever those dreams are, he will.'

'Hush, you'll wake him.' Eleanor tucked the blanket in tighter but James gave a sweep of his hand and the blanket slipped again. 'Why can't the blanket stay tucked in?'

'James is a born fighter and stubborn. He wants what he wants and the world needs to be remade that way,' Ben remarked, coming to put his arms about her waist. 'Takes after his mother.'

'His father.'

He laughed. At the sound of Ben's laugh Romeo looked up from where he lay, guarding the cradle.

'Both of us, then. We know he comes by it honestly.'

Eleanor leant back in his arms. 'He is his own person, though.'

'He always has been. He came into the world determined to make his mark.'

Eleanor put her hands over Ben's. 'He's been his own person since the very beginning.'

The pregnancy had been different from her first pregnancy. She couldn't explain it exactly. Her body had felt different—not as bloated or tender—and she had not been able to look at a piece of cheese without being queasy. Even so she had not dared to believe until she'd felt a hard kick to her bladder. Ben and she had been playing a game of chess, and she'd been so startled that she had allowed him to take her queen. But once she'd told him and her stomach had begun to move they had both believed.

She knew the day James had been born was one of the happiest days of their lives—even if it had been traumatic for Ben. Despite Eleanor's assurances he had become irate, and had refused to leave the room until he knew that both of them were safe and well.

'And I am very lucky to have you both in my life,' Ben rumbled in her ear.

'Not luck but skill.' Eleanor thought back to the long-ago spring day when she had wondered what the right words to get a man to marry you were. She decided that words didn't matter. Actions did.

She turned and captured Ben's lips. He brought his arms around her. And they stood there in the circle of their happiness.

* * * * *

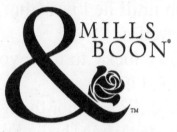